A STORM OF GLASS AND STARS

ALSO BY MARION BLACKWOOD

Marion Blackwood has written lots of books across multiple series, and new books are constantly added to her catalogue. To see the most recently updated list of books, please visit: www.marionblackwood.com

CONTENT WARNINGS

The Oncoming Storm series contains quite a lot of violence and morally questionable actions. If you have specific triggers, you can find the full list of content warnings at: www.marionblackwood.com/content-warnings

A STORM OF GLASS AND STARS

THE ONCOMING STORM: BOOK FOUR

MARION BLACKWOOD

First edition

ISBN 978-91-986386-7-7 (hardcover)
ISBN 978-91-986386-6-0 (paperback)
ISBN 978-91-986386-5-3 (ebook)

Editing by Julia Gibbs
Book cover design by ebooklaunch.com

www.marionblackwood.com

*For everyone with a heart covered
in black ice and metal spikes*

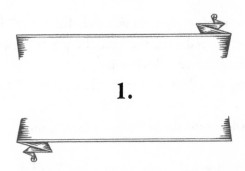

1.

The descent into madness is a slow one. It happens gradually. You don't just go to bed completely sane one day and then wake up batshit crazy the next morning. Trust me, I would know. However, an interesting side effect of that gradual deterioration is that you don't actually realize that you're losing your mind. Until it's already gone. It's like not noticing that you've aged because you see yourself in the mirror every day. Then suddenly, it's all too late.

A pebble tumbled over the stones further up the street. My ears pricked up. The soft clattering was followed by muffled footsteps. I opened my eyes. *Finally*.

Uncrossing my legs, I jumped down from the wall I'd been sitting on. Darkness blanketed the alley around me but the silent night betrayed my stalker's movements by sound. It was only one person and they were sneaking along the wall up ahead. I drew the hunting knives from the small of my back. Of course, I could have just thrown a blade at them from the shadows, killing them before they even got close. But what would be the fun in that?

"Aren't you gonna introduce yourself?" I called into the warm night air.

For a moment, everything was still. Then, a tall lanky man emerged and moved into the moonlit patch between us. A curved dagger gleamed in his hand.

"Planning to stab that in my back, were you?" I nodded at the blade.

A sly smile spread across the man's face. "Courtesy of the Rat King."

"Seriously, doesn't that man ever learn? You'd think that after the last five dead bodies I left for him, he would've realized that shit like this doesn't work on me."

"He's never sent me before."

I rolled my eyes. "Said by every overconfident fool ever, right before they died."

The fact that I had said something similar more than once in my life was of course entirely irrelevant. After all, *I* was still alive.

Anger bloomed in the lanky man's eyes and he gripped the dagger tighter in his hand. Arrogance. It worked every time. I gave the man a patronizing smirk and twitched my fingers at him. He launched himself across the stones.

His curved dagger swished through the air as he swiped at my ribs. I twisted to the side and rammed an elbow into his wrist. A grunt escaped his throat and his arm snapped downwards but he managed to keep a hold of the blade. Yanking it back up in an arc, he forced me to jump back to avoid being gutted by the sharp edge. Adrenaline thrummed through my body.

Metal clashed as I blocked a strike to my head. While his knife hand was trapped, I drew my other blade down his forearm. He sucked in a sharp breath. Shoving my knife away, he threw out an arm. Blood smeared across my face as his wounded forearm connected with my cheekbones. I blinked and stumbled to the side.

Not giving me a moment to get my bearings, he darted towards me. Throwing up an arm, I narrowly managed to redirect the thrust meant for my throat. His knife hand sailed past harmlessly over my shoulder instead of through my windpipe. Using the brief moment of surprise as my attacker realized that his dagger hadn't ended up where he thought it would, I struck.

A startled huff sounded. Followed by a wet sliding sound as I withdrew the hunting knife buried in his heart. Since his previous momentum from the missed stab had brought him forwards, he continued in that direction and crashed right into me. The weight of the dead man knocked me off my feet and I slammed back first into the stones with his corpse on top of me. Blood pooled onto my chest.

Drawing a deep breath, I shoved him off me and sat up. After another glance at my dead attacker, I pushed to my feet.

Looking down at the body, I snickered and shook my head. "Said by every overconfident fool ever right before they died, indeed."

Energy and excitement from the fight bounced around inside of me. I tipped my head up towards the rooftops. Better make the most of it. After wiping off my hunting knives and sticking them back in their holsters, I climbed up the side of the nearest building.

Wind whipped through my hair as I sprinted across the roof and took aim for the next building. That moment of weightlessness as I flew through the air before I landed on the tiles again filled me with exhilaration. I continued towards the next one.

The adrenaline rush from the fight, amplified by the rooftop run, kept me going for a while but eventually wore off. When it finally fizzled out and died, I found myself on the east side of the city walls. I climbed the stairs in silence. The elation had given way to a hollow numbness but I knew that would be replaced soon as well. Pity.

When I reached the top, I found the battlements empty. Of course. No sane person would be strolling the walls at this time of night. Placing my hands on the cool stones forming a barrier at the edge of the walkway, I drew myself up. On the other side of the wall, the harbor waited in darkness. I let my legs dangle over the side as I watched the waves and the ships bobbing in the water.

Mist rolled in from the sea and covered the harbor in a shroud of white. I took a deep breath. The smell of seaweed, fog, and old wood greeted me. Drawing my legs up underneath me, I continued watching the night.

Eventually, an orange sun peeked over the horizon, its pale tendrils chasing the mist away. I studied it in the detached sort of way that a butcher looks at an animal they're about to carve up. Only when the sun had risen completely from the sea did I manage to pull myself out of the stupor. I blinked and shook my head violently. Was it morning already?

My stiff legs protested when I finally unfurled them and jumped down from the wall. Normal people would be flooding the streets now that the sun was up so it was best to use the roofs to get back. Still trying to get my mind in working order, I made my way to the rooftops and then continued on towards Norah's school.

Since another damn day had already started, the school yard was full of squealing children. I rubbed my temples at the noise before climbing down the side of the opposite building. How Norah managed it was beyond me. Especially now that Liam pitched in with his earnings from the hatmakers' shop, which had opened the doors for even more kids. I shook my head as I strode through the gate towards the side entrance.

"Oh gods, are you alright, Miss?"

I frowned down at the boy who had stopped dead in my path. "Of course I'm alright. Why wouldn't I be?"

The young student stared at me, eyes wide, for another moment before whirling around and running towards the building. "Miss Norah! Miss Norah!"

Heaving a deep sigh, I continued towards the door. As I was saying, how Norah managed to stand these strange creatures was a mystery to me. I shook my head again but before I reached the sanctuary of the staffrooms, the boy reappeared with the aforementioned teacher in tow.

"Miss Norah, look! There's a woman covered in blood!" he called, pulling her along by the hand.

Blood? What blood? The beautiful teacher came to a screeching halt when she saw me. Bending down, she said something to the concerned boy and sent him away before stalking towards me. I looked down at my body. Oh. Right. The fight and the stabbing. That blood.

"Inside," was all she said.

I trailed after her until we were out of sight. Norah was a very kind person but she was also fiercely protective of her students and her school. I had a feeling that an admonishment was coming and I didn't want to hear it so I decided to get ahead of it.

"Look, I'm sorry," I said. "I didn't realize that I was covered in blood. Otherwise, I'd never have let myself get spotted by the kids."

The Pernish teacher frowned at me. "How could you not know that you were covered in blood?"

Good question. And one that I didn't have a satisfactory answer to so I just shrugged.

"It's been a rough night."

Norah pinched the bridge of her nose. "I know that you've been... struggling lately and I know I said that you could stay here until you figured things out but..." She trailed off and looked up at me with sad eyes. "Maybe it's best if you started looking for a place of your own?"

There was already so much pain ripping my heart to shreds that the hurt from her statement barely registered. And besides, she was right. I'd been slipping up quite a lot lately. Coming back to the school in all states and at all hours. She had said it the very first time I met her. *Whatever trouble you might get yourselves into, you leave my students and my school out of it.*

"Yeah." Releasing a long exhale, I skirted around her and made for my room. "I'll be out before the school day is over."

"Wait. I didn't mean it like that."

Stopping briefly, I turned around. "I know. You're a kind person, Norah. Thanks for letting me stay this long. I know I'm not the easiest of people to live with." I gave her a small smile. "I understand what Liam sees in you."

Before she could answer, I spun on my heel and disappeared down the corridor. Norah was right. It had been six months since Shade had won the election and Liam had announced that he was staying in Pernula. Six months of confused numbness and pain. It was time to pack up my things and leave.

ON THE OTHER SIDE OF the fence, horses meandered in the afternoon sun. Since my chat with Norah that morning, I had managed to successfully avoid Liam, get some sleep, eat something, and gather up all my belongings. Not that it was much to gather. Everything fit nicely in the backpack currently resting on the ground next to me. It was mostly weapons, blackout powder, exploding orbs, and things like that. But also a map, compass, and other stuff one might need to survive the great outdoors.

"Planning to leave without saying goodbye?"

My body performed an involuntary jerk at the sudden sound. I narrowed my eyes at the assassin who had appeared seemingly out of thin air.

"You know, one of these days you really gotta tell me how you do that."

Shade just raised his eyebrows while taking up position next to me.

"Find me like this, I mean."

"This is my city now." The Master of the Assassins' Guild and new General of Pernula nodded at the gigantic double doors set into the city wall. "Don't you think I have spies at the main gate?"

"Yeah, I'm pretty sure you've got spies at more than the main gate," I grumbled.

For a moment, we both simply watched the horses in the pen wander back and forth. And the gray one being readied in the courtyard as well, of course. The one I had just bought.

"You're leaving?" Shade asked again.

"Yeah."

"Why?"

Twisting around, I met his gaze head on. "I don't fit in here. Liam is living happily ever after with Norah at the school. Elaran and the elves are establishing connections with the other wood elves. And you're running the freaking city." I heaved a deep sigh and ran my fingers through my hair. "I have nothing. I can't go back to Keutunan. I tried that. It's too empty. The guild is empty, the Mad Archer is empty, the whole city is empty without Liam." I let my arms drop. "It's too fucking empty. I can't be there. Too many memories. So yeah, I'm leaving."

Shade's intelligent black eyes studied me intently. "Where are you going?"

"To find the Storm Casters."

"Do you even know where to start?"

"No. But I'll figure it out." I lifted one shoulder in a shrug and gave him a tired smile. "I always do."

A large black horse snorted and trotted by in front of us. We leaned against the fence in silence for another minute before Shade broke the somber stillness that had settled.

"Are you coming back?"

"I don't know," I answered honestly. "What is there to come back to? Everyone already has a life. Everyone except me. I'm the odd one out. There's no place for me here."

A range of emotions flew past in Shade's dark eyes and he opened his mouth. For a moment, it looked like he was about to say something but then he closed it again and that unreadable mask descended on his face.

I bent down and picked up my backpack. After slinging it over my shoulder, I turned to the silent assassin. "Goodbye, Shade."

It took a few seconds but then he finally replied. "Goodbye, the Oncoming Storm."

Without a second look back, I strode over to the gray horse and climbed up. Haela's lessons had paid off. I did actually know how to ride a horse now. So I dug my heels into the mare's sides and trotted out the main gate. Dust swirled around its hooves as I left the city of Pernula, along with everything and everyone I had ever known, behind.

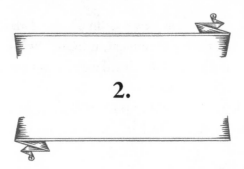

2.

Buildings rose in the distance. I arched my back and stretched it as much as I could while on horseback. Popping sounds came from my stiff bones. Thanks to elves' rigorous lessons, I might know how to ride, make a fire, and do other outdoorsy stuff but it didn't mean that I had to like it.

"That's it," I muttered to the grasslands around me. "No more sleeping on the ground outside."

It sounds so romantic. Sleeping out in the open with a blanket of stars. But what no one tells you is that there's sand everywhere, lurking animals, and that vast night sky full of glittering stars only serves to remind you how small and insignificant you are. How alone you are. I squinted at the houses growing larger in front of me. Whatever this town was, I was staying there until someone could point me in the direction of the Storm Casters.

A worn wooden sign painted with faded red letters greeted me as I reached the town.

"Welcome to Travelers' Rest," I read aloud.

Interesting. It was written in my language. Well, in the elven language, I suppose, but it was also my native tongue. Earlier, I had gotten a feeling that the elven language was some kind of lingua franca on this continent and this further confirmed my theory.

Travelers' Rest was a surprisingly fitting name for this quaint town. Clusters of brightly painted buildings spread out in front of me as I rode along the dirt road. The colorful houses mingled nicely with the grasslands surrounding the town, as well as the plants and flowers growing by the doors and windows. It did indeed look like a place where people could rest.

"Hey, you!" I called to a man pushing a small cart along the road.

"Oh, welcome, traveler." He smiled at me.

"Is there a tavern or something where I can rent a room?"

"Oh, of course." He wiped his brow with the back of his hand. "This is Travelers' Rest, after all." Taking his hand from his forehead, he pointed further down the road. "If you continue down there, you'll find a large square with a well in the middle. To your right is a three-story building with a sign that says *The Sleeping Horse*. That's the tavern I'd recommend."

I lifted a hand at him and urged my horse on. "Thanks!"

The man had spoken true. The wide road led to a dirt square with a stone well in the middle. Sun beamed down on me as I steered towards the tall building on my right. A wooden sign swung in the warm breeze, displaying a white horse lying in a field of grass underneath the tavern's name. I reined in my gray mare and climbed off outside the front door.

It looked like there was a stable next to the tavern but I figured that I needed to pay before I could put her in there so, for the moment, I tied her by the water basin outside. She snorted at me.

"Yeah, I know." I stroked her neck while she bent down to drink. "You'll get out of the sun soon. Just gotta pay first."

While my horse gulped down water, I moved to the front door. A wide room filled with tables and chairs met me when I stepped across the threshold. Taking a moment to study my surroundings, I noticed that there was also a long bar on the right while a fireplace occupied a spot on the opposite wall. It was unlit, of course, since it was almost summer and both the days and nights were warm at this time of year.

"Welcome to The Sleeping Horse," a middle-aged woman with short curly hair said. "What can I get you?"

I let my eyes glide over the handful of patrons already seated at the tables before turning my attention to the woman. "Yeah, I wanna rent a room. And I need to stable my horse too."

"Of course." She gave me a warm smile. "Any room preferences?"

"Top floor, if you have."

That way, if unwanted trouble came looking for me it was easier to disappear up on the roof. The woman with the curly blond hair nodded and went in search of a key. She reappeared a moment later with a thick metal one but didn't hand it over.

"How long are you staying?"

I shrugged. "Don't know yet."

She cleared her throat. "It's just... we take payment in advance."

Ah. Of course they did. Having someone stay for weeks and realize that they had no money only when it was time to leave was no way to run a business.

"I'll pay for a week in advance then." I gave her another shrug. "And then I'll just keep doing that until I'm ready to leave."

A bright smile spread across her plump face. "That works well."

While we were finishing up our money transaction, a girl with brown hair in wild curls burst through the door at the back of the tavern. The other patrons looked up in alarm but then went back to eating and drinking when they saw who it was.

"Mom!" she called. "Have you seen the beautiful gray mare outside?"

The tavern hostess chuckled. "That would be this young lady's horse."

Brown eyes sparkled when the girl turned to me. "What's her name?"

"Silver," I replied. "Or so they said when I bought her, at least."

"See to it that Silver is stabled, brushed, and fed, would you?" the middle-aged woman said before the girl could fire off any more questions.

"Of course!" She flew out the door again.

Shaking her head, the woman in front of me gave me another smile. "That whirlwind of a girl is my daughter Livia. She loves horses. So don't worry, yours will be well taken care of." She jerked back and blinked at me like a surprised owl. "Oh dear, I've quite forgotten to introduce myself, haven't I? I'm Merina. My husband is Hestor. You'll probably meet him later this afternoon. And then we also have an older daughter, Meera. You will hear her tonight."

"Hear her?"

Merina handed over the key and winked at me. "Wait and see."

Not being in the mood for guessing games, I simply thanked her and took the offered key. I had spotted the staircase to the left of the entrance when I arrived so I found my room on the top floor without issue.

It wasn't much to cheer for. A bed, desk and chair, and a set of drawers. But at least I had a mattress, blanket, and pillow. And a door I could lock. I had slept in better rooms but I had also slept in a lot worse. This would do. After locking the door behind me, I dropped my pack on the floor and flopped down on the bed. This would do nicely, indeed.

Traveling on horseback and sleeping outdoors had taken its toll on my city girl disposition so I spent the rest of the day trying to get the exhaustion out of my body. It didn't do much, though. My mind refused to turn off and pain dripped from my heart. I tossed and turned restlessly in my bed until late afternoon before finally giving up and stalking down the stairs.

At this time of day, the tavern was full of people. I watched them as I made my way to the bar. Some looked like travelers, their dusty clothes betraying them, but others appeared to be locals who came here to drink at the end of another workday.

"What do you want?"

I blinked at the brown-haired man behind the bar. "What?"

"To drink?" He motioned behind him. "We have ale and wine..." Trailing off, he studied my startled expression. "Unless you fancy something stronger?"

Oh. Right. What did I want to drink? Of course that was what he had meant.

Words spoken on a ship by a certain smuggler had beaten mercilessly against my brain for months now. *What do you want? For you?* Zaina had asked. *I don't know*, I had replied. *I don't know what I want for me.* For so long, all I had ever wanted was to keep Liam safe and happy. That had been my purpose in life. But now Liam *was* safe and happy and had a life of his own. He didn't need me anymore. What was my purpose in life now?

Realizing that the man I presumed to be Merina's husband, Hestor, was still waiting for an answer, I shoved my heartache and confusion aside and shook my head to clear it. It only partially worked.

"I'll have an ale. And a shot." I drummed my fingers on the bar. "Actually, make that two."

Hestor was gracious enough not to judge and instead simply nodded. "Coming right up."

All my visible knives lay packed away safely in my room because I had wanted to survey the crowd first, without drawing too much attention. However, that meant I couldn't scare away people from the table I wanted so I had to settle for a less ideally placed one. It was not by the wall, which I would've preferred, but at least it was at the back of the room so I could keep an eye on the other patrons.

Ale sloshed over the top of the mug as I placed it and the two shot glasses on the table. Flicking spilled ale off my fingers, I sat down and took a long drink. It was decent. Not as good as the Mad Archer's, of course, but nothing ever was. A cold fist gripped my heart at the thought of the Mad Archer and all the wonderful times I'd spend there with Liam. I slammed up the walls around my heart and downed the first shot.

Afternoon turned into evening while I exercised my skills in self-medication. Concerned brown eyes studied the rather vast collection of empty glasses on my table when Hestor brought me yet another shot, but he didn't comment. The alcohol helped dull the hurt a bit but didn't chase it away completely. I kept trying anyway.

A woman's distressed yelp pulled me back to the present. I squinted at the source. Some tables away, a heavily muscled man was laughing and catcalling a woman in a blue dress. From the position of her hands, he had no doubt put his fingers where they didn't belong. When she scurried away, he roared again while his friends slapped the table in excitement. Glaring at him, I emptied another glass. Men.

He tried the same thing with other women passing by his table. Briefly, I wondered why no one said anything. Bulging muscles rippled under a dusty shirt when he swung his thick limbs around to reach for another woman's bottom. He was big and, given the state of his clothes, a traveler. Yeah. That was why. They probably just hoped that he would leave soon enough on his own.

"Meera! Meera!" a rhythmic chanting unexpectedly rose from the gathered crowd.

The excited calls were followed by clapping, cheering, and table slapping. Puzzled, I turned in every direction to figure out what in Nemanan's name had brought this on. My eyes fell on a gorgeous young woman with long blond hair and blue eyes. Meera. A memory from earlier floated to the front of my brain. Hadn't that been the name of the tavern keepers' eldest daughter?

When the stunning woman climbed onto a short stool by the bar, the room fell silent. Everyone watched her with eager eyes. She opened her mouth. A voice as soft as royal silk drifted through the room as Meera sang. It was hauntingly beautiful. The song was a sad one and it, combined with her otherworldly voice, produced something so raw it threatened to destroy me. I didn't think there was anything left to break in my heart, but whatever it was that had managed to remain intact, shattered that night in the tavern.

What was the point of anything? All I had ever done was bring violence and death to the people I cared about. Rain. Liam. They would have been so much better off without me. I had wanted to protect them but the thing they had needed protection from was me. And now they were gone. My whole life, I had persevered through all the awful things I'd been through because I had wanted to keep my friends safe. That was what I had lived for. What was there left to live for now?

Meera's heartbreaking tunes came to an end. The whole tavern broke out in cheers but I could only stare blankly ahead while searing agony and a profound sense of loss ripped my soul to shreds.

"Thank you," the beautiful singer said to the crowd. "You're too kind."

I couldn't keep feeling this way. Emptying the rest of my glasses, I tried desperately to dull the pain. I had to do something.

"Come here, you," the muscled man said and grabbed a hold of Meera's arm. He drew her closer. "That was beautiful. Any chance of a private concert?"

Discomfort was evident on her face as she carefully pried her arm from his grip and slid away. "I'm afraid not."

My eyes narrowed. Him. Given everything I'd seen this night, he would have no qualms about laying a hand on a woman. Placing my palms on the table full of glasses and spilled drinks, I pushed myself up. The edges of my vision were blurry. Ignoring it, I stalked towards his table in a far clumsier fashion than I would've preferred. Once I reached it, I pretended to stumble and slammed right into him.

"Hey! Watch it," I snapped.

The man turned gray eyes full of annoyance and incredulity on me. "Watch it? You're the one who should watch it."

"Not my fault that you flap your arms around like a retarded seagull."

Shocked silence fell over the room for a moment. Everyone stared at me. Then, chairs scraped against the floor as he and his companions shot to their feet. Now that he was standing, I had to crane my neck to meet his eyes.

"You're gonna apologize for that," he warned. "Now."

"Yeah, not gonna happen." I flicked my hand in an arrogant gesture. "So why don't you take a walk."

Fire roared in his eyes. "Apologize. Now."

"Or what? You're gonna hit me?" Quick as a snake, I gave his stubbled cheek a hard slap. "Like that?"

His arm shot out and grabbed the front of my shirt. Hauling me forward by my collar, he leaned down and opened his mouth to no doubt growl threats in my face.

A loud bang echoed. Hestor put down the two metal rods he had just slammed together. "If you are going to fight, you do it outside. And any blood on the sheets will be added to your bill. Is that clear?"

Despite only being of average height and build, Hestor commanded enough respect to make the muscled man comply. He released my shirt and shoved me towards the front door. I gave him an arrogant grin as I exited the building and took up position on the sandy ground outside.

"Last chance to back out." He cracked his knuckles.

"Why? You afraid you'll lose?"

Scattered chuckles broke out from the crowd that had filed out behind us. Anger flashed in my opponent's eyes. He took a step forward and swung a fist at my face. I ducked it and slammed my knuckles into his side. Pain shot up my wrist. With all his muscles, the huge man barely registered the strike and instead threw an elbow into my cheek. My head snapped to the side. I took a step back to steady myself but didn't get far before a blow struck my jaw. I crashed to the ground.

"Had enough?" my assailant jeered.

Pressing a hand to my forehead, I blinked repeatedly until the scene came back into focus. I climbed to my feet again.

Darting forward, I feigned a direction change and aimed for his jaw. He didn't fall for it. His large hand flew up and gripped my fist before it connected. With my hand trapped, and my other arm too slow to react, I was defenseless as he backhanded me across the mouth. Pulling back again, he drove his hand into my stomach. I collapsed to the street.

"Stay down!" the man called.

Short ragged breaths made it out of my throat as I pushed myself onto my knees. Pain rolled over my body. Wheezing, I climbed to my feet.

"I said stay down!" he bellowed and planted a boot in my side.

The kick flipped me over on my back. For a few seconds, I just lay there but then I gathered the rest of my strength and started pushing myself back up. My opponent grabbed my shirt and yanked me up only to deliver a heavy blow to my face. When he let go, I slumped back down.

"Don't you ever disrespect me again," the muscled man said before stomping back inside.

The crowd followed him. I heard their footsteps more than saw them because I couldn't manage to lift my head. Everything ached. Rolling over on my side briefly, I coughed blood onto the sand before flopping onto my back again.

Every muscle and every bone pounded from the beating. I savored the feeling. Physical pain was good. Another cough racked my body and I spit more blood onto the street. This kind of hurt was much better than the excruciating agony clawing inside my chest. Physical pain I could handle. Mental, on the other hand, was much harder to cope with.

"Are you trying to get yourself killed?"

I opened my eyes to find a face framed by wild brown curls looking down on me.

"I don't know."

"It sure looked like it," Livia said and held out her hand. "You must've known you couldn't beat him."

Taking her hand, I let her help me to my feet. "Oh, I could have. If I wanted to."

She held my elbow as I stumbled to the door. "Why didn't you want to?"

As we made slow progress up the stairs, I fell silent. How did one explain to a twelve-year-old that the goal hadn't been to win? It had been to feel something. Anything. I could've stabbed him straight away and ended it before it began but I had wanted him to beat me up. I had wanted pain I could deal with instead of the horrible internal one I otherwise felt. But there was no way to explain that to a child so I kept quiet while she helped me onto my bed. I stared blankly into the ceiling. What was I supposed to do now?

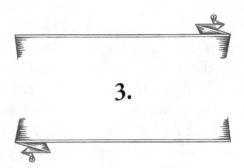

3.

Sleep eluded me for hours. It wasn't until dawn reached its tendrils through the shutters of my room that I finally dozed off. Nightmares plagued my dreams. I woke up exhausted at midday but I couldn't bring myself to get out of bed. Instead, I remained lying there, staring unseeing into the wall for another few hours.

Late that afternoon, I finally managed to muster enough energy to tear my gaze from the wooden planks and climb to my feet. Every one of my limbs throbbed when I made my way downstairs. I had to hold on to the railing and take the steps one at a time but it was worth it because it kept my mind off other topics.

"Ale," I said to Hestor while bracing myself on the bar. "And whatever you have to eat."

After accepting my payment, he filled up a mug and handed it to me. "Livia will bring the food over in a few minutes." He hesitated for a moment. "There is a doctor here that–"

"I'll live." I took the mug and made for a table at the back.

Since it was still early afternoon, the tavern was far from full which meant I could choose almost any table I wanted. I picked one at the back where I could see the whole room and have my back protected by the wall.

A couple of minutes later, Livia popped out of the kitchen and ran over to my table with a plate in her hand. She placed the steaming meal in front of me but didn't leave.

"Thanks," I said and shoveled a spoonful of food into my mouth.

It was some type of stew or other but I didn't much care which kind. Livia was still standing by my table. I eyed her suspiciously. She turned around to leave but then immediately whirled back around again and drew out the chair next to mine. Wood creaked as she plopped down on it. Drawing herself up so that she sat cross-legged on the seat, she peered at me.

"So, where are you headed?" she asked.

"Don't know." I shoved more stew into my mouth.

"Then you've come to the right place for sure." She beamed at me. "Did you know that Travelers' Rest sits exactly in the middle between Pernula, Sker, and Beccus? Well, it does. And then of course there's Frustaz just a little more south of Beccus. But they're occupied by the star elves of course. Beccus and Frustaz, I mean. So if you have beef with the star elves then you shouldn't be heading there. Are you wanted or something? I'm not. Wanted, I mean. Or scared. Of the star elves, that is. I don't think they'll come here. Or if they do, I'm–"

"Do you ever, like, take a breath?" I interrupted. Astonishment filled my eyes as I stared at her. "Did you even breathe once while saying all that?"

Livia scrunched up her face in thought. Then she shook her head so vigorously her brown curls danced around her face. "No."

Not being able to help myself, I released a chuckle. "That mouth ever get you into trouble?"

"Yeah. Lots." She grinned at me.

I snorted. "I can relate."

A large group of travelers wandered through the door. Chairs and tables scraped against the wooden floor as they rearranged the furniture so they could all sit together. After swallowing the last bit of stew, I leaned back and rested my head against the dark wood of the wall panel.

"So," Livia began and pinched her lip, "if you don't know where you're going, how do you know where you're going?"

I frowned at her. "What?"

"What's it you're looking for?"

"Oh, uhm..." I hesitated but then decided that I had nothing to lose by being honest. "I'm looking for the Storm Casters. You ever met one?"

"Ashaana?" She shook her head. "No. I don't know anyone who has." A grin spread across her young face. "I'd really wanna, though. They seem kinda cool."

"So you have no idea where they are?"

"Nope." Livia lifted her narrow shoulders in a shrug. "You could ask people in town but I don't think they know either."

"Livia!" Merina's voice rose from the kitchen. "Stop bothering the young lady and come help me with these plates."

Mischief sparkled in her brown eyes as the enthusiastic girl grimaced at me. "Gotta go." She jumped off the chair and raced back behind the bar.

I shook my head at her retreating back. Had I ever been that way? Innocent, excited, and full of life. I felt like I had been old even when I was young. Maybe in another place at another time, things would've been different. Maybe.

As the afternoon turned into night, I graduated from ale to stronger liquor. Hestor thankfully didn't comment on my constant calls for refills but his brown eyes were tinged with worry. I ignored it and emptied another glass.

The huge man who had beaten the living daylights out of me last night showed up with his squad after the sun had set. He cast a challenging stare my way but I only glared back at him. Since my body was still pulsating with pain from his blows yesterday, there was no need to fight him again so soon.

I watched him through narrowed eyes as he continued catcalling the women passing by his table and continued reaching for places his hands had no business touching. When Meera arrived, he rose and sidled up next to her. Her beautiful face was full of discomfort as she tried to separate herself from his hulking shape. Only when Hestor approached and said some wisely chosen words to him did he sit down again.

Deciding that I'd had quite enough of people, I braced myself on the table and pushed out of my chair. The room swayed before me. I shook my head to clear it but it only served to make me even more dizzy so I wove through the tables towards the staircase on unsteady feet.

Something shot out in front of me. Because of the severe state of intoxication, my reflexes were too slow so I tripped over it and stumbled to the side. Raised voices called out in annoyance as something sloshed and splattered onto the wooden boards.

Looking down, I realized that I had tripped over the muscled man's outstretched leg. Malice shone in his gray eyes when I turned to him. He gave me a satisfied grin. Oh I had definitely had enough of people for today.

The huge man shot to his feet and shoved his mug in my face. "You spilled my ale." He jerked his head downwards. "All over my boots."

"It's your own fault," I muttered. "You did it on purpose."

"Clean it up."

I answered with a derisive snort. "I don't think so."

A heavy fist slammed into my stomach. I dropped to my knees. While I was still trying to get air back into my lungs, a large hand gripped the back of my neck and shoved my head towards the floor.

"I said *clean it up*." He pushed my face closer to his boots. "Get out your tongue and lick it up."

Fury fierce enough to rival the demons of hell flashed through my body. The darkness surged from my soul and I gave into it gladly. Tendrils of black smoke shot out around me and deafening thunder boomed inside the dark tavern. My attacker snatched his hand back.

With deliberately slow moves, I climbed to my feet. Death and insanity raged in my now black eyes as I leveled them on the tall man in front of me. He flinched and took a step back. All around us, the room was dead silent as everyone held their breaths and waited for what would happen next.

"Don't you ever disrespect me again," I growled, throwing his own words back in his face.

Before he could respond, I closed the short distance between us. Shooting a stiletto into my hand, I rammed it into his chest. A surprised grunt escaped his throat. I yanked the blade back. The rest of the tavern watched in stunned silence as he toppled backwards, a red stain spreading across his shirt. His companions seemed stuck between wanting to kill me and wanting to run for their lives. I ignored them and strode to the bar.

"For the blood." I slid a couple of pearls across the counter.

Hestor placed a hand over them but said nothing. No one moved as I stalked back to the stairs and returned to my room. Strength drained from my body with every step but I managed to make it to my room and lock the door before I passed out.

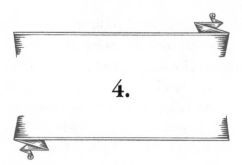

4.

Animals of the night played their nocturnal songs outside my window. Given the position of the moon, I had been out less than an hour. I swung my legs over the side of the bed and sat up. Dark smoke still swirled around me. Not nearly as much as before but it was still visible. My eyes were black as well. Interesting. Usually when I woke up, the darkness had returned to the deep pits of my soul. But not this time.

Well, the cat was out of the bag now. The time for surveying the crowd without drawing attention was over. I reached for my bag and the knives packed away in there. The time for once again being a one-woman army had come.

After strapping on all my knives, I descended the stairs again. Since the darkness was still here, I might as well make the most of it and ask people about the Storm Casters. Something told me that they'd be more inclined to give a truthful answer when they were faced with a real life Ashaana.

Rough hands shoved me to the side as soon as both my feet were off the stairs. I flew out the open front door. Tumbling down on the ground, I came to a halt a few strides from the entrance to the tavern.

"You killed our friend," a man with short black hair said. "Shouldn't have done that."

I threw them an annoyed look while climbing to my feet and dusting myself off. "I'm gonna give you one chance to back away."

Three more men appeared behind the black-haired one. After nodding at each other, they moved forward.

"I take it that's a no then?" I lifted my eyebrows at them. "Suit yourselves."

Lightning crackled over my skin. I fed the raging storm inside me with more fury. Black clouds swirled around me. The men were brave, though, I had to give them that, because they kept advancing on me anyway. I drew two throwing knives. Thunder boomed as I flicked them towards my attackers.

Surprise mixed with fear in the faces of the remaining two when their partners dropped dead. Their steps faltered. I drew two more knives as dark mist bloomed around me.

"Should've backed away."

Terror had immobilized them so they didn't stand a chance when I hurled the blades at their throats. Dull thuds sounded across the area as they joined their dead friends on the street. I shook my head. Idiots. After yanking my throwing knives from their lifeless bodies, I wiped them off and returned them to my shoulder holsters. Weariness crept up on me.

Shaking my head again, I tried to get rid of it. It didn't work. I squinted at the scene around me right before my knees buckled. Sand coated my cheek as I passed out on the dirt road next to my victims.

A HAND GRAZED MY BODY. My eyes shot open. Stiletto blades already in my hands, I flew to my feet.

"Ain't done nothing! Ain't taken nothing!" a man called as he sprinted away with his hands raised over his head.

Turning in every direction, I tried to make sense of my surroundings. Four dead bodies on the ground. Black smoke still twisting around me. The Sleeping Horse a few strides away. Right. The fight. Tilting my head up, I checked the position of the moon.

"Huh, haven't been out that long," I mumbled before heaving a deep sigh. "I need a drink."

After taking another bracing breath, I strode through the tavern door. Cheerful chatter and laughter met me inside but it all fell silent when I made it into the room. With eyes still black as death, I turned to Hestor at the bar.

"An ale. And keep the shots coming."

He nodded. His hand fumbled while filling the ale mug. I took it and stalked to the table I had sat at earlier. It was now occupied by another couple but they scrambled out of the way when they saw me coming. Wood creaked as I dropped into the chair and slammed the mug down on the table.

Once the rest of the patrons understood that I was only there to drink and not to kill anyone, conversation started back up. Hesitantly and discreetly at first, but it soon grew in strength again. Their merriment did not rub off on me but I kept watching them as I drank anyway. Meera kept bringing me new glasses as soon as the ones on my table were empty.

Horses whinnied and snorted outside. My table was close to the door at the back of the tavern so I could hear when riders tied their horses there. The thick metal rings banged against the wooden wall every time. However, this time there was no metallic noise. Only neighing animals. The door banged open.

"Ey, nobody moves!" a man's voice shouted as he barreled through the back entrance.

Three more men and a woman bust in behind him. They all brandished loaded crossbows. Several of the tavern's occupants shot up from their chairs and made as if to reach for weapons.

"I said sit your asses back down!" the young man shouted again. He ran a hand through his matted brown hair and flashed a toothy grin. "Or we gonna have some dead bodies droppin' real soon."

Taking a long drink of ale, I rolled my eyes. *Seriously?* Why did everything always have to happen on the same bloody day?

The two blond men moved their crossbow bolts between different parts of the crowd until everyone had sat back down. Still grinning, the leader moved towards the bar. The woman and the remaining man took up position behind him.

"Now then, old man," the brown-haired man said to Hestor. "Hand over them money."

The tavern keeper glared at him, but faced with two crossbows he could do nothing except reach for the money pouches stored behind the counter. Livia's young face peeked out of the kitchen door but was quickly pulled back by her mother. Next to a large table of six, Meera stood frozen with a pitcher of wine in her hand.

The leader snatched up the pouches with greedy hands as soon as Hestor held them out. When he turned around, his toothy grin widened. Meera took a step back once she noticed that his gaze had fallen on her.

"Now what have we here?" he said. "Ain't you a beauty."

After securing the pouches to his belt, he took a step towards the beautiful singer. Her father roared and darted around the counter but was stopped by the crossbow-wielding man in front of him. Wood vibrated as he slammed Hestor's face into the bar. While twisting his arm behind his back, the robber placed the crossbow bolt against the tavern keeper's neck.

The leader continued his trek towards Meera. She backed away until she hit the far wall. Terror bloomed in her blue eyes.

"Now, darlin', don't be afraid," he cooed. "You gonna come with us."

Metal dinged against wood as Meera dropped the pitcher she'd been holding when the brown-haired robber's hand snaked around her wrist. He pulled her towards him.

"No, please," she begged. "Please, don't."

The man shoved her in front of him and jerked his head to his partners. They all started moving towards the back door. By the bar, Hestor shouted into the wood while Meera shrieked and whimpered in the toothy man's grip. Closing my eyes briefly, I heaved an exasperated sigh. Why couldn't people just let me drink in peace? At least, that's what I told myself was the reason I shot to my feet.

Five surprised robbers stared at the black-eyed girl who had slunk along the wall and now blocked their way out. I met their gaze with an even stare.

"Get your hands off her, drop the money, and get the hell out right now." I swept hard eyes over the five of them. "Or you all die."

The leader laughed and nodded in my direction. "Who is this freak?"

"Out!" I screamed. Thunder punctuated the word. "Or die."

"Look at her. Look. Smoke's coming out of her." The man with the toothy grin snickered. "Ain't this the weirdest shit you've ever seen?"

Dark clouds exploded around us. Terrified shrieks and scraping furniture filled the room as the tavern's patrons dove for cover when lightning flashed and deafening thunder echoed off the walls. I drew my hunting knives. With the black smoke obscuring everyone's vision, the attackers didn't stand a chance. Blades slashed through flesh and wet gurgles mingled with the screaming. Dull thuds sounded as bodies dropped.

When the dark mist finally withdrew and the occupants peeked out from under the tables, they found five dead robbers and a Storm Caster standing in the middle of the carnage. I wiped my hunting knives on the dead leader's pants. After sticking the blades back in their sheaths, I returned to my table by the wall.

All eyes in the room watched me as I sat down and picked up my mug. Leaning back and crossing my ankles, I went back to drinking my ale in peace. The silence was so loud it was deafening. I wasn't even sure anyone breathed while they tried to process what had just happened. Then, the spell broke and Hestor ran over to Meera.

The blond woman flung herself into her father's arms while tears streamed down her face. He stroked her long flowing hair while making soothing sounds. Black swirls twisted around my arms as I picked up a shot glass and emptied it into my mouth. I was so tired. By Nemanan, was it even possible to be this tired?

When I reached down to put the glass back on the table, I had to blink repeatedly to have a clear view of the tabletop. The glass clattered and toppled over when the surface turned out to be further down than expected. My fingers fumbled as I tried to straighten it. Darkness pressed in from the corner of my eyes and before I had managed to get the glass upright again, I slumped forward and blacked out on the table.

FINGERS HOVERED OVER my body. My mind snapped to attention and my hand shot out and grabbed the person's wrist. A startled yelp sounded. I blinked at the room around me and found Hestor standing next to my table which was still filled with toppled shot glasses and spilled alcohol. Exhaling deeply, I let go of his wrist.

"Are you okay?" Hestor asked.

"No."

He looked at me, concern filling his eyes.

I gave him a tired smile. "But it's alright. I haven't been okay in quite some time."

His kind brown eyes met my still black ones. "What's your name?"

"People call me the Oncoming Storm."

A small laugh bubbled from his chest. "I can see why." He placed a hand on my shoulder. "Thank you for what you did today. Please know that you are welcome to stay here as long as you like."

Dipping my chin, I gave him a smile. "Thanks. Oh, and you don't happen to know where I can find other Storm Casters, do you?"

Hestor shook his head. "I'm afraid not. But I'll keep an ear out and let you know if I hear anything."

"Thanks." I placed my palms on the wooden tabletop and pushed to my feet. "I really gotta go sleep somewhere that isn't a table."

The tavern keeper chuckled and patted me on the shoulder before heading back to the bar. All around us, people still ate and drank. The bodies of the dead robbers were nowhere to be seen and the only trace of the fight was the splatters of blood that Merina was mopping off the planks. People watched me warily as I passed their tables.

What a day this had turned into. Three fights and ten dead bodies in the span of a few hours. No wonder I was exhausted. And then there was of course the darkness. Black smoke still snaked around my limbs and it always left me drained after I'd used it. This time, however, it appeared as though it refused to leave. As I reached my room I couldn't help wondering if it was here to stay forever.

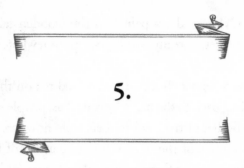

5.

Days turned into weeks but I had no idea exactly how long it had been since I arrived in the quaint town of Travelers' Rest. My existence had whittled down to three states. Drunk out of my mind. Physical pain and bloody fights shrouded in a cloud of black haze. And unconsciousness. Given that I was often blacking out several times a day and that I was barely conscious even when I was awake, it was difficult to tell how much time had passed.

I watched the dark smoke play over my skin before tilting my head up to gaze at the sky. Stars glittered in the heavens and decorated the dark blue night in silver dust. I wondered if Liam was watching the same stars. Had he thought about me while I'd been gone? I hoped so. And at the same time, not. I had left my best friend without saying goodbye because I knew that he would try to stop me. He was probably still mad about that.

While drumming my fingers on the roof tiles, I considered what to do next. I might not know exactly how much time I'd spent in Travelers' Rest but I knew it was a lot. Every person I'd come across, I'd asked about the Storm Casters. Hestor and Merina had done the same in their tavern. No one knew anything.

Warm winds blew across the rooftops. I took a deep breath. Maybe it was time to move on. The answers weren't going to come to me, as it had turned out, so maybe it was time I started looking for them myself again. I nodded at the empty night. Yes. It was time to leave.

Climbing back in through the window, I started packing up my belongings. Once everything was safely stored in my backpack, I slunk down the stairs and approached Merina at the bar. A handful of patrons still lingered in the tavern, drinking the night away.

"You're leaving," she stated.

"Yeah." I gave her a sad smile. "Time to move on. I've paid for the rest of the week. Keep it. And tell Livia and the others I said goodbye, will you?"

Merina nodded. "Livia will miss you. And Silver." When I said nothing, she went on. "Good luck with everything."

After nodding back, I turned and strode towards the front entrance. The door was yanked open. I froze. So did the person who had just stepped across the threshold.

"What the hell are you doing here?" I blurted out.

Elaran drew his eyebrows down. "What do you think? Looking for you."

His yellow eyes flicked over my body, assessing my appearance. I knew what they found. Eyes black as death, a thin coat of dark mist twisting around me, and bruises in various stages of healing covering my cheekbones and jaw. Elaran crossed his arms. If he was shocked by the state I was in, he hid it well.

"Reports have been trickling in to Pernula about a madwoman covered in black smoke and lightning raising hell in

Travelers' Rest," the elf said. "We all knew it could only be one person so Shade–"

"Shade," I interrupted and blew out an annoyed breath. "Of course. So he sent you here to... what? Straighten me out?" Shaking my head, I spun around and stalked towards the back exit instead. "I think I liked it better when you two were trying to kill each other."

Curious eyes followed me from every occupied table as I stomped through the room. Merina had watched the exchange from behind the counter and when I passed her, she leaned forward.

"Do you need help?" she asked in a quiet voice.

Knowing that Elaran and his elven super senses would've heard her anyway, I didn't bother keeping my voice down when I replied. "No, I'm alright. Thanks, Merina. Him and I go way back. He's just a really annoying one, is all."

Elaran muttered something under his breath while following me towards the back of the room. I probably couldn't outrun him but that didn't mean I couldn't damn well try. Yanking the door open, I strode out into the empty stabling area outside. A man appeared from the shadows.

"Oh for Nemanan's sake!" I huffed and threw my arms in the air.

Shade ran his eyes up and down my body. "You look like hell."

Behind me, Elaran had exited the tavern and closed the back door. No chance to retreat that way. I stalked forward, intending to skirt around the assassin and head for the stable, but as soon as I got close, Shade took a step to the side and blocked my path.

He grabbed my chin and tilted my face to the side so that the bruises became more visible. "You need to stop this."

I slapped his hand away. "I don't need to do anything. And besides, why do you care if I drink myself to death or get my throat slit in some street fight?"

Strange emotions flashed over Shade's face but I was too pissed off to decipher them. After another couple of seconds, they were gone and that usual unreadable mask of his had settled on his face.

"I don't," he countered. "I care that you're making trouble for Pernula. Your little storm cloud theatrics have started to draw attention. In case you didn't know, we're very close to star elf-occupied territory and they're known to investigate reports of potential magic users." Shade scowled at me. "Pernula and Sker are the only unoccupied countries left. Do you understand that? We can't afford to draw the star elves' attention here so you need to calm the fuck down."

Flicking a hand dismissively, I took a step forward, intending to bypass him. "I don't take orders from you."

Steel scraped against scabbards as Shade drew his twin swords. I rolled my eyes.

"Seriously?" I muttered but dropped my backpack and yanked the hunting knives from the small of my back.

That distinct ringing of swords being drawn echoed behind me as well. I whirled around to find Elaran with his two elven swords in his hands. He had taken quite a shine to those blades since receiving them from Zaina all those months ago and now he always wore both his massive black bow across his back and the two swords at his hips. As if he needed any more weapons to be deadly.

"*Seriously?*" I repeated with even more force and flicked my gaze between the two fighters. Shaking my head, I blew out an annoyed breath. "Well, let's get on with it then."

Shade and Elaran started circling me while I crouched into an attack position. Without warning, they both sprang forward. I ducked and twisted out of reach as their swords whizzed through the air. Moving in terrifyingly synchronized tandem, they whirled around and darted past each other until they both could approach from either side. Feigning another direction change, they both flashed forward and swung a sword at me.

Throwing up my arms, I managed to block both strikes with my hunting knives but my victory was short-lived. Since both my hands were busy blocking the swords, I could do nothing as Elaran and Shade used their free arms to slam a fist down on my wrists. The knives flew from my hands and clattered to the ground.

With a blade from each fighter against my throat, they backed me into the wall. One of the thick metal rings used to tie up horses dug into my back as Elaran shoved me the last bit into the wooden planks. I glared at them.

"What are you gonna do now? Huh? Kill me?"

Shade returned his swords to his shoulders and reached down for something in his bag. After straightening again, he closed in on me and leaned forward until he was almost pressed against me. I scowled at him from over the edge of Elaran's blade. Then I felt something around my wrists. *No way.* However, I didn't react fast enough because a metallic click sounded. Shade withdrew and Elaran removed his sword from my throat. I stared at them wide-eyed.

"You handcuffed me?" I yanked at the manacles locking my wrists to the thick metal ring behind my back. My voice rose in anger and disbelief. "You fucking handcuffed me?"

Shade took a firm grip on my jaw and forced me to look at him. "You are out of control."

"You bastard!" I snapped. "I will kill you for this."

"I'm sure you will try. And it will end exactly like this next time too." He let go of me and turned around. "Now stay here while we get everything sorted before we leave."

"You son of a bitch!" I screamed as Shade and Elaran disappeared around the corner towards the front of the house. Metal clanked as I pulled against my restraints. "I will kill you! Do you hear me?"

As soon as they were gone, my fingers went in search of the lockpicks I'd sewn into the back of my belt. After prying them loose, I got to work on the locks. Once I was free, I stalked over to my dropped knives and after having snatched them up, I grabbed my backpack and made for the front of the tavern.

The dirt square on the other side was empty except for Elaran, Shade, and their two horses. A strong wind blew a cloud of dust across the area. Or maybe it was me? Anger coursed through me like a deadly current. How dared he? How dared he shackle me to a bloody wall? While gripping the hunting knives so hard the handles almost snapped, I advanced on them.

"You thought you could handcuff me?" Lightning crackled over my skin and the dark clouds grew around me. "I'm a thief. Don't you think the first thing I learned was how to get out of handcuffs?"

Uncertainty filled their eyes as both of them moved away from the horses. Elaran held up his hands in an appeasing gesture as he approached me.

"Calm down. You're not yourself right now."

"Get out of my way," I growled, my eyes locked on the assassin behind him.

The elf refused to move. He continued straight towards me but before he could say anything else, I cut him off.

"I said *get out of my way*!" Thunder boomed in the huge clouds around me and a strong wind pushed Elaran aside.

He seemed as surprised as I was to see him standing several strides away from his original position. I had no idea if I was responsible for that, but at that moment I didn't care. My mind was lost to a torrent of fury. The black mist pressed in on me and I disappeared into its deadly embrace. I launched myself at the assassin.

A voice called to me. Saying my name. It sounded very far away but I was sure it was talking to me. I swore I knew that voice from somewhere.

"Storm!" the voice said again.

It sounded urgent. Frightened. I tried to remember where I was and what was going on but holding on to a single thought was as slippery as holding a wet eel. At last, my vision started to return. When the black haze had finally disappeared, my mind had trouble processing the scene around me.

Elaran stood next to me with his hands raised. They hovered over my shoulder as if he wanted to touch it but couldn't quite bring himself to do it. When he kept repeating my name, I realized that he was the source of the scared voice.

In front of me, Shade stood pressed against the wall with a knife to his throat. The expression in his eyes was an odd one. He looked... afraid. I squinted at the weapon causing such strange emotions. The blade was connected to a hand. Blood trickled down Shade's pale neck. Blood caused by a shallow wound made by a sharp edge pushed into his skin. A sharp edge *I* was pushing into his skin. Reality slammed back down on me like a block of stone. What had I done?

Horrified, I jerked back and dropped the knife as if it had burned me. Stumbling back another step, I stared at him with wide eyes. And then something unexpected happened. For the first time in... weeks? Months? The darkness snapped back and disappeared into the deep pits of my soul.

"I almost killed you," I stammered. Raking my fingers through my hair, I raised my voice to a shout. "By all the gods, I almost killed you!"

Shade's black eyes softened as he looked at me. Even Elaran's usually grumpy features took on a look of sympathy. Shaking my head, I put a hand over my mouth and ran over to the corner of the building. I barely made it there before I threw up. And then again. And again.

Once the convulsing had stopped, I leaned against the wall and wiped a hand over my mouth. For a while, I just stood there, trying to wrap my mind around what I had almost done. When I failed that, I drew a deep breath and turned around to face my mistakes. I looked from face to face. Immense relief flooded through me when neither of them flinched at my gaze. I walked back towards them on unsteady feet.

Shade placed his hands on my shoulders when I reached them. "Are you alright?"

A weary laugh bubbled from my throat. "Am I alright?" I drew two fingers beneath the thin red line on his throat. Even stronger relief surged through my body when he didn't draw back from my touch. "I almost killed you. I should be the one asking you that." I held his gaze steadily. "I'm sorry."

"Wait. Did you just apologize?" A mischievous grin spread across his mouth as he let go of my shoulders and turned to Elaran. "Did you hear that? Storm apologized. Has she ever done that to you before?"

The elf shook his head. "No."

"Me neither. This is something for the history books."

I gave Shade's shoulder a push. "It's not funny! I could've killed you."

"Yeah, right." The Master Assassin smirked at me. "As if I'd let that happen."

Not being able to help myself, I released a soft chuckle and shook my head.

Elaran gave my shoulder a quick squeeze. "Glad you're yourself again."

Before I could respond, he wandered back to his horse. Despite everything they'd seen, everything I'd done, neither of them was angry with me. Or afraid of me. I didn't know which was more astonishing.

Unfortunately, the same couldn't be said for me. *I* was afraid of me. Of what I could do. Clearly, I had even less control over the darkness than I thought. That was dangerous. And Elaran had it all wrong. I still wasn't myself again. Pain continued to bleed from my heart and that profound loss of identity still plagued me, swallowing my soul like a vortex. How long before

I needed alcohol or physical pain to dull it again? How long before I lost myself in the darkness again?

"Let's get back to Pernula before the star elves come knocking, shall we?" Shade's mouth drew into a lopsided smile as he strode towards his horse.

I nodded. "Yeah."

After adjusting my backpack, I went to retrieve my missing knife. Right after I slid it back in its sheath, movement in the corner of my eye made me freeze. The three of us exchanged a glance. Without a word, we all clustered together in tight formation. No one drew weapons. Yet. But Elaran's palms rested on the pommels of his swords and I felt the comforting weight of the stilettos in my sleeves. To my right, I was sure Shade did something similar.

From the deep shadows around us, tall figures approached. They didn't appear to be carrying weapons but the three of us remained alert anyway. A shocked gasp rose from Elaran's throat.

"What?" I hissed.

But before he could explain what his superior eyesight had revealed, the mysterious group of people exited the shadows, making it possible for me to see them as well. My mouth dropped open.

Elves in intricately decorated white armor moved gracefully through the night. The silver decorations carved into their breastplates accentuated the long silvery white hair that flowed freely or was held back by a simple tie. Pale violet eyes met me as I stared into the face of the closest one.

"Star elves?" I whispered.

"Yeah," Shade breathed.

Everyone stopped a few strides away except for a serious-looking elf who appeared to be in charge. He took one more step towards us before coming to a halt.

His violet eyes found mine. "You are Ashaana."

Since I wasn't sure if being a Storm Caster would help us or get us killed, I decided that the best course of action was to say nothing.

The leader of the star elves fixed me with an iron stare. "There is no point in denying it. We all saw what you did just now." He swept his gaze to my companions. "The question is, are you Ashaana as well?"

Shade and Elaran seemed to be of a similar mind to me because they remained silent. When in doubt, it was always best to neither confirm nor deny anything. The authoritative star elf raised his eyebrows expectantly. When he finally understood that no answer was forthcoming, he shook his head and gave us an irritated flick of his wrist.

"I guess we will find out," he muttered just as something made of glass shattered behind us.

We all whirled around while reaching for our weapons. None of us made it. A purple mist rose and enveloped us from all sides. I only had time to register the glass shard lying on the dusty ground before I, too, found myself face down on that same surface. The last thing I saw before the black void swallowed me was elves in white armor closing in on us.

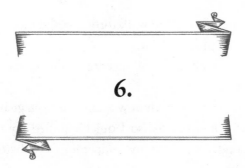

6.

A jolt sent me flying into the metal wall. When the carriage's wheel dropped down on the other side of the surprise speed bump, I had to brace myself on the floor to avoid getting tossed in the other direction.

I was seated at the back wall of what I assumed to be a prisoner transport carriage since the door opposite me was locked shut. Only a small window to my left illuminated the space. I swept my gaze over the assassin under the window and the elf opposite him before reaching for a pair of lockpicks.

The manacles clicked open within a matter of seconds. I placed them on the floor soundlessly while Shade did the same with his own handcuffs.

Elaran raised his still shackled wrists. "A little help?"

The Master Assassin scooted over to the elf while I staved off a chuckle. Once Elaran was free of his restraints as well, I stood up and peered out the window. Jagged rocks rose in hulking shapes a short distance away. It was the perfect place to disappear to when running from one's pursuers.

"Can't you just pick the lock on the door too?" Elaran muttered.

"No." I frowned at him. "The lock is on the outside. So unless you can walk through solid metal, there's no way to pick it. Not to mention that if we could walk through solid metal, we would have no need to pick the lock."

The grumpy elf drew his eyebrows down. "A simple no would've sufficed."

I glanced outside the window again. An elven guard in white armor walked right outside so I quickly pulled my head back. Turning around, I met both my companions' eyes before flicking a hand dismissively.

"It's not my fault that you ask such stupid questions," I said.

Elaran shot to his feet. "What did you say?"

"You heard me."

The tall elf took a step towards me and raised his voice. "I'm so sick of your arrogance! It's your fault that we're in this mess."

"He's right," Shade added. "If it weren't for you and your storm cloud fights, the star elves would never have found us." Raking his fingers through his black hair, he released a loud groan and raised his voice to a shout. "You're so damn careless!"

"Hey!" the guard outside called. "Quiet down in there."

Ignoring him, Shade and Elaran both advanced on me.

"My fault?" I yelled at them while retreating towards the back of the carriage. My back hit the wall with a soft thud. "I never asked you to come! If you'd just stayed away this wouldn't be a problem. But no, you just had to be the heroes."

The Master of the Assassins' Guild slammed a fist into the metal next to my head, making the whole wall vibrate. "Watch your mouth!"

Involuntarily, I jerked away a little.

"I said *quiet down*," the star elf outside the window called again.

But his command fell on deaf ears as both Shade and Elaran turned murderous eyes on me. However, before they could do anything, I decided to act first. Putting one hand to the assassin's chest, I shoved him backwards while I aimed a fist at the elf's jaw. Shade stumbled back a step but before my blow connected, Elaran's hand shot out and grabbed my wrist. I barely managed to raise my other arm in defense before his own fist sped towards me.

Loud groans drifted out through the carriage window and mixed with the dull thuds of strikes hitting metal and body parts as both Shade and Elaran attacked me. Throwing up my arms to protect my head, I crouched down against the back wall. The shouts from outside was drowned out by the noise around me but I heard the clanking of keys and bolts by the door.

"Break it up!" someone bellowed from the front of the carriage.

Three elves climbed in through the now open door and stalked towards us. The first two headed for the attackers on either side of me while the last one continued straight towards me.

As one, Shade and Elaran whirled around and drove a fist right into jaws of their respective star elves. Two heads snapped to the side and hit the metal wall. In the second it took the last guard to realize what had happened, I rammed a knee into his groin. He doubled over and was met by Elaran's fist.

"Let's go," Shade hissed.

Without casting a single look back at the three unconscious star elves, we darted from the carriage and sprinted towards the jagged rocks on our left. Clamor and raised voices could be heard from the guards at the front. We all ignored them as we sprinted to safety.

Dark gray rock formations rose around us. Since we had no idea where it led, we were forced to continue running blindly through the stone forest in the hopes of losing our hunters. After a while, Elaran skidded to a halt and drew us in behind a large boulder. My heart slammed against my ribs. While the elf peeked back out to check for pursuers, I tried to get my breathing under control.

"Weren't you supposed to pull your punches?" I muttered at Elaran while massaging my sore shoulder.

He frowned down at me, confusion evident on his face. "That *was* me pulling my punches."

I stared at him. "Oh."

Though I suppose I couldn't complain too much. The fake fight had been my idea, after all. But man, was I glad it hadn't been real. If it hadn't just been a ruse to get the guards to open the door and those two had actually been attacking me, I would probably have ended up with broken bones.

"Besides, you kind of deserved that," Shade added with a teasing smirk. "It actually *is* your fault that we were captured." He gave me a lazy shrug. "But you also got us out of there so now we're even."

Since I wasn't entirely sure if he was joking or not, I just snorted in reply. Regardless of which, I was glad he considered our score settled because being indebted to the Master of the Assassins' Guild was never a good position to find yourself in.

"Yeah that's all well and good but what do we do now?" Elaran demanded. "We don't know how to get back to Pernula."

"They took all our weapons so we can't make a stand," Shade said. "We'll just have to keep running north and then we'll take it from there."

Raised voices came from somewhere behind us. We all exchanged a glance.

Elaran jerked his head. "Let's go."

Shade and I took off after him. Moonlight illuminated our path but navigating through the sharp rocks turned out to be much more difficult than we expected. It was like running in a maze. Suddenly, a dead end would appear out of nowhere and other times, the trail between the large stones would just lead around in circles. Blood pounded in my ears. The star elves were practically snapping at our heels.

"They're gaining on us," Shade pressed out between heavy breaths. "We'll never make it like this."

Making a split-second decision, I screeched to a halt on top of a jagged ridge and swung towards our attackers. "Go!" I called over my shoulder. "I'll hold them off."

"Stop that," the assassin snapped. "You've already made up for your mistake. You're forgiven! Alright? You don't have anything to prove." He yanked at the back of my clothes. "Now come on."

Reluctantly turning back around, I let out a frustrated groan and did as he said. Gravel crunched beneath our feet and rolled down the slope as we sprinted down on the other side. I threw a glance over my shoulder. The star elves had stopped atop the ridge and were pulling something from behind their backs. Shit.

"Bows!" I called. "They're gonna fire."

Projectiles whizzed through the air just as we made it down the hill. We dove for cover. Sharp rocks scraped my skin as I rolled in behind the closest boulder and hunkered down. My heart thumped in my chest.

Glass shattered against stone. I jerked up in time to see purple mist well from the broken crystal orbs tied to every arrow around us. It engulfed the whole area in seconds. *Not again.* Irritation burned through me but there was nothing I could do. Slumping to the ground, my mind disappeared into nothingness for the second time that night. For Nemanan's sake, could we never catch a break?

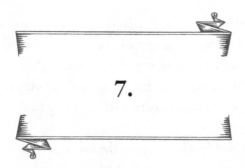

7.

Brilliant white light filled my vision. I shot up and scrambled backwards to what I thought was safety. The surface disappeared beneath my right hand and I tumbled down in heap of tangled cloth.

"Ow," I muttered while trying to disentangle my limbs from the sheets.

Smooth walls and a shining floor matched the furniture in nuances of white. Even the bed I had just fallen off was in that same pale hue. I frowned at it. Straightening, I dropped the bundle of sheets back on the mattress and started forward. My body felt unnaturally light. It took one more confused second to realize why. I stopped dead in my tracks.

My clothes. Whipping my head down, I stared in shock at my body. Someone had removed my clothes and dressed me in... in what? I pinched the thin fabric and pulled at it. A nightgown? Dread welled through me like an icy creek. Someone had stripped me and put me in a white nightdress. I wrapped my arms around me to stave off the feeling of violation while my mind refused to process the situation.

The floor was cold under my bare feet as I stalked towards the large wooden closet pushed up against the opposite wall. Yanking the doors open, I scoured the space for my trusted thief clothes. A mountain of white dresses met me. Panic shot up my spine. I tore through the rest of the room in a mad search for anything that belonged to me. Shirts, pants, vest, boots. Knives. Lockpicks. Stopping in the middle of the now very messy room, I ran my hands through my hair while trying to slow my racing heart. There was no sign of any of it.

When I had finally accepted the fact that all my belongings were gone and that someone had undressed me, the other screams of alarm at last made it to the front of my mind. Where was I? I darted to the window. As my eyes roamed over the scene, I couldn't help letting out a gasp.

Dark gray cliffs stretched from the shining white walls before dropping into the sea beyond. A smooth path had been cut into the rock leading all the way down through the precipices until it disappeared from view and the glittering waves painted gold by the late afternoon sun took its place. I gawked at it.

Wherever it was, it was beautiful. But beauty often hid danger. Shaking my head, I tore my gaze from the stunning view and made for the door. Before I opened it, I bent down to check for shadows under it. Nothing. I straightened and placed my hand on the cool metal handle. If it indeed was locked, I was about to find out.

It slid down without resistance. *Huh*. After drawing a soft breath, I opened a tiny crack in the door. A white corridor appeared on the other side. Flicking my eyes around the empty space, I pushed open the door a little further. My breath hitched. *Shit*.

Silver-decorated armor had materialized right in front of the gap. Raising my eyes, I found a male star elf standing there. Everything from his strong jawline to his posture dripped with authority when his dark violet eyes stared down on me. I cleared my throat and straightened.

"I take it I'm in star elf lands?" I said in a light tone as if I was out for a stroll in the park and not a prisoner in an unknown location.

"Yes, we're in the City of Glass." When I only looked back at him with a bewildered expression on my face, he went on. "In Tkeister. Though you might know it as Star Home."

I didn't recognize any of those names but I didn't want to admit that so I just nodded.

"I will alert Queen Nimlithil that you're awake." The star elf in his spotless white armor let his eyes travel over my body. "You might want to put on some clothes."

Resisting the urge to punch him in the throat, I crossed my arms over my chest and scowled at him. "Well, I'm not the one who decided to wear this in the first place."

"Just do as you're told."

Before I could inform him that I don't specialize in doing as I'm told, he pushed the door shut in my face.

"Rude," I muttered after finishing a rather lengthy string of profanities directed at the elf behind the door.

As much as I loathed taking orders, I had to concede that he did have a point. If I was going to meet the queen of the star elves, I probably shouldn't do it wearing a thin nightgown. The only problem was of course that there was nothing to wear except more damn dresses. I glared at the selection in the closet before picking the plainest one.

There was a mirror on the other side of the wardrobe, but I refused to look in it after putting on the white dress and shoes. I already knew I looked silly in this outfit so there was no need to confirm the fact. Instead, I took to pacing the room.

While I was still trying to figure out how to best play this, the door was pulled open. A beautiful elven woman glided into the room with graceful steps. Her silvery white hair cascaded down around her slender shoulders and accentuated the well-tailored dress of the same color while her loose curls mingled with the headdress made of silver and clear gems. I had once described Faye as liquid starlight but, in all honesty, she had nothing on this woman.

"Queen Nimlithil of Tkeister, queen of the star elves, protector of Tkeiwed, Wegh, Frustaz, and Beccus, and savior of Weraldi," the rude elven guard from before announced as he took up position behind the queen.

Lifting a hand, I gave her a little wave. "The Oncoming Storm, queen of bad decisions, protector of herself, and savior of unguarded valuables."

The guard looked at me like I had just slapped his grandma. Whatever he had expected me to say, that had apparently not been it. His dark violet eyes flashed with displeasure.

Now that I had time to actually study two different star elves up close, I noticed that the color of their hair and eyes weren't identical. The guard's eyes were of a dark violet color while the violet in the queen's eyes was much paler. Their hair sported similar differences with the guard's silver hair being much darker.

"Have you no manners?" he demanded. "When meeting a queen, you bow and then introduce yourself with your real name."

"Yeah, I don't bow." I lifted my shoulders in a nonchalant shrug. "And the Oncoming Storm is my real name."

"It is quite alright, Hadraeth," Queen Nimlithil said to her guard before turning back to me. "You will have to forgive my Guard Captain. He does not realize that you are only acting this way because you are scared and confused." She gave me a kind smile. "I understand."

I was about to point out that I was always like this but changed my mind at the last second. If I wanted to find out where Elaran and Shade were, it was probably best if I didn't offend the ruler of this country. I tipped my head in a quick nod.

"Speaking of being confused," I began. "Where are my friends?"

"They are safe," the star elf queen said. "You will see them tonight. I am sure you have a lot of questions so how about accompanying me for a walk?"

"Sure," I said because I knew I couldn't exactly refuse. And I did have questions.

The Captain of the Queen's Guard, Hadraeth, seemed to disapprove of my casual reply because he narrowed his eyes at me, but he remained silent as he followed us out the door.

Soft rugs made of fine silver threads muffled our steps in the spotless corridor. Mounted on the smooth white walls were intricate candle holders that complemented the carpets in color while the white paintings added to the crisp and clean atmosphere. Almost all hallways we traversed looked the same but I noted every twist and turn on my mental map as we made our way upwards.

A million questions swirled in my mind but there was one that took precedence so I decided to ask it straight away.

"Why am I here?"

"We save wayward souls like you," she replied with a kind smile as we ascended another gleaming staircase. "We can show you a better life."

"A better life?" I frowned at her. "As a prisoner?"

The queen stopped on the steps and looked down at me in surprise. "You are not a prisoner."

"Then I want to leave."

Her well-manicured eyebrows scrunched up as a look of absolute bafflement blew past on her face. "Why would you want to leave?" She started out again. "Come. I will show you the marvel that is the City of Glass."

Fresh air whirled in and filled my lungs when Queen Nimlithil opened the door to a platform. Stepping outside, I let out an involuntary gasp. We were standing on a balcony high up on one side of the castle where you could see the rest of the structure. Soft curving domes and twisting arches gleamed in the sun. Turning my head, I took in the area around it. A large city seemingly made from the same strange material sprawled beneath it and glittered like a white sea. It was breathtaking.

"Welcome to Starhaven," the elegant queen said and motioned at the castle. "The jewel of our city."

Now I understood why the star elf capital was called the City of Glass. The material that everything was built of looked like frosted glass.

"Is it not beautiful?" Nimlithil continued. "This is what we want to bring to everyone. Beauty and peace."

My white dress fluttered in the wind. "Peace? Aren't you the ones waging war and conquering the whole continent?"

"We are trying to save Weraldi. Not destroy it."

Ah. So Weraldi was the name of the continent. I hadn't known that since people usually referred to it as simply *the continent*. Except the star elves, apparently.

"I'd say bringing death and violence to people is classified as destroying, not saving." I shrugged. "But maybe that's just me."

Behind me, Hadraeth fumed but the queen just smiled at me as if I was a particularly slow child she was trying to educate.

"Do you know why I declared pistols outlawed across all of Weraldi?"

I shook my head.

"Because all they do is bring death and violence." She stroked a graceful hand over the balcony railing. "Sword fighting and archery has an art to it but with firearms, you do not even need any skills. You simply point and pull the trigger. They can only fire one bullet now but how long until someone invents one that can fire, say, ten bullets?"

That was indeed a terrifying thought.

"Imagine the death and destruction that would bring," Queen Nimlithil said, her voice filled with distress. "Countries fight and kill to get ahead of each other and what does this technological development lead to? They are cutting down the forests, polluting the water, destroying arable land." She flicked a hand and clicked her tongue in disgust. "We do not conquer, as you said, we are freeing cities of immoral leaders and giving them peace and a bright future."

I opened my mouth but then closed it again. As much as I didn't want to admit it, she did have a point. But I still wasn't sure how I felt. Was stopping progress really the best way to go? It had brought a lot of good things too, after all. Zaina's question from all those months ago popped up in my head again. *What do you want?* I had no idea what I wanted or what I thought about everything I had learned about the star elves this afternoon.

Queen Nimlithil seemed to understand because she placed an elegant hand on my arm. "You need time to take this all in. Captain Hadraeth will escort you back to your room and I will see you again at the banquet."

"Banquet? What banquet?" I asked but the star elf queen was already gliding away, her sparkling dress billowing behind her.

The wind had blown strands of dark silver hair in front of Hadraeth's shoulders. Grabbing his long flowing hair in a fist, he flipped it back behind him again before jerking his chin at me.

"Let's go."

I scowled at the rude elf but followed him down the stairs anyway. My mind kept spinning the whole way back. This was not at all how I had pictured the star elves. Queen Nimlithil actually did have some pretty convincing arguments for what they were doing. As we rounded the corner of yet another white hallway, I shook my head.

If the star elves' actions were justified or not wasn't important. My concern was for three things: Shade, Elaran, and getting the hell out of here. As my scheming mind filled in more spots on my mental map, I wondered if my friends were spending their time doing the same before this banquet we were apparently forced to attend.

Oh, who was I kidding? It was Shade and Elaran. Of course they were scheming and strategizing as well. The entrance to my room appeared further down a long corridor filled with more white doors. I dared a quick smile. The star elves would never know what hit them.

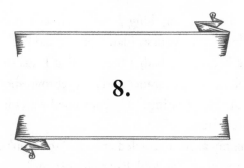

8.

Three sharp knocks broke my scheming session. I strode to the door and yanked it open. A silver-haired elf with a neutral expression on his long face met me outside.

"The banquet is about to start," he announced. "Please follow me."

Without waiting for a reply, he swung around and started down the corridor. The door behind me closed with a soft click. Even if I'd actually had a key, I wouldn't have bothered locking it because nothing in there was mine anyway.

"One moment, please," the elf said as he stopped outside the white door next to mine and rapped his knuckles on it.

It was shoved open. "What?" demanded a voice I recognized very well.

"The banquet is about to start," the star elf with the long face announced once again. "Please follow me."

Elaran gave him a curt nod and stalked across the threshold. I looked him up and down. The tight side braid he always wore gathered up the hair on his right side but the rest of his auburn hair fell down his back and left shoulder, painting the white shirt with silver buttons in stark contrast. White pants and shoes completed the outfit.

I stared at him. "What the hell are you wearing?"

It was so unlike anything I had ever seen him in that I couldn't help myself. At first, Elaran just jerked back in surprise at the sound because he hadn't realized that I was there as well. Then he took in my appearance and his eyebrows shot up.

"What are *you* wearing?" He continued watching me, eyes wide. "Is that a dress?"

Crossing my arms, I scowled at him. "You don't look like a woodsman anymore. You look like a city person."

He drew his eyebrows down and huffed with indignation at such an insult, but before he could counter, three quick knocks sounded at the next door. Realizing that our escort had already made it there, we exchanged a look and jogged to catch up.

After the star elf had repeated the same announcement for the third time, a black-haired man wearing a well-tailored white suit stepped out the door. Coming to a halt a few paces away, I studied him. As with Elaran, I had never seen Shade wear that color before. I preferred him in black but I couldn't deny that he looked just fine in that suit as well. Catching myself, I shook my head vigorously. How ridiculous. Who was I to prefer him in anything?

Shade's dark eyebrows arched upwards when he saw us. Saw me. "Are you wearing a dress?"

"Wanna switch?" I muttered before crossing my arms over the plain white fabric. "There wasn't anything else to wear."

"Of course there are only dresses in your closet," our guide interrupted. "Women should not wear pants. It is indecent." He cast me a befuddled look before motioning with his hand. "Now, please follow me."

A culture where women were not allowed to wear what they wanted. Oh, joy. I blew out a sigh and stalked after him with Elaran and Shade next to me.

None of us said anything as we moved through the gleaming halls. Occasionally, we would meet other star elves who were heading in the same direction we were. They didn't appear surprised to see us. Maybe that whole thing about often taking in wayward souls, as Queen Nimlithil had put it, had actually been the truth.

Before long, a vast dining room became visible in the distance. When we crossed into the room filled with long tables and cushioned chairs, I had to resist shielding my eyes.

All the furniture was made of white wood, and both the cushions and the tablecloths were of the same color. Candelabras and ornate decorations created from silver and white gems adorned the space. And then there were the elves. Hair colors spanned from dark silver to pure white and every single piece of garment in the room fit that color scheme as well.

I shook my head. "What in Nemanan's name is their obsession with white and silver?"

Next to me, Shade's mouth twitched into a quick lopsided smile but Elaran just continued scowling at the scene around us. Our guide kept his long face completely neutral as he ignored my comment and led us to the front of the room. Merry chatter hung over the hall.

Shade nudged an elbow in my arm and jerked his head up.

Craning my neck, I tipped my head back to see what it was. *Whoa.* I let out a low whistle. The dome that covered the banquet hall was made of glass. Not of the frosted kind that appeared to be present everywhere else, though. Here, it was completely see-through and glittering stars shone against the dark night outside the crystal ceiling. Okay, that was kind of cool.

The star elf escorting us came to a halt. I flicked my eyes over the area. A high table with room for only one was positioned by the wall in front of us and then all the other tables branched out from there. Our guide had stopped at the one closest to the high table.

"This will be your seat," he said and motioned between Elaran and a white chair. After taking a quick step to the side in order to skip the seat right next to it, he patted the back of another chair. "And this is you."

Shade took up position behind the indicated furniture just as the star elf turned to me.

"And you," he began while rounding the table, "you will sit here."

It was close to Elaran and Shade but not directly opposite either of them. Whatever seating arrangements these people had, it appeared as though there were some very specific rules behind it.

"Your table companions will arrive shortly." And with that, the star elf escort with the long face twirled around and glided back through the room.

The three of us exchanged a look.

"What now?" I asked.

Elaran shrugged at me from across the table. "I don't know."

All around us, more star elves trickled in and took up position behind the remaining chairs. A well-dressed couple claimed the seats only a few strides away. Rippling giggles floated through the air as the female elf laughed at something her partner had said. I studied them. It wouldn't be long before whoever was going to occupy the spots between us showed up as well.

"Did you meet Queen Nimlithil?" Shade asked, keeping his voice low. When he watched us both nod, he went on. "What did you tell her?"

"Only my name," I said.

The assassin gave me a quick nod. "Same. Elaran?"

"My name." He furrowed his brows. "And where I'm from."

A whole group of star elves in beautiful dresses and suits were rapidly making their way towards us.

Shade flicked his gaze between us. "Good. Try to keep it that way."

We didn't have time to reply because our table companions had reached us, so we settled for a brief nod.

"You must be Mother's special guests," said a gorgeous elf with loose curls cascading around her, while she glided towards the chair next to Elaran.

Mother? Wait. Did that mean...?

"Yes, they are, Princess Illeasia," a familiar voice said. "I met them all earlier this afternoon."

I narrowed my eyes slightly as Captain Hadraeth stopped behind the chair next to mine. The princess behind the chair opposite him fired off a sparkling smile.

"It was a rhetorical question, Hadraeth." She winked at the now embarrassed-looking guard. "Who else would they be?"

"Of course, Princess Illeasia," he said and dipped his head. "Forgive me."

While she and the Guard Captain had stated the obvious, I had taken the time to study her more closely. Yep. There was no question about it. This was Queen Nimlithil's daughter. In terms of looks, they were almost identical with the same shade of silvery white hair, pale violet eyes, and elegant features. But there was one difference.

Where the queen had exuded power with every graceful step, this princess emitted something else. It took another few seconds before I realized what it was. Life. Her whole being practically sparkled with the joy of living.

"I think it was a considerate clarification," another female elf said as she planted herself by the empty chair between Elaran and Shade. "Captain Hadraeth is always so kind."

"Yes, of course you're right, Nelyssae," Princess Illeasia said before turning her head and sending an apologetic smile in the captain's direction. "I didn't mean it like that."

Nelyssae beamed at him but the Captain of the Guards appeared to only have eyes for the princess. When she didn't receive the reaction she had hoped for, Nelyssae flicked her straight white hair back behind her shoulder. Her pale violet eyes settled on me.

"Oh, by the Stars," she exclaimed and put a hand over her full lips. "Did no one help you dress for this banquet?"

I glanced between my perfectly average body in the plain dress and her gem- and silver-decorated gown and the luscious figure it accentuated.

"Uhm..." I so eloquently replied while swatting at the insecurity sneaking up behind me.

"Poor thing." Nelyssae ran a delicate hand over the gleaming jewelry around her neck. "No wonder you're so badly dressed. I promise, we will get someone to help you next time." She scrunched up her manicured eyebrows while scrutinizing the rest of my body. "And to find some makeup to cover those awful bruises."

Not sure whether to thank her or stab her, I ended up settling for a frown. When a few other elven ladies giggled further down the table, I couldn't help thinking that it was me they were laughing about.

"I think the dress is rather elegant in its simplicity," a male elf said as he claimed the last remaining seat. The one on my other side. He turned to me. "Hello. I am Niadhir."

"The Oncoming Storm," I replied automatically.

His pale violet eyes filled with confusion. "Pardon?"

"My name. It's the Oncoming Storm."

A quite unladylike snort sounded from Nelyssae before she covered her mouth with the back of her hand and broke into giggles. Anger pulsated through my body. It was only by sheer force of will that I kept the black out of my eyes.

"Lords and ladies!" a voice called from somewhere down the room before I could say something highly inappropriate to the rude lady. "Queen Nimlithil."

Silence fell over the vast hall as the queen of the star elves glided through the room. The train of her bejeweled dress swooshed as it trailed behind her on the floor. When she reached the carved chair by the high table, she lifted an elegant hand and smiled at the gathered elves.

"Welcome, my friends," she said, "to another beautiful evening. We have three guests of honor here today. Let us show them the grace and splendor that is Starhaven." She swept her arms outwards. "Please be seated."

Chairs scraped and clothes rustled as the entire banquet hall took their seats. Shade, Elaran, and I exchanged a glance.

Whatever we were in for, we had to keep it together. Anxiety bubbled through me. Social gatherings weren't exactly my forte and now I was seated with both the Princess of Tkeister and the Captain of the Guard. Slipping up now would be terrible for us.

After dropping into the chair, I studied the array of utensils in front of me. I didn't even know what I was supposed to do with half of them. Wasn't one fork and knife enough to eat with? When I raised my eyes, I found Lady Nelyssae giving me a smile as beautiful as it was malicious. And then there was her. Yep. This was definitely going to be an interesting dinner.

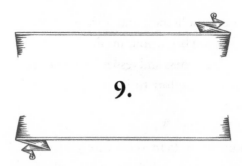

9.

Heavenly scents drifted across the room. I turned my head to find smartly-dressed elves weaving through the tables while carrying large silver trays. They started by placing a plate in front of Queen Nimlithil and once she had given them a nod of approval, they continued down the tables.

I squinted suspiciously at the small silver plate being placed before me. There was salad on there, of that much I was sure, and also something that looked like cheese. Fried cheese. After another brief glance over the numerous utensils around the dish, I concluded that I still had no idea which ones to use so I just picked up a random fork from somewhere in the middle.

"What are you doing?" Lady Nelyssae hissed.

Stopping with the fork hovering halfway to the strange cheese, I frowned at her. "Eating?"

"You don't eat until everyone at the table has received their food."

"What in Nemanan's name does their food have to do with mine?"

On my left, Captain Hadraeth harrumphed. "You have no manners. First when greeting Queen Nimlithil, and now this."

Before I could retort, the elf to my right, Niadhir, placed a hand on my arm and supplied an answer to my original question.

"It is a gesture of politeness and a show of respect to wait for everyone before you begin your meal."

Of course. Politeness and respect, my two greatest strengths. It took considerable effort to keep the sarcasm from my voice when I replied.

"Right. Obviously."

Returning my fork to the white tablecloth, I waited for everyone else to receive their food as well. Shade cast me an amused look. He just had time to see the scowl I directed at him in reply before Lady Nelyssae reclaimed his attention with a question. On the white-haired lady's other side, Elaran and Princess Illeasia were deep in discussion. I flicked my gaze between the two people flanking me.

To my left, a serious-looking guard in immaculate armor and on the other side, a scholarly-looking elf in a crisp white suit with his hair tied back by a silver ring. Out of the two, the one on my right seemed like the easiest interrogation target. I turned to Niadhir.

"Queen Nimlithil said that she often takes in what she called *wayward* souls," I said. "Have you met any of them?"

"Oh, of course," Niadhir replied. "I have met all of them."

Lifting a hand, I motioned at the room full of elves. "Where are they now? There are only star elves in here as far as I can tell."

"They have left. As they all do, when they are ready. Queen Nimlithil helps them find their purpose in life and once they have, they return to their homes to fulfill it." He gave me a kind smile. "What about you? What is your purpose in life?"

A cold fist gripped my heart, squeezing out more blood from the wounds in it. When we'd been captured by these star elves, my mind had snapped into survival mode and the pain bleeding from my heart had receded to a muted dripping. If nothing else, getting ambushed and kidnapped had been a great distraction from the burning anguish inside my soul. But now it was back.

"I, uhm..." I began.

Fortunately, I was saved from having to reply because everyone at our table had at last received their food. Princess Illeasia lifted her glass goblet.

"To the beauty and grace of the stars," she said.

"To the beauty and grace of the stars," the rest of the table echoed while raising their own glasses.

Elaran, Shade, and I exchanged a look but lifted our crystal goblets as well. The pale liquid inside tasted sweet and flowery. It had to be some kind of wine. After returning the glass to the table, I picked up a random fork from the middle of the row next to my plate and stabbed at the fried cheese.

Giggling rang out from across the table. I flicked my eyes up to find Nelyssae covering her lips with the back of her hand again. Scowling, I continued my attack on the piece of cheese. More snickering rose from Nelyssae.

"What?" I demanded, slamming the fork back on the table.

All the star elves around me drew back a little in surprise at my violent outburst. Niadhir recovered first and placed a hand on my arm again.

"That is not the right fork for this course." He pointed at the fork and knife at the very end of the row. "As a rule, you start here and then work your way in."

Obviously. Because gods forbid we got to the point of the meal where we actually ate something. No, first we had to wait for everyone else to get their food and then we had to catalogue every single piece of cutlery on the table to make sure we used the almost identical utensils in the right order. Why had that not been my first conclusion?

However, instead of informing my table companions about that, I plastered a smile on my face and turned to Niadhir. "Thanks."

The rest of the banquet continued in much the same fashion. Me trying to figure out what was on my plate and how I was supposed to eat it without making a fool of myself, while Nelyssae and her friends down the table snickered behind their jewel-bedecked hands. When she wasn't busy making me feel like an uninvited goat, Nelyssae was chirping and giggling in Shade's ear.

The Master Assassin had a look of calm composure on his face as he replied to her queries with skillfully vague answers. Elaran, on the other hand, seemed to actually enjoy himself. At the edge of the table, he and Princess Illeasia spent most of the night with their heads together, discussing one thing or another. My eyebrows shot up when I realized that the grumpy elf had even smiled several times.

Hadraeth said nothing during the whole dinner. He only switched between gazing at the princess and glaring at Elaran and then back again. Shaking my head, I turned my attention back to Niadhir.

"So, do you choose your leaders too then?" I asked.

I had spent the night trying to learn as much as I could about the star elves. If we were going to escape, we'd need every advantage. But my interrogation had been less successful than I expected because most of Niadhir's answers had been rather vague. I wondered if it was due to my own incredibly ambiguous replies to his questions.

"Don't be daft," Lady Nelyssae cut in from across the table. "The queen's eldest daughter inherits the crown. As it should be."

"Obviously," I said, sarcasm dripping from my voice. "Because it's not like I've visited four different nations, all with their own different way of choosing the next leader." I flashed her an insincere smile. "But of course your way is the only logical way."

Around me, the table fell silent. Glasses and utensils clinked from further away while the star elves next to me tried to figure out if I was being ironic or not. From my tone of voice I thought that had been obvious, but apparently these people didn't have sarcasm ingrained in their whole being the way I had. However, before they could figure it out, Queen Nimlithil rose from her chair.

Furniture scraped against the polished floor as the rest of the banquet hall hurried to do the same. In her hand, the queen held a small glass. It looked almost like a simple shot glass but with more elegant curves. I squinted down at the identical one in front of my plate.

A servant had appeared and placed it there a few minutes ago but since no one else had touched theirs, I hadn't either. Now, everyone picked it up and raised it in the direction of their queen. After one last suspicious glance at it, I did the same. When the clear liquid moved it almost looked like a faint shimmer of color swirled inside it.

"My friends, thank you for another wonderful evening." Queen Nimlithil raised her glass a little further. "To the beauty and grace of the stars."

"To the beauty and grace of the stars," the whole room replied before tipping their glass to their lips.

Shrugging, I downed mine as well. A surprisingly refreshing taste exploded in my mouth. It was actually rather good and a perfect way to end the meal, even though the aftertaste was a bit strange.

"Would you like to accompany me on an evening stroll?" Niadhir asked and held out his arm.

"Oh, uhm..." I began and cast a quick glance at Shade and Elaran. From the look of it, the assassin was being asked something similar by Nelyssae. As was Elaran by the princess. "Sure," I finished.

That would give me another chance to get information out of him. On my other side, Captain Hadraeth threw one last glare at the auburn-haired wood elf taking the princess' arm before stalking off across the room. I wondered what his deal was.

From across the table, Shade locked eyes with me. "Elaran," he said in a light and conversational tone before taking the arm of Nelyssae and strolling away.

The elf in question stared in confusion at the assassin's retreating back but I had understood the message and for now, that was enough. Taking Niadhir's offered arm, we left the befuddled wood elf and the sparkling princess behind.

Being escorted in this way was not something I particularly enjoyed because it made me feel weak and helpless. Like someone who needed to be protected. And I had never, in my whole life, been a person who needed someone else to defend me. *I* was the one other people needed protection from.

But for now, I had to follow their customs if I was to get the information I needed. Burying the irritation deep inside me, I put on my best friendly face and turned to Niadhir. It was time for some more interrogation.

10.

Stars glittered above me. The vast rooftop we strolled along looked more like a sculpted garden than anything else. Manicured bushes and small trees in silver pots had been artfully placed across the frosted glass while paths between them provided privacy. I took a deep breath. The cool night air smelled of jasmine and roses.

"What is it that you do for a living?" Niadhir asked.

I blinked to clear my head. "I'm, uhm... I'm a procurer of goods. Of a sort."

"Oh, so you sell wares to merchants?"

"You could say that." I wiped the grin from my face before he could see it. "What about you?"

Niadhir ran his fingers through the green leaves of a bush as we passed. "I am a scholar. In fact, I am one of Tkeister's *foremost* scholars."

"Hmm."

Not one for modesty, this elf. When he turned and peered down at me with his face full of surprise and disappointment, I realized that he had expected a different reaction to his statement.

"Impressive," I quickly amended.

He seemed satisfied because he smiled at me. "If you want, you could accompany me to the library tomorrow."

"Sure." I blinked repeatedly again to clear my head. "Yeah, that would be great." Stopping in front of a white bench, I pressed a hand to my forehead. "Can we sit down? I'm not feeling so good."

"Of course," Niadhir said and sat down next to me. "After the food and drink and adapting to a new environment, it is understandable that you are tired."

He was right, there had been a lot of new circumstances to navigate, but I wasn't sure that was the reason. I had been in overwhelming situations before but had never reacted like this. It felt as though thick fog was pressing in on my consciousness. At the beginning of our walk, it had been faint but now my normally sharp mind was growing duller with each passing minute. Even the darkness felt very far away.

"Are you alright?" Niadhir turned pale violet eyes full of concern on me.

"No," I answered honestly.

This was dangerous. Without a clear head, there was no telling what I could reveal. I had to get out of there. The elf placed a hand on my arm and gave me an encouraging smile. He asked me something. I looked at him for a moment and then opened my mouth to reply.

THE WHITE DOOR TO MY room appeared in front of me. Panic flashed through my body like lightning. How had we gotten here?

"It was so nice to get to know you, Storm," Niadhir said as he let go of my arm.

Hadn't I told him that my name was the Oncoming Storm? How did he know that other people called me Storm? Realizing that he was still waiting for a reply, I gave my head a quick shake and pulled myself together.

"Yeah, you too."

"I will see you tomorrow, then."

"What?"

He gave me a patient smile. "When we go to the library."

"Right. Yes, of course." I cleared my throat. "See you tomorrow."

Before he could reply, I yanked open the door and slipped inside. Once it was closed behind me, I slid down the door and rested the back of my head against the cool white material. A lock clicked shut above me. *Not a prisoner, huh?* I drew my knees up to my chest.

For a while, I just sat there on the floor, waiting for the last of the strange dampening sensation to disappear from my mind. For what I was going to do next, I needed a clear head. Once I was satisfied that my brain worked as normal again, I pushed off from the floor and strode to the window.

That intoxicating scent of jasmine and roses drifted into my room when I threw open the window. Sticking my head out, I analyzed the situation. We were high up. Very high up. And at the end of that steep drop, cliffs made of dark stone waited. After adding 'not falling down the building' to my to-do list, I took a hold of the frame and climbed through.

Wind pulled at my white dress. Still standing on the windowsill, I made a quick decision and ditched my inconvenient shoes. They thudded to the floor after I kicked them back in through the window. Feeling much steadier on my feet, I moved to the edge of the windowsill.

It wasn't that far to the next one but I would still have to leave the relative safety of the long rectangular slab and free climb across the wall to reach it. Fortunately for me, the shiny material that the castle was built from wasn't as smooth as it looked. Dents and bumps were mixed with tiny cracks in the wall. Taking a deep breath of cool night air, I reached for the closest one.

The strange material was cold against my skin as I placed my hand on it. Adrenaline surged through me when both feet left the windowsill and I was only using the wall's uneven surface to remain in the land of the living. My heart beat rapidly in my chest. It was exhilarating.

A strong gust snatched at me. I pressed myself harder into the frosted material to avoid being flung away. Scrambling around on the side of a building was so much harder in a dress than in my normal burglar-friendly clothes. I cursed the star elves' limited view of fashion for the hundredth time. When the wind finally died down, I continued my climb. Cold glass appeared under my feet as I reached the next windowsill. Crouching down, I peered in through the window.

Elaran was sitting on the bed with his back towards me. Using a tiny spoon I had stolen during dinner, I lifted the latch and edged open the window. My feet hit the floor soundlessly.

The grumpy elf on the bed still hadn't noticed me. I studied him. With his face buried in his hands like that, he looked exhausted. Vulnerable. Like he had given up. I had never seen him like that before and I had no idea what the appropriate thing to say would be.

"Your room is bigger than mine," I simply stated instead.

"Gah!" Elaran yelped and shot up from the mattress. Whirling around, he crouched into a fight stance before realizing that it was me. "What the hell is wrong with you? Sneaking up on people like this." He whipped his head from side to side. "Where did you even come from?"

I hiked a thumb over my shoulder. "The window."

"The window." The grumpy elf stalked over to the offending building feature. "Of course you came through the bloody window." He stuck his head out before letting out another yelp and stumbling backwards.

Shade jumped through and landed silently on the floor. His black eyes met mine. "I see you understood my message."

"Of course I did."

"What bloody message?" Elaran raked his hands through his hair and threw an exasperated stare at the assassin.

"At dinner." Shade moved away from the window and dropped into the chair by the white desk. "When I said *Elaran* I meant: *we meet at Elaran's room after we're done*. Because your room is in the middle."

The elf drew his eyebrows down and crossed his arms. "And you actually expected me to infer all of that from just my name?"

Amusement played in the assassin's dark eyes. Shaking his head, Elaran stalked over to the bed and sat down while muttering something under his breath about skulking underworlders.

"Alright, we need to talk about a few things," Shade said.

Striding across the room, I plopped down on the bed next to Elaran. "Yeah."

The grumpy elf scowled at me. "There's a whole room here. We don't have to sit right on top of each other."

"Then move over."

Muttering under his breath again, he scooted from the middle of the bed to the side closest to the headboard. I drew my legs up and crossed them underneath me. After smoothing the white dress over my thighs, I turned serious eyes on my two friends.

"After dinner, I went to some rooftop garden with the scholar, Niadhir." I let out a long exhale. "I can't remember what we talked about."

Shade and Elaran exchanged a look.

"Same," the assassin said.

The elf leaned back on his palms. "Yeah, me neither."

"You think we were drugged?" I asked.

"Most likely." Shade ran a hand along his jaw. "It has to have happened sometime during the dinner." Dropping his arm, he flicked calculating eyes between us. "How much training have you had in withstanding advanced interrogation techniques?"

I wasn't sure whether to chuckle or sigh in exasperation. "Yeah, uh, none."

"I grew up in Tkeideru," Elaran announced as if that was explanation enough that no such ridiculous skills would have been needed there.

The Master Assassin clicked his tongue. "Yeah, I expected as much. But that's not our top priority right now. So drop that because now we need to figure out how to escape from here."

"You're giving orders again," Elaran stated with a frown directed at the self-proclaimed dictator.

"Yeah, and what do you mean drop it?" I shot up from the bed and took to pacing the room. "If we don't remember what we said, we could've said anything! It could be a huge problem."

The auburn-haired archer backed me up with a nod. "She's right. What if we told them everything? All our secrets?" He rubbed his temples. "They might know that the two of us aren't Storm Casters. They might know that you're the General of Pernula. They might–"

"Stop panicking!" Shade cut off. Using his whole arm, he pointed from me to the bed. "And you, sit down."

Raising my chin, I crossed my arms and remained standing firmly on the floor. The Master of the Assassins' Guild blew out an exasperated breath and shook his head.

"You might not have been trained to withstand interrogation techniques like these," he began. "But the two of you are the most distrusting people I know. I highly doubt you would've just blabbered on about anything." Leaning back in the chair, he crossed his ankles. "And besides, making someone answer is just half of it. You also need to know the right questions to ask. So yeah, calm down and let's talk about our escape plan."

Reluctantly admitting that he did have a point, I gave him a short nod. Elaran did the same. I wanted to sit down for our discussion but I didn't want him to think I did it because he told me to, so I waited until I judged an appropriate amount of time had passed since his arrogant command before strolling over to the bed and sitting down again. When Shade's mouth twitched in amusement, I knew he had seen right through me. Damn assassin.

"So, the plan," I said once I'd drawn my legs up underneath me again.

We spent the first part of our strategy meeting sharing what we had learned about the star elves from our respective dinner companions. It wasn't much, all things considered. But it was enough to get us started at least.

Shade pressed his fingers together, forming a little triangle, and tapped them against his chin. "So, what we know is basically this then. We're locked in our rooms but the corridors aren't patrolled a lot. The stairs, on the other hand, are heavily guarded."

"Yeah, and we need the stairs to get to the ground floor," I added. "Which is where all the exits are."

"No, we don't necessarily need the stairs," the infuriatingly smug assassin contradicted. "What it means is that we will have to find another way down."

"And we also know that the queen is pulling all the strings," Elaran cut in before my eye roll could turn into something more tangible.

"Correct. And we learned that the princess will inherit the crown so she has to have some pull too." Shade turned to the elf. "She seemed to like you."

Elaran nodded. "Yeah. She's actually pretty nice."

"For someone who kidnaps and drugs people," I filled in.

The bed creaked as the archer shook his head and leaned back on his palms again. I shifted my weight on the mattress.

"Our best shot of finding out something important is probably through her, so keep being friendly with her." Shade moved his eyes from Elaran to me. "And you'll keep trying to get information from this Niadhir fellow. I'll keep trying with Lady Nelyssae."

I rolled my eyes.

"What?" he demanded.

Befriending the gorgeous and elegant Lady Nelyssae, what a sacrifice on his part. Really taking one for the team. However, when the assassin met my gaze with raised eyebrows, I just waved a hand in front of my face.

"Nothing." I looked between the two of them. "So, the plan is to figure out the plan later."

Elaran threw a scowl in my direction. "Yes. We can't break out without a proper plan because we'll likely only get one chance at this. How can you not get that?"

"I didn't say I didn't get it." I pushed off from the bed and stalked back and forth across the polished floor. "I said it's annoying and I don't like it. The formal dinners and the pompous ladies snickering behind their hands. The five hundred different forks. And this!" Flicking my hands, I motioned up and down the white dress. "I've never felt this out of place in all my life."

Yellow and black eyes softened when my friends looked at me. I wanted to slap them both. I didn't want their sympathy. What I wanted was to get my clothes and my knives back and then get the hell out. Raking my fingers through my hair, I tipped my head back and let out a long breath. It wasn't their fault that we were here so I shouldn't be getting angry at them.

"The plan is to continue gathering intel until we can figure out how to get to the ground floor without being caught by all the guards," I amended. "Got it."

When I tilted my head back down, I found Elaran and Shade nodding at me. After nodding back, I strode to the window. With one hand on the frame, I turned back to the assassin and the archer.

"As soon as you find something out, let me know. I wanna get out of here as fast as possible."

Without waiting for a reply, I climbed out the window and into the flower-scented night.

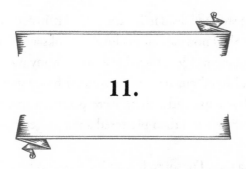

11.

Rows upon rows of bookcases crowded the whole room. Studying the multicolored spines, I realized that this was probably one of very few rooms in Starhaven that wasn't entirely white and silver. The walls and floor were of course made of that strange frosted glass, and all the furniture was a mix of white wood and silver, but at least the rather vast collection of books added some color to it.

"Is it not beautiful?" Niadhir's handsome face beamed with enthusiasm.

My eyes drifted over the large tables covered in stacks of books that broke up the long rows of bookcases. "Yeah, sure."

He seemed a bit disappointed with my lukewarm reply but led me further into the library anyway. No natural light made it inside because there were no windows. Instead, countless candles in glass containers illuminated the vast space smelling of dust and old books. It made me feel as if I was entering a place separate from the rest of the world. A place where time somehow stood still. I shook off the strange feeling.

"So, this is where you work?" I asked.

"Yes, this is where I spend most of my time." His mouth drew into a small smile. "My own little kingdom."

I chuckled. "Don't let the queen hear you say that."

Niadhir stopped dead in his tracks and frowned down at me. "Why not? She knows about my love of books and research."

For a moment, I just stared at him with my mouth slightly open. Man. Literal much? I mean, I didn't have much of a sense of humor but apparently, there were people worse than me. I cleared my throat and then plastered an apologetic smile on my face.

"It was a joke. I'm sorry. It wasn't a very good one."

"Oh," the humor-challenged scholar said before forcing out a dry laugh.

This situation was making even my social awkwardness feel awkward so I decided to switch topic. Lifting a hand, I motioned at the empty tables around us.

"Is it usually this empty?"

Having recovered from the failed joke, Niadhir waved me forward and started out again. "No, there are usually a few more people here. We are a bit early today."

When we reached a large table overlaid with books and scrolls, the scholar stopped and pulled out a chair made of white wood. I stared between him and the piece of furniture. Niadhir pointed a graceful hand at the chair.

"Please have a seat," he clarified when I still didn't move.

"Oh, uhm, okay." I moved towards the offered seat.

He pushed the chair in behind me, making me jerk a little in surprise. Resisting the urge to inform him that I did know how to sit down on a chair by myself, I just smoothed my dress in silence. Niadhir rounded the table and sat down to my left. After picking up an already open book, he started reading. I glanced between him and the rest of the room. What was I supposed to do now?

Minutes dragged on while the scholar continued studying the text. Other elves started trickling in through the door, filling the tables around us or browsing the bookshelves. I drummed my fingers restlessly on the wooden tabletop but stopped when Niadhir threw me a sharp look. Did he actually expect me to just sit there? What a waste of time.

"So, do you mind if I just take a look around?" I asked with as much politeness as I could muster.

The engrossed scholar looked up from his book and blinked at me. "Oh. Yes, of course."

He had barely finished the sentence before I shot up from the chair and strode away. My white dress billowed behind me as I made for the closest wall. While I was here, I might as well see if I could find some kind of exit. Doubtful. But still worth a shot.

Most of the wall space was covered by those white wooden bookcases and if one of them hid a secret passage, I would have to pull on thousands of books before finding it. It also seemed quite unlikely that there would be a hidden door here. These star elves didn't seem like the kind of people who built clandestine passageways behind their library walls. But then again, you never know.

While I made my way around the room, I pulled on random books just in case. Nothing happened. Eventually, I arrived at the very back of the room. Stacks of books had been pushed in front of what looked like the edge of a very tall door. Actually, *stacks* wasn't quite accurate. *Towers* was more like it. They were so tall they reached all the way up and covered part of the ceiling. I flicked my gaze over the huge mounds.

"Well, hello secret door to a potential exit," I said to myself.

Lifting my dress, I stepped over the closest pile and began carefully weaving my way through the books. If I could just made it to the back and push some of those books out of the way, I could see if it really was a door.

Clattering rose behind me. I squeezed my eyes shut before edging around to see what had caused it. A soft groan escaped my throat. The hem of my dress had gotten caught in a pile and made the topmost books fall down on the floor. Not for the first time, I cursed this ridiculous garment and wished for my own clothes back. I wondered if this was what it was like for normal people. Not knowing how to sneak and hide and spy without getting caught. Yeah, I was so not made to be a civilian.

Hoping that no one had heard my mishap, I continued towards what I hoped was a door. The tower hiding it stared down at me in challenge. I didn't have time to move it one book at a time so I would have to push the whole stack to the side and hope that it didn't create a chain reaction that brought everything down around my head. Taking a deep breath, I placed my hands on the nearest pile and pushed.

The tower swayed above me. Stopping briefly, I sent a quick prayer to Nemanan. This had better work. I continued edging the pile to the side.

"Excuse me," a voice said from behind. "What are you doing?"

Shit. Transforming my face into a look of innocence, I turned around to face the source of the voice. A male elf in a silver-colored shirt stared at me with eyebrows raised.

"I found an interesting book," I lied. "I just wanted to get it."

He looked at me with a dubious expression on his face. "Who are you here with?"

"Niadhir."

"Ah okay, I see." He nodded at the book stacks around me. "Be careful not to topple those."

"Yes, of course." I gave him an apologetic smile. "I'm almost done."

My heart pattered nervously in my chest but the suspicious elf seemed to accept my explanation because he wandered off after one final nod. I heaved a deep sigh. It was time to get this done before someone else showed up and started asking questions.

Putting my palms back on the frayed spines, I pushed the pile of books to the side. All the other stacks next to it moved as well until I could finally make out the object behind them. It was a door. Only, it didn't actually lead anywhere. A loose door stood leaning against the wall instead of attached to it. Irritation burned through me. Why put a spare door here? Cadentia, Goddess of Luck, sure had a strange sense of humor.

After one last murderous glare at the slab of wood, I hiked my dress up and started climbing back out. Damn them for getting my hopes up. When I finally made it out of the maze of book piles, I took a moment to smoothen my clothes. Tipping off Niadhir to my odd activities wouldn't be ideal. At last satisfied that no trace of my climbing remained, I turned around.

I drew in a sharp breath between my teeth. A female elf with dark violet eyes and silver hair stood right in front of me. Her dress, with sharp lines and no decorations, was hanging still around her as if she had been standing there for a while and not just walked up to me.

"Who are you?" I blurted out.

"Maesia," she said in low voice. "You are the Oncoming Storm."

"Yeah," I replied hesitantly.

"Be careful what you plan to do."

I narrowed my eyes at her. "Are you threatening me?"

Soft footsteps and a rustle of clothing sounded behind me. I whipped around just as Niadhir rounded the bookshelf.

"Were you talking to someone?" he asked, his brows slightly furrowed.

"I..." I began and looked back at Maesia. Only, she wasn't there anymore. Shaking my head, I decided it was best to not admit that I was apparently talking to people no one else could see. "No, I was just commenting to myself about how many books there are here."

Niadhir seemed unconvinced but didn't push the matter. "Yes, my colleague said he found you here, looking for a book. Which book was it?"

Scrambling to think of something that made sense, I said the first thing that popped up into my head. "I thought I saw a book about the Storm Casters."

"I see." He motioned for me to follow. "Come with me."

Thankful that he appeared to have bought it, I trailed behind him back to his table. Wood creaked as I dropped into my chair and squinted at the items now placed on the table in front of my seat. It was some kind of round frame with a white piece of cloth stretched over it and a small silver box.

"I realized that you did not have anything with which to occupy yourself while I continued my studies," Niadhir supplied. "So I had these brought for you."

Opening the lid, I peered inside. "What am I supposed to with these?" I picked up a small silver needle and frowned at it. "You can't stab anyone with this."

"By the Stars, why would you want to stab anyone?" Niadhir exclaimed, shock evident on his delicate features.

Oh. Whoops. My lips parted but only uncertain noise made it out. How was I supposed to explain myself out of that comment? Fortunately, I didn't have to because Niadhir did it for me.

"It is fine, I understand." He gave me a patient smile. "I understand why you would say something like that. Given your nature."

I frowned at him. "My nature?"

"Yes, with you being a Storm Caster." When my frown only deepened, he went on. "From what I understand, you do not know anything about what that entails."

My mind turned suspicious. How had he known that? Had he just deduced that from my lie about looking for a book on the Storm Casters and the confused look on my face when he talked about my nature? Or had I told him that yesterday during the conversation I couldn't remember?

"No," I replied honestly because I also desperately wanted to learn more about it.

"Would you like me to tell you?"

I managed a smile. "Yes, I would."

"Great!" His pale violet eyes sparkled with scholarly excitement. "I will tell you a bit more about it then." He motioned at the cloth in front of me. "Feel free to start your embroidery while I talk. The spools of thread are underneath."

Start my embroidery. Did I seriously look like someone who spent their free time doing embroidery? Struggling mightily not to roll my eyes, I instead forced a smile and picked up the box of needles. After a satisfied nod, Niadhir began his lecture.

"Storm Casters, or Ashaana, as your people as also called, are not born. They are made."

Tipping out the box of needles on the table to get a better look, I glanced up at him. "How?"

"It is a quite distressing process." His concerned eyes found mine. "Are you sure you want to know?"

"Yes."

The scholar knitted his fingers and placed them on the table. Leaning forward, I waited for him to start. My heart thumped in my chest. I was finally about to find out who and what I was.

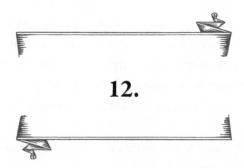

12.

Niadhir cleared his throat. "Well, then. Storm Casters are created by making a deal with a demon from hell. The person in question summons a demon and then proceeds to sell his or her soul to the demon in exchange for power."

My mouth dropping open slightly, I stared at him. He gave me a grave nod. Dread and hopelessness washed over me as if I was drowning in a frozen black lake. I had made a deal with a demon. By all the gods. I had sold my soul. No wonder I only left death and destruction in my wake.

"It often happens when the person is experiencing extreme emotions in their childhood," Niadhir went on. "Such as fury, pain, or grief."

Memories of Rain bleeding to death in a dark alley flashed through my mind. The coppery tang of blood. My heart being ripped to shreds when the light faded from her brown eyes. Deafening screams about vengeance echoing into the night.

Fresh pain from Rain's death wormed together with the feelings of rootlessness and the loss of identity. I slammed up the walls around my already battered heart before it shattered completely.

"Yeah, I remember a time like that," was all I said.

The serious scholar gave me a knowing nod. "After the person has sold their soul, they receive powers similar to that of a thunderstorm. Black clouds, lightning, thunder." He pushed strands of silvery white hair back behind his pointed ears and fixed me with a piercing gaze. "I am sure you are familiar with the concept."

Breaking his stare, I lowered my eyes to the pile of needles on the table before me. "Yeah."

"The problem, though," he continued, "is that no one who receives these powers is actually able to control them. Since they have a demonic source, the powers always end up controlling the person instead of the other way around. I am sure you have experienced that as well."

Picking up a handful of needles, I started sorting through them while trying not to think about all the times the darkness had claimed me without my permission. Especially the last time. Shade's frightened eyes. Elaran's pleading voice. The blood running down the assassin's throat as I pressed the edge of my blade into it with the intention of killing him.

"I have," I finally replied.

Niadhir leaned back in his white chair and placed his hands in his lap. "That is why there are almost no Storm Casters left. Most of them either die in a storm of their own making or commit suicide because they accidentally killed a loved one."

An iron fist squeezed my heart so hard and I had to close my eyes to stave off the pain. If I had killed Shade that day, I would probably have done the same. I wouldn't have been able to live with myself if I had woken up from that black haze to find him on the ground with his throat slit and the bloody knife in my hand.

Opening my eyes again, I forced out a long breath. "So that's it then? That's what my life will come down to? Dying by my own hand? The only question being whether I do it before or after I kill someone I love."

"Not necessarily." His concerned eyes found mine. "There is a third option. But it is not something to be considered lightly." The worried scholar spread his hands in a helpless gesture. "Are you sure you want me to continue? I see that you are already distressed. Perhaps we should take a break?"

"No. I want to know."

A pair of star elves passed by our table, discussing something about astronomy, while Niadhir considered in silence whether he should continue or not. I picked up a few needles and turned them over in my hands. At last, the concerned scholar leaned forward on the table again.

"Very well." The chair creaked as he shifted his weight. "The third option is to get rid of the Storm Caster powers."

I looked up and stared at him with raised eyebrows. "Get rid of them?"

"Yes. There is a ritual that we can perform here in the City of Glass that will purge the demonic powers from you." He motioned at the book-filled room around us. "Here in this library, in fact. But as I mentioned, it is not a decision to be made lightly. The ritual is complicated and once done, it can never be undone."

Using the side of my hand, I swept the needles into a neat pile before picking up the box again. I chewed the inside of my cheek while I returned them to the silver box and snapped the lid shut.

"That's why you brought me here," I stated at last. "Some of the wayward souls you bring here are Storm Casters."

"Yes." Niadhir gave me a sincere nod. "We do not want you to commit suicide or kill someone you love any more than you do. Despite what the rest of Weraldi thinks of us, all we want is a world free of pain and sorrow."

I studied his face, trying to find hidden deception in the pale violet irises. He wasn't lying. The sincerity in his eyes when he had explained what the star elves really wanted told me that he was speaking the truth. They did want a world free of pain and sorrow. I furrowed my brows. That was not at all what I had expected.

Niadhir reached over and placed a hand on my arm. "Do not be afraid. We would never force the ritual on anyone. And besides, it cannot even be completed if the person does not give up their powers willingly." He let go and leaned back again. "We simply wanted you to know that there is an alternative. If you want it."

"I, uhm..." I began. "I need time to think."

"Of course." He rose from the chair and held out his arm. "I will take you back to your room."

Pushing off from the table, I stood up as well. I still didn't like being escorted in this way but I took his offered arm anyway. My mind was spinning so much the whole way back to my room that I almost forgot to execute my plan. We were right outside Shade's door when I finally remembered. Placing my right foot behind my left, I tripped on purpose and tumbled to the floor.

"Oh, by the Stars!" Niadhir exclaimed. "Are you alright?"

While moving my arm as if to brace myself on the floor, I threw two needles under Shade's door. "Yes, I'm fine. Sorry. My mind was somewhere else." I took his outstretched hand and climbed to my feet.

"Understandable considering everything you have learned today." He looked me up and down with concerned eyes. "Are you sure you are alright?"

"Yeah, I'm alright," I replied as we started out again. "I just need some rest."

"I understand. I will come and collect you for dinner."

"Alright. See you later then."

Not waiting for a reply this time either, I slunk into my room and closed the door behind me. The lock clicked shut. Turning around to face the silver mechanism, I let a grin spread across my face as I pulled out two more needles that I had hidden in my sleeves. Ha! Good luck keeping me locked up now.

After one last smug look at the door, I strode to the white desk by the window and sat down. I would only need to bend them in a few strategic places and then I would have a pair of makeshift lockpicks. And so would Shade.

Since I could only pretend to trip once without raising suspicion, I'd had to choose between Elaran and Shade. It had been an easy decision considering that the grumpy elf could neither make lockpicks out of needles nor actually pick locks.

I bent down over the sharp metal pieces and got to work. My mind was still as tangled as a nest of snakes, though. I had finally learned what being a Storm Caster meant but now that I knew, I wasn't sure I wanted to know. Whatever I had expected, this hadn't been it. I had sold my soul to a demon from hell in order to get revenge. Talk about making irrevocable life decisions at the tender age of eleven.

Pushing those concerns to the back of my mind, I refocused my efforts on the makeshift lockpicks. What mattered now was getting out of here. Getting Shade and Elaran out of here. Because whatever was going on in Starhaven, it was bigger than them simply wanting to save a Storm Caster. Otherwise, why would they keep us locked up? No, I could deal with my demonic powers and everything else that entailed after all this was over. I blew out a humorless laugh. If there was an *after* for me, that is.

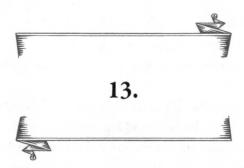

13.

Soft clicks echoed from the lock on my door. I whipped my head from the closet I'd been scouring for something more burglar-friendly to wear, and blew out the candle. Darkness fell around me as I darted across the room. The sound stopped just as I skidded to a halt behind the wall next to the door. I watched the silver handle intently. It edged downwards. Someone was breaking into my room.

The handle reached the bottom with a quiet snap. My heart pattered against my ribs. Light spilled onto the floor as the door was pulled open a tiny crack. A shadow appeared in the illuminated area. I crouched down and got ready.

In the span of a second, the tall figure had slunk through and drawn the door shut. I lunged. A surprised hiss sounded as I grabbed a hold of the intruder's clothes and yanked them towards me. Their body plowed into mine with a force I hadn't expected while they hooked a leg behind my kneecap and pulled forward. We both tumbled to the floor in a heap of tangled limbs.

Struggling to get the upper hand, I pushed off from the floor and tried to roll on top of my attacker. I only managed to get to my knees before I was yanked to the side and slammed to the floor again. A huff escaped my throat as my breath was knocked out of me. While I'd been busy trying to breathe, my opponent had used the second of grace to wedge me against the floor.

"Did you really think you would win that?" Shade's voice said.

Squinting against the darkness around us, I found the Master Assassin's athletic body straddling my chest while his strong hands pinned my arms to the floor above my head. He leaned down over me until I could see the smirk on his face.

Of course it was him. Who else would it be? Damn assassin.

"Yeah, I would've won that. You just got lucky I stumbled there in the beginning."

Shade's hot breath drifted over my face as he let out a chuckle. "Uh-huh. Whatever you need to tell yourself."

I pulled against the fingers locking my wrists to the cool floor. "You gonna let me up?"

His black eyes glittered. "When you admit you can never beat me."

Rolling my eyes, I shook my head just as an idea flashed into my brain. I drove my knee into his backside. With him leaning this far over me, he was completely defenseless against the sudden push and rolled right over my head. Shooting to my feet, I gave him a quick rise and fall of my eyebrows.

I grinned at him. "You were saying?"

My eyes had adjusted enough to the dark that I could see the stunned expression that swept over his handsome features as he climbed to his feet. Shaking his head, he released an impressed chuckle. While the Master Assassin came to terms with being outsmarted, I strode to the desk and lit the candle again. Light flickered to life against the smooth white walls.

"So, did you want something?" My mouth drew into another grin. "Or did you just come here to prove once again that you really can't take me on your own?"

"Yeah we'll see about that," Shade promised. "But no, I came here to tell you that I might've found a way out."

I stared at him. "What? Why didn't you just say that from the beginning?"

"Because someone decided to attack me before I'd even opened my mouth."

"Whatever."

Shade moved towards me so that we wouldn't have to shout across the whole room. Crossing his arms, he leaned his shoulder against the closet door. "There's some kind of chute built into the wall outside a small room filled with cleaning supplies. I'm thinking it's been used to dump trash without having to lug around a stinking sack through these spotless halls."

"Can it fit a person?" I jerked my head towards the wall separating my room from Elaran's. "An elf?"

"Yeah, that's not the problem. The problem is that we have no idea where it leads."

"Can't we just slide down the chute to check?"

"And if it leads to nailed-up metal plate?"

I scrunched up my eyebrows. "Good point."

Shade peeled his shoulder off the white wood and approached me. His hand brushed against my ribs as he reached behind my back to grab a sheet of paper and a pen from the desk. An involuntary shiver coursed through me. While Shade put pen to paper, I shook my head to clear it of ridiculous thoughts.

First he drew a map of the corridors, marking where the chute was, and then he started drawing something else. I frowned at it. Was that a flower?

"There's a symbol on it." He pointed to the flower. "It looks like this. I'm guessing, or hoping rather, that the other side of the slide has that symbol on it too."

"So, we find where it ends and we might find our way down the stairs," I summarized.

"Yeah, so you're going to have to get that Niadhir fellow to take you to the lower levels so you can see if you can find it. I've talked to Elaran and he'll do the same with the princess."

Crossing my arms, I blew out a breath. "And you with Lady Nelyssae."

"Yeah."

"Alright." I pushed off the desk I'd been leaning my hip again. "I'll do a sweep of this floor tonight."

"I've already swept it. That's how I found the chute."

"Good for you. I'm gonna sweep it too."

Shade's mouth drew into a lopsided smile. "Of course you are."

After a long look at me, he turned and made for the door. Light from the flickering candle played in his dark hair. When he got to the door, he paused for a moment with his hand on the silver handle. He turned back to me with a smile.

"Oh, and thanks for the lockpicks. How did you even get them?"

I drew my eyebrows down. "Niadhir thought I might enjoy embroidery."

A surprised laugh bubbled from his throat. "Which is something you excel at, I'm sure."

"I'm good at stabbing things at least."

"There is that." He gave me a quick rise and fall of his eyebrows. "And at swiping unattended needles, it seems."

"That too."

Shade gave me another lopsided smile. "See you tomorrow."

When the door had clicked shut behind the Master Assassin, I pulled out my own lockpicks. Since I had given up on finding any clothes in that infernal closet that were better suited for sneaking, I had to settle for the ones I was wearing. I cast a glance over my shoulder. The moon peeked through the window.

Dinner had long since come and gone, so by now most star elves should be asleep. It was the perfect time to skulk around the halls undetected. After slipping out the door, I relocked it behind me. Time to see that chute Shade had found with my own eyes. Maybe we really did have a chance at escaping. I tiptoed down the hall. All we had to do was find the other side.

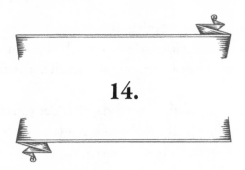

14.

"A what now?" I stared at Niadhir, skepticism swirling around in my dark green eyes.

"A ball. Tonight." He raised his pale eyebrows at me. "Have you never been to a ball?"

I very narrowly prevented myself from informing him that my only experience with balls was breaking into the attendees' houses and stealing their valuables while they were away.

"Uhm, no," I replied instead.

Niadhir's face lit up. "Then this will be a wonderful introduction to it! I asked some of the ladies to help you dress for it." He picked up his book again and continued reading with a wide smile on his face. "This will be perfect."

Perfect. Right. Me at a ball. In a dress. Dancing. What could possibly go wrong? I stabbed at the white fabric as if I was using a knife and not a needle. The sharp instrument left a big hole. Not caring how ugly it looked, I yanked the silver thread through.

The past week had been an endless series of trying to get Niadhir to take me to the lower levels, failing most of the time, and instead having to spend the day embroidering while he studied some text or other. On those rare occasions when he had agreed to show me a few other parts of the castle, I had searched fervently for a hatch similar to the one we had found on our floor. So far, I had been unsuccessful.

Shade and I had kept up the tradition of sneaking into Elaran's room once every day to share the latest news. If it was late at night, we used the door, and if it was earlier in the evening, we climbed in through the window. The grumpy elf never got quite used to suddenly finding us in there but didn't complain because he didn't want to be the one scrambling across the side of a building or picking locks.

I drummed my fingers against the frame that kept the embroidered cloth taut. None of us had found the end of the chute yet. Or any other way out. If we were going to escape, I had to convince Niadhir to show me more of the castle. Stabbing the needle through the mess of threads again, I continued running schemes in my head.

Afternoon wore on as I plotted in silence until I finally decided that faking an interest in Starhaven's history and architecture was my best bet. Say what you will about needlework but it was actually a pretty good way of clearing one's mind.

"Ready to go?"

Startled out of my schemes, I looked up to find Niadhir standing next to me with his arm out. I placed the wooden frame and the needle back on the table. "Yeah."

Book-filled aisles twisted before us as we made our way out of the library. Almost every time Niadhir passed another star elf in this sacred place of his, they acknowledged him with a nod. After the first few days, I had come to the conclusion that he hadn't lied. He probably was one of the foremost scholars here.

"I've been admiring Starhaven's extraordinary design," I lied as we left the library behind and moved into the white corridor beyond. "It must've been built by some great architects." Looking up at him, I gave him an innocent smile. "I would love to see more of it."

"You have?" His violet eyes sparkled. "Yes, it was indeed built by very talented architects. In fact, it..."

As the excited scholar launched into a rather extensive recounting of all the great star elves responsible for designing and building the castle, I turned my attention level down to the lowest possible. I said *mm-hmm* and *aha* at the right places while waiting for him to tell me that he would take me on a tour. When we at last arrived outside my door, we still hadn't gotten to that part.

"So, could you take me to see some more of it?" I interrupted and gave him a light shrug. "Maybe tomorrow?"

Niadhir paused mid-sentence and blinked at me, making him look like a startled deer. "Oh, of course. I apologize. I got slightly carried away." He shook his head. "Of course I will show you some more of it tomorrow."

"Great!" I detached myself from his arm and pushed down the handle to my room. "See you tomorrow then."

"No. I will see you tonight."

"What?"

He gave me a patient smile. "The ball. The ladies I mentioned should arrive shortly and help you get ready. And I will come back later and escort you there."

Damn. The ball. I had already forgotten about that. Or maybe I had simply tried to suppress the knowledge because I would rather face a squad of Silver Cloaks than attend it.

"Right, yeah. See you later then."

Having closed the door behind me, I stalked across the room and flopped down on the bed. The soft mattress shifted under my body. I draped an arm over my eyes and let out an endless string of profanities. Why in Nemanan's name would anyone want to go to a ball? What did people even do there? I hadn't a clue and I was in no mood to find out but a knock still sounded from the door. Much sooner than I would've liked, I might add.

Rolling off the fluffy covers, I stomped over to the door and shoved it open. Three startled star elves blinked at me. When I just continued staring at them in silence, the one at the front finally cleared her throat and spoke up.

"We're here to help you get ready for the ball." She motioned at my room. "May we come in?"

"If you must." I turned around and stalked to the middle of the room. Drawing my eyebrows down, I crossed my arms. "I do know how to put on clothes by myself, you know."

The three elegant elves exchanged a look. I studied them through narrowed eyes. If they were going to the party themselves, they were very plainly dressed. Well, for star elves anyway.

They all wore simple white dresses and had their hair pulled back in a loose knot. Niadhir had referred to them as *ladies* but from what I'd seen this past week, he was also a very formal person who valued tradition and propriety, so he might've said it to be polite. I let my eyes glide over them again. Yeah. These three *ladies* most likely worked in the castle.

"Fine," I muttered while massaging my forehead. It wasn't their fault that I was forced to attend this ridiculous thing and that they had been ordered to help my ungrateful ass. "Let's get on with it then and do... whatever it is that you do."

Relief blew across their features. The leader smiled, pulled out the chair from the desk, and motioned for me to sit down while the one with the dark violet eyes placed bottles and tins on the table. White hair bobbed in front of me as the third one swept through the room before stopping in front of the closet. Oh I was not going to like this.

Time dragged on with all the hurry of a particularly lame snail while the three star elves pulled at my hair, covered the rest of my fading bruises with makeup, and stuffed my limbs into clothes I would never have worn voluntarily.

"And you're done," the leader beamed at me.

"You look beautiful," the one with the white hair added. She took a few graceful steps to the mirror and held out her arm. "Come see for yourself."

I groaned. "Do I have to?"

All three ladies let out a pleasant-sounding laugh and nodded at me. Reluctantly giving in to their suggestion, I started towards the full-length mirror by the wardrobe. Fabric swished around me as I moved. The star elf with the dark purple eyes stepped in front of the reflective panel so that I wouldn't see anything until I was positioned right in front of it.

"Are you ready?" she asked with a mischievous smile on her face.

I shook my head. "No." I wasn't sure I wanted to see this.

She laughed again and took a quick step to the side. I stared at the person in the mirror. I say *person* because whoever it was that stared back, it wasn't me.

The dark brown hair I usually wore in a braid now cascaded down my upper back. Silver pins with white gems decorated it. My body had been laced into a silver-colored dress with a tight bodice and flowing skirt, also adorned with the same precious stones, while the makeup not only covered the faint bruises but also added color to my cheeks. Glittering jewelry covered the skin above my cleavage and around my wrists.

Light glinted off me as I turned and squinted at my reflection. "By Nemanan, if I tried to burgle a house in this sparkly spectacle, I'd set off alarms from a hundred strides away."

Surprised laughter erupted from the three elves. "Why would you want to burgle a house?"

"Never mind." Clearing my throat, I cast one last look in the mirror before turning away. "I feel like a different person."

The three star elves giggled and thanked me as if it had been a compliment. The right clothes can add to your spirit and enhance your personality. Others clothes, diminish it. And then there are some that try to change it completely. These were of the third kind. When you wear something that doesn't fit who you are as a person, others can usually tell. I tried to swallow the dread rising in my throat. People were definitely going to laugh at me.

However, the ladies who had dressed me looked so happy and satisfied with the result that I decided not to share any of that with them. Instead, I followed them to the door in silence.

When their white skirts had finally disappeared into the hallway, all I wanted to do was rip everything off. With a deep sigh, I settled for simply closing the door. It had barely shut before a knock sounded on the wood. Mustering all the strength

I had, I wiped every trace of my emotions from my face and pushed open the door again.

"Oh by the Stars!" Niadhir exclaimed. "You look gorgeous!"

"Well, I didn't..." I trailed off when I realized what he'd said. "Wait, what?"

The scholar was dressed in a crisp white suit with silver details and the plain silver ring gathering up his hair had been replaced with a gem-covered one. He raised his eyebrows slightly as if he was confused about why I was surprised.

"Of course!" He gave me a bright smile. "The way you look tonight... you look more beautiful than ever before."

Heat radiated from my face as a blush settled on my cheeks. No one had ever told me I was beautiful before. It was an odd feeling. Not sure how to respond, I just stepped into the corridor next to him and drew the door shut behind me.

Niadhir held out his arm. "Shall we?"

Nodding, I took his arm and started forward, silver skirts swishing around my legs. We moved in the direction of the banquet hall we had dined in exactly one week ago.

"Last week was the banquet and now there's a ball," I said. "Is there always something like that happening on this day of the week?"

"Yes." A wistful smile blew across his lips. "We like to celebrate the beautiful aspects of life."

"I can tell."

A stream of people in elaborate outfits carried us ever closer to the vast room with the glass dome. Chatter and anticipation hung in the air. My heart thumped in my chest. I had done a lot of nerve-racking things in my life–assassinated a king, tricked an invading army, manipulated an election in a foreign country–but this ball beat them all. Killing, cheating, and manipulating were everyday staples for me. No matter how high the stakes. But this...

"I have no frame of reference for this," I mumbled while blood continued pounding in my ears.

Niadhir frowned down at me. "Pardon?"

Gem-covered bracelets clinked when I waved a hand in front of my face, telling him to disregard my strange comment. I glanced down at them before running a hand over the elaborate necklace lying heavy on my chest. Man, I had never worn this much jewelry before. Well, except for when carrying it off after a heist, of course.

The grand entrance to the banquet hall appeared before me. Wishing that I was wearing battle armor instead of this flowing dress was an exercise in futility but I couldn't help myself. As we reached the huge double doors, I sucked in a deep breath. This was going to be rough.

15.

Light filled the ballroom. Thousands of candles flickered in silver candelabras and mingled with the pale moonlight streaming in from the crystal dome. I ran a hand over the statue next to me. It wasn't ice. The intricately carved swan was made of glass. In fact, everywhere I looked, decorations of frosted and clear glass, silver, and precious white stones adorned the vast hall. It was like a winter fairy tale landscape.

"Wow," I mumbled.

Niadhir patted me on the hand and gave me a smile before leading me into the mass of star elves in elaborate outfits.

The banquet tables from last week had been rearranged to create seating arrangements along the edges while the middle of the room was left empty. Panic flashed through me when I realized what it was. A dancefloor. I glanced at the people around me, forming glimmering islands on the smooth floor. Excited murmuring hung over the area. At least no one was dancing. Yet.

"Princess Illeasia," Niadhir said as a pair of familiar faces appeared in the crowd. "You look beautiful as ever."

"You're too kind," the gorgeous princess in her sparkling dress replied and inclined her head, making her gem-covered headdress glint in the starlight.

"And... I beg your pardon but I seem to have forgotten your name," the scholar continued.

The auburn-haired elf next to her flicked his eyes around the room. "Elaran."

He looked about as uncomfortable in his white suit as I felt in my elaborate dress but I had a feeling that the worried glance hadn't been because of that. Following his gaze, I found the source of his uneasiness.

A few strides away, Captain Hadraeth in his ceremonial armor stood glowering at the wood elf. When he noticed that I was watching him, his dark violet eyes locked on me in a challenging stare. I narrowed my eyes at him. What was his problem?

"Right, Storm?" Niadhir's voice cut through my musings.

"What?" I tore my gaze from the strange Guard Captain and turned back to the small talk I hadn't been paying attention to.

The soft-spoken scholar gave me a patient smile. I knew he did it to be nice but every time he smiled at me in that way, I felt like a halfwit child. It made me want to stab him.

"I was just telling Princess Illeasia and Elaran that you have been practicing embroidery and that your needlework is improving," he explained.

Elaran didn't even try to hide his amusement. His yellow eyes practically glittered with it when he met my gaze. I threw him a scorching scowl.

"What's this I hear about embroidery?" a smug voice said.

Around us, the crowd shifted to let a stunning couple pass. Shade gracefully wove through the chatting people with a breathtaking star elf on his arm. Lady Nelyssae's white and silver dress both accentuated her curvy feminine form as well as complemented the assassin's suit. Fire from the candelabra next to her glinted off the jewelry in her hair and around her neck. When they stopped in front of us, Shade ran his eyes up and down my body but before he could say anything, I cut him off.

"I swear, if you say anything about the dress or the hair, or any of it, I'll pull out one of these hairpins and stab you in the neck."

Niadhir whirled on me, aghast. "That was a very unkind thing to say."

Feeling like a student being admonished, I averted my gaze and drew my eyebrows down. "Well, I'm an unkind person."

"Do not say that." The silver-haired scholar patted my hand again. "I am sure that is not true."

Confusion had passed over Shade's face at my comment but it was gone now as he and Elaran exchanged a look before sending a synchronized smirk my way. I flicked my eyes to the ceiling in exasperation and shook my head.

A hushed silence fell over the crowd. I had to balance on my tiptoes and crane my neck in order to see what all the tall elves around me were looking at. In the middle of the dancefloor, Queen Nimlithil stood, her silver dress pooling around her on the frosted glass.

"Welcome, my friends," she called across the glittering sea of people. "Tonight, we celebrate the beauty and light of the stars. Let it always guide our path." After putting her hands together in two graceful claps, she spread her arms wide. "Enjoy."

Hauntingly beautiful notes from violins and harps floated through the air. Clothes rustled as the elves around us moved towards the empty space in the middle of the domed hall. I glanced at Niadhir. *Please don't ask me to dance. Please don't ask me to dance.*

The polite scholar held out his hand. "Would you care to dance?"

Damn. No, I most certainly didn't want to dance. I had no idea how to. And besides, there was a reason I hadn't faked a deadly illness just to get out of this, and instead actually agreed to go tonight. This high-ceilinged hall was on the ground floor. It was the perfect excuse to start searching for the end of the chute without the restrictions that came with a guided tour by Niadhir.

"I'm afraid I don't know how to dance," I said in my best polite voice. "And I feel a bit flushed. All the excitement, you see." Spying a set of glass doors leading to some kind of balcony, I waved a hand in that direction. "I just need to get some air."

"I will accompany you," he replied.

Placing a light hand on his arm, I gave him a reassuring smile. "No, no need. I'll be right back."

When he was about to protest, I shot Shade a pointed look. Thankfully, the scheming assassin caught on and took a casual step forward and spoke up as if he had just spotted something surprising. The movement blocked Niadhir's view long enough for me to slip into the crowd.

I lifted a white shawl from an inattentive lady nearby and draped it over my head. My dark hair might as well be a beacon in this sea of pale colors but with that covered, it would be easier to disappear. The sparkly spectacle I was wearing actually helped me blend in. My mouth twisted into a wry smile. How about that?

Weaving expertly through the bodies, I stepped out of the way as an elf in white armor approached a group of giggling ladies. He bowed and offered one of them his hand just as I slipped behind their backs.

This setting, in these clothes, and with these people, might've been the most uncomfortable event I'd ever experienced but despite it all, I was still excellent at slinking unnoticed through a mass of bodies. I just had to adjust my thinking. Instead of staying in the shadows while wearing dark clothes, I merged with the light. It worked. Though, I still preferred the darkness.

Cool night air met me as I glided past the decorated glass doors that had been thrown open to reveal a grand terrace. Dark green bushes covered in white flowers had been placed in silver pots throughout the space. I snuck towards the railing on the left.

Placing my hands on the chilled material, I peered into the darkness beyond. We had to be at the back of the castle because those dark gray cliffs I could see from my window stretched out before me like a forbidden sea. We could probably disappear there if we left at night. The only problem was of course how in Nemanan's name we would get here in the first place.

"Storm?" Niadhir's voice drifted across the balcony.

Shit. I ducked in behind the closest bush. He had already found me. Jasmine-scented flowers and green leaves hid me from view as I skirted around the plant in step with the pursuing scholar. Once he was behind the large pot, I bolted for the door.

Warmth and noise from a room full of people enveloped me as I disappeared into the banquet hall again. I wove towards the side of the room. The terrace didn't help our escape plan because we still needed a way to get down to this level unnoticed and our best chance at that was the chute Shade had found.

A nondescript door became visible against the wall in front of me. It might be some kind of servants' corridor. And we all knew that those usually ran to all manners of places in a castle. I sidled up next to the door. Sweeping my gaze across the room, I made sure that no one was watching as I pushed down the handle. Just as Niadhir appeared from the balcony, I slid inside and drew the door shut behind me.

Silence pressed against my ears. After all the chatter, laughter, and music in the ballroom, the sudden stillness was almost eerie. Turning around, I studied my surroundings. Wall-mounted candles cast the empty corridor in warm light. I had to see what it looked like further in.

The door was yanked open. I whirled around, ready for a fight even in these inconvenient clothes, but didn't have time to do anything before I was shoved backwards.

"Move!" Elaran said.

Backpedaling quickly, I managed to stay on my feet as the grumpy elf barreled through the door and closed it behind him.

"What was that for?" I hissed once I'd regained my balance.

Elaran scowled at me. "It's your own fault for stopping right inside the door. You never thought that maybe someone else needed to get through in a hurry?"

Crossing my arms, I clicked my tongue. "No."

The auburn-haired archer shook his head and waved an impatient hand, telling me to start moving. I gave him a rather unladylike grimace in reply. Elbowing past me, he stalked down the hallway while muttering curses under his breath.

We snuck further into the servants' corridor until a metal plate located in the wall on our left drew our attention. Elaran and I exchanged a glance. Crouching down, I traced the flower stamped into it with my fingers.

"It's the same symbol," I stated. "It's gotta be the end of the chute, right?"

The elf dropped to a knee next to me. "Only one way to find out."

Two simple latches secured the top of the plate to the wall. Lifting them open, we edged it outwards. Nothing came tumbling out so we continued lowering the metal sheet until we could place it on the ground with the bottom part still attached to the white wall. A handle stuck out of both sides of the plate.

Elaran waved an impatient hand at me. "Check it out."

"I'm not sticking my head in there!"

"Of course you are." My grumpy friend rose and crossed his arms. "Skulking around places no one should know about is your area of expertise."

"If we ever run into a moose or a bear or something, I'm gonna push you to the front and repeat that back to you," I muttered while sticking my head through the opening in the wall. The square-shaped hole sloped upwards. "It's definitely built to slide stuff downwards. The drop isn't too steep." I crawled a little further in. "But it's impossible to tell where it leads because I can't climb it. Not in this dress."

Skirts rustled as I drew back and got to my feet again. Next to me, Elaran frowned at the hole for a minute before replacing the metal plate over it.

"If we sabotage the latches now, we could just slide down it tonight," he said.

"It's not the same chute," a voice announced.

We both whirled around to find Shade striding towards us.

Elaran shook his head at the assassin. "Always with the dramatic entrances."

I arched an eyebrow at the elf. "You're one to talk."

The Master Assassin flashed us both a lopsided smile before nodding to the metal plate. "That's not the same chute as the one we found. It can't be. We're way too far into the other side of the castle for it to be the same one. Most likely, they have a whole network of these throughout the building."

"So we've gotta either find the start of this one or the end of the other." I sucked my teeth. "Given that the start of this one is in another wing, I'd say finding the end of the other is the priority."

"I agree," Shade said while Elaran backed us up with a nod. The assassin turned his intelligent eyes on me. "Niadhir is in a full-blown panic because he can't find you."

I snorted. "Bet he is." Raising my eyebrows, I nodded at the both of them. "How did you even get away from your companions?"

Shade smirked at me. "You're not the only one who knows how to disappear into a crowd."

"No, she most certainly is not," an authoritative voice said as Queen Nimlithil materialized in the corridor. She fixed us with a knowing stare. "But I would expect nothing less from the head ranger of Tkeideru and a man who is both the Master of the Assassins' Guild and the new General of Pernula."

Silence hung heavy over the hallway. Not only had the queen found us skulking about in a place we shouldn't be in, she also knew who we really were. How were we supposed to explain our way out of this?

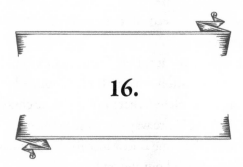

16.

Elaran had apparently no intention of trying to placate her with excuses because he crossed his arms and drew his eyebrows down while demanding, "How did you know that?"

The elegant queen turned her pale violet eyes on the ranger and gave him a patient smile. "You told me."

He dropped his arms and took a step back. "What?"

"Yes. After the banquet last week, I happened upon you and my daughter outside on the terrace. I asked you to tell me more about yourself and your companions, and you did."

Dread tumbled down my stomach like a bag of rocks but years of training helped me keep a calm outward appearance. A quick glance at the impassive mask on Shade's face told me that he was doing the same. Our friend the wood elf, on the other hand, wasn't as good at lying. Sweat trickled down his temple.

"Why are we here?" I cut in before he could say something that would screw us even worse.

"In this servants' corridor?" Queen Nimlithil arched a well-manicured brow at me. "I was just about to ask you the same."

"No, here in this castle." I swept my arms towards the pale unadorned walls in an exasperated gesture. "Why–"

"Did Niadhir not tell you?" A befuddled look blew across the queen's face. "There are almost no Storm Casters left because their demonic power has caused them to either die in a storm of their own making or commit suicide because they accidentally killed a loved one. You are here because we want to offer you an alternative." She scrunched up her eyebrows. "I was under the impression that Niadhir had already explained that."

Godsdamn it. I hadn't told Shade and Elaran about that yet because I needed time to process that information myself first. Their eyes burned holes in me but I refused to meet them. That was a conversation for another place and another time.

"Yeah, he did," I challenged the queen instead. "And that explains why I'm here but you have obviously known for a week already that these two ain't Storm Casters. If that's the only reason we're here, then you can just let them go home and I can stay here."

Queen Nimlithil let out a soft exhale. "After everything you have been told by others, I understand that you are suspicious of our intentions. But believe me when I tell you that the reason you are here is because we want a world free of pain and suffering. I have also experienced unfathomable pain, and I would not wish it upon anyone."

"You've experienced unfathomable pain?" I scoffed. "I seriously doubt that."

She drew herself up to her full height. "My husband was assassinated."

"Oh." For a moment, her last comment distracted me from the piece of information she had let slip before that. I narrowed my eyes at her. "Wait... you said *the reason you are here*. So there *is* another reason we're here?"

"It is high time we rejoined the ball," she announced abruptly, completely ignoring my comment and ushering us forward. "I am sure that your respective partners are beside themselves with worry."

One brief glance at each other was enough to convey that the three of us would be continuing this conversation in Elaran's room as soon as this party was over. Grabbing a fistful of my skirts, I hiked them up so that I could move better before following the queen's long silver train back into the ballroom.

Noise assaulted my ears when I stepped across the threshold. It took a moment to get my bearings in the room packed with people chatting, laughing, and dancing to the otherworldly string music. Scanning the crowd, I quickly found a certain scholar hurrying towards me. Lady Nelyssae followed him.

"Mother," a surprised voice said from my other side. "What's going on?"

"Nothing, my dear," the queen said and gave Illeasia's arm a gentle squeeze. "Enjoy the dance."

Princess Illeasia watched her mother disappear into the room again before turning to Elaran with concerned eyes. "Are you alright?"

Startled, the auburn-haired archer drew back slightly. "Uhm, yes."

"Good." A genuine smile, you know one of those that reaches the eyes and makes them sparkle, settled on her face. "Do you want to dance?"

"I... uhm..."

"Come on." Her violet eyes twinkled as she took the astonished ranger by the hand and drew him towards the dancefloor.

Shade and I chuckled at the terrified expression on his face just as our two partners caught up with us. Niadhir smoothed his hair and drew himself up to his full height in front of me.

"You gave me a terrible fright, Storm. I thought something had happened to you." He looked down on me with stern eyes. "Please do not do that again."

"Yeah, uhm, sorry." I gave him a light shrug. "Just took a wrong turn."

The scholar seemed unconvinced but he didn't get a chance to comment because Lady Nelyssae pushed past him and planted herself in front of Shade.

With one hand on her cocked hip and the other twirling a strand of glossy white hair, she pouted her luscious lips. "Aren't you going to ask me to dance?"

The Master Assassin held her gaze and offered her a hand. "Would you like to dance?"

A high-pitched squeal rose from her throat as she took his hand and twirled around. I glowered at their retreating backs while they made their way towards the dancefloor.

"Now that you have gotten a little fresh air, would you care to dance as well?" Niadhir asked next to me.

With my eyes still locked on the assassin and the gorgeous lady weaving through the crowd, I crossed my arms. "I don't dance."

"Oh." The disappointment in his voice was so strong that even my cold black heart softened.

Loosening my frown, I turned to face him. "But how about we get something to drink?"

His eyes recovered some of the light they had held before my curt comment had snuffed it out and he offered me his arm. "I would like that. This way, please."

Once again submitting to being escorted, I took his arm and followed him around the edge of the dancing couples. They all seemed to move in a prearranged pattern. It wasn't just each couple dancing by themselves but instead larger groups had formed and they stepped in similar directions back and forth across the smooth white floor, twirling and trading partners for a moment.

"Here we are."

Niadhir let go of my arm and bent towards a table covered in white silk and gems. Picking up two crystal goblets from a silver tray, he offered me one. I took it and squinted at the sparkly liquid inside. After lifting my shoulders in a brief shrug, I tipped the glass towards my lips and took a large gulp.

"To the beauty and grace of the stars," Niadhir said next to me and held up his glass as if I hadn't already started drinking.

Coughing, I swallowed the sparkly wine I already had in my mouth before flashing him a sheepish grin. "Right, yeah, to the stars and all that."

Man, this was so not my scene. Instead of looking at the disapproving expression on Niadhir's face, I turned back to the dancers. In the centermost group, Elaran and Princess Illeasia were engaged in a synchronized dance. The princess seemed to know what she was doing but the wood elf was flapping about like a disoriented seagull. When he accidentally stepped right into another couple, making them stumbled backwards, the princess placed a hand on his arm and leaned into his chest while doubled over with laughter. Joy and life radiated like sunlight from her whole body.

My eyebrows shot up. By all the gods, was Elaran... laughing? The normally grumpy elf shook his head ruefully at the giggling princess while a wide smile decorated his face. A warm fuzzy feeling that had nothing to do with the sparkling drink spread through my chest. Happiness suited him.

"Did your tutors never instruct you in the art of dancing?" Niadhir's voice interrupted my musings.

"What? No." I cleared my throat and took another sip of wine. "My education had a... different focus."

"Such as?"

"Oh, you know, a bit of this and a bit of that."

A little further down from the princess and the ranger, another couple swayed to the violin notes floating through the starlit hall. I glared at Nelyssae as she squirmed in front of Shade and brushed her curves against his athletic body. They moved in perfect step with the music and the other dancers.

Irritation bubbled through me. Of course the damn assassin knew how to dance. Was there anything he didn't excel at? His smug voice drifted through my head. *It's not about having the need. It's about being prepared for every eventuality.* Fuming, I drew my eyebrows down. At least I knew how to ride and how to make a fire now. Did I really have to add dancing to that damn list too?

Shade leaned forward and, with lips brushing her ear, whispered something to her. She drew back and swatted his muscular chest with the back of her hand while a sultry smile spread across her features. I stared daggers at her.

"Fine!" I banged the half-empty glass down on the table. "Let's dance then."

Niadhir blinked like a startled bird at my violent outburst but composed himself quickly. After placing his crystal goblet on the white silk in a much calmer fashion, he held out his hand and gave me a satisfied smile. I slammed my palm onto his and dragged him towards Shade and Nelyssae.

"Storm," the scholar said in a gentle voice. "In a dance, it is the man who leads."

"I am not a follower. I am a leader."

Niadhir drew back and stared at me as if I had just informed him that I liked running around the city naked during a full moon. Realizing that it had been the wrong reply, I gave my head a quick shake and transformed my features into an apologetic look.

"I'm sorry." I smiled up at him. "I don't know where that came from. Of course it's the man who leads."

The confused look stayed on his face for another moment but as soon as we reached the dancefloor, it disappeared and he started instructing me on how to stand and move in step with the music. He lost me about three sentences into the explanation but I nodded at the appropriate times anyway. I was sure I would figure it out regardless. I mean, compared to the complexities of breaking into a mansion, how hard could a little dancing be?

Very difficult, apparently. A startled yelp rang out as I twirled in the wrong direction and stumbled right into a lady in a voluminous silver dress. Nelyssae snickered behind her hand to my left. Ignoring her, I tried to catch up with the rest of the dancers and ran over to where Niadhir had disappeared to in the ever-moving line of people. Once I finally made it back, I tried again.

The crowd spun together and formed several smaller groups. Me and three other ladies ended up in a ring with our hands together in the middle, moving slowly around like the petals of a flower. One of them was Nelyssae. A haughty smirk dripped from her lips as she flicked eyes brimming with superiority over my halting steps. I narrowed my eyes at her but before I could spit out the curses brewing on my tongue, the dancers shifted again and formed new groups of four.

Sprinting to the one with only three in it, I managed to rejoin them before we were left too far behind. A star elf in a pure white dress with sharp lines met my gaze from across the interlocked hands.

"You shouldn't be here," Maesia said, her face stern and eyes hard. "This is not the place for you."

Surprised, I simply stared at the strange elf I'd met in the library the other day. That time she had threatened me and now she was outright telling me that I had no place here.

"What the hell have I ever done to you?" I shot back.

Only silence met me. I shook my head as the group broke apart again. Two long lines formed. One had all the ladies and the other one all the men. Skidding to a halt in the space left for me, I barely managed to take my place before the whole row of ladies moved forward.

Niadhir gave me a proud smile as I got close. "You are doing well."

"Thanks," I mumbled as we touched hands before all the ladies backed away again.

Next to the scholar, Shade tore his eyes from Nelyssae and glanced at me. Amusement played over his lips. I sent him a murderous stare. If I'd had a knife at that moment, I would've thrown it at him. Damn assassin.

My foot stepped on something soft and slipped. The noise of fabric tearing sounded below me. I managed a panicked look down just before the train of the dress I'd accidentally stepped on was yanked away. The heavy dress I wore apparently wanted me to fall because it pulled me further off balance when it tipped to the side. Despite my arms flailing like a deranged windmill, I tumbled to the frosted glass floor in a heap of silver and white.

That treacherous skirt rustled in the air before flapping down on the floor. I closed my eyes. Humiliation burned through my whole body like wildfire. All around me, silence had fallen. I didn't want to open my eyes to face the embarrassment, so for a moment I just stayed there, fervently praying to Nemanan that a chasm would open in the floor and swallow me.

Malicious giggles rang out somewhere above me. When I finally allowed my vision to return, I found Lady Nelyssae and her posse pointing and laughing at me. I shot to my feet.

"If I were you, I would shut my mouth right now," I said in a voice laced with fury and madness. "Before anyone gets hurt."

The smug ladies flinched and stopped snickering. Death and insanity tried to claw its way out of my soul and it was only by sheer force of will that I kept the darkness from exploding.

"By the Stars," Niadhir said and stepped in front of me. "What is going on? Come with me."

He placed a hand on my arm and led me from the disaster on the dancefloor. Since I was too mortified and pissed off to protest, I allowed him to lead me to an unoccupied table by the wall. Yanking out a chair, I dropped into it. The delicate wooden thing creaked in distress at being handled in such a rough way.

Niadhir lowered himself into the one next to me and placed a soft hand on my arm. "What happened?"

"I stepped on a damn dress and fell over," I muttered and crossed my arms. "Didn't you see that?"

The dancing had resumed in the middle of the room, and for a moment only the breathtaking tunes of harps and violins sounded. At last, Niadhir opened his mouth again.

"Are you alright?"

"Never better." I nodded at the tables on the other side of the room. "Could use a drink, though."

He gave my arm a quick squeeze before rising. "Of course. I will be right back."

While the polite scholar went in search of some much-needed alcohol, I tried desperately to mend my shattered self-esteem. I hadn't thought it possible to feel even more out of place than I already did, but boy had I been wrong. Every day felt like I was part of a well-rehearsed play, only I was a last-minute stand-in from the bottom of the list and someone had forgotten to actually give me the script so all I did was blunder in and out of every scene with no clue of what to say or do.

Before I had even arrived in this strange place, I had felt lost and now all I wanted to do was go to bed, pull the cover over my head, and hide from the world.

Insistent words from long ago stabbed into my brain. *What do you want?*

I gave myself a mental slap. Hiding? What the hell kind of weak loser talk was that? I shouldn't be hiding. The world was the one that should be hiding from me.

As I watched Niadhir weave his way back towards me, I shook my head vigorously and slammed my mental armor back in place. Right now, I just needed to survive the night. Light from the candelabras glinted off the crystal goblets in the scholar's hands. My mouth twisted into a wry smile. And the contents of those glasses would definitely help with that.

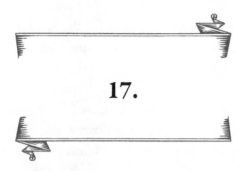

17.

Flower-scented winds whipped through my hair. I felt loads lighter. As soon as I'd gotten back to my room and closed it in Niadhir's face, I had practically ripped off that ridiculous dress and those sparkly hairpins. After putting on the plainest clothes in the closet and pulling back my hair in a simple braid, I had kicked off my shoes and climbed onto the windowsill.

The cool night air against my skin was a blessing after the heat I'd endured in that ballroom packed with dancing people and lit candles. Elaran's window had been left open so once I made it across the wall, I jumped right into his room.

He jerked back a little in surprise when I landed on the floor. The assassin leaning against the wall right next to the window, however, only twisted his head to look at me with a serious expression on his face.

"What's this business about Storm Casters dying?" Shade said without preamble.

"With everything that's happened tonight, that's where you want to start?" After a confused shake of my head, I flicked a hand dismissively and clicked my tongue. "It's none of your business."

Taking a step forward, I aimed for the bed Elaran currently occupied but only made it that one stride before the assassin's arm shot out in front of me.

"I asked you a question."

"And I said it's none of your business." I shoved his arm away.

His hand snaked around my wrist and he whirled me around, trapping me against the wall instead. "It *is* my business. Our business. If you're dying, I... we..." He trailed off before repeating, "It is our business."

Tilting my head back, I stared into his intense black eyes before moving my gaze to Elaran. The wood elf watched me in silence. I blew out an irritated breath and crossed my arms.

"Apparently, I sold my soul to a demon when I was eleven in exchange for power. So there is that. But everyone who's done that has ended up either killing themselves in a storm they created because they can't control the demonic powers, or taking their own life because they accidentally killed someone they cared about." I nodded at the assassin. "Like I almost did to you in Travelers' Rest." Glaring at him, I made as if to slink away. "Satisfied?"

The Master Assassin put a hand below my throat and pushed me back into the wall. "Not so fast."

A range of emotions drifted across his handsome face. Most of them far too serious for my liking. I couldn't handle a grave conversation about the implications of having sold my soul or the prospects of dying in some horrible way. Fortunately, whatever the assassin had seen in my face, he seemed to have understood that. Relief flooded through my chest when a teasing grin spread across his lips instead. Right now, I would take teasing over just about anything.

Shade's black eyes glittered as he met my gaze. "Did you just admit that you care about me?"

"What? No. I..." I huffed and drew my eyebrows down. "I never said that."

From atop the white covers, Elaran chuckled. "He's got you pushed into a corner now, doesn't he?"

Deciding to get out of that corner, literally and figuratively, I ducked under Shade's arm and took refuge on the bed next to the amused elf. "You're idiots. Both of you."

The black-eyed assassin shot me another satisfied grin before striding over to the chair by the desk. It scraped against the floor as he dragged it into position and dropped into it.

"Queen Nimlithil said she had an alternative for you," he picked up. "What's that about?"

"Apparently, there's a way to get rid of it."

He raised his eyebrows. "You're not seriously considering it, are you?"

"No. I don't know." I let out a long exhale. "What matters is getting out of here. Until then, I can't spare the brain capacity to think about it." Shade looked like he was about to protest so I changed the subject before he could. "They know who we are."

The mattress bounced up and down underneath me as Elaran shifted his weight.

"Thanks to me, it seems." He shook his head, discomfort clear on his face. "How could I have let that slip?"

"Yeah it's not like you were drugged or anything." Picking up a fluffy white pillow, I threw it at him. "Let it go. The important thing is, we now know they know and that they're keeping us here for a reason."

"You're saying we didn't know we were here for a reason before that?" Shade arched an eyebrow at me.

I groaned and scowled at him. "Shut up. I'm saying that we now have confirmation they're up to something more than just *rescuing wayward souls*, as they call it."

Shade tipped his head to the right and studied me for a moment. "Fair enough."

Air full of jasmine and roses blew in through the window, making the white curtains flutter. Elaran leaned forward.

"We also found out that Princess Illeasia had nothing to do with the drugged interrogation," he said.

"We don't know that." I frowned at him. "Just because the queen said she was the one who asked you stuff doesn't mean the princess wasn't involved."

The auburn-haired archer ran a hand over his tight side-braid. "I don't think she was. She's... different. There's no dishonesty or deception in her eyes. I don't think she's involved in whatever it is that her mother is doing. She's just... her."

"If you say so." I rolled my eyes. "Just be careful when–"

"Of course I'm careful," he cut off. "It's not like I'm going to go tell her all our plans or anything. I'm just saying that she's probably not a threat."

Holding up my hands, I signaled that I didn't want to argue. Shade drummed his fingers on the desk next to him.

"We need to find the end of that chute," the assassin said. "The one we found today might've been useless because it's in a different part of the castle, but it did confirm that they use them for something and that they're locked by latches from the outside." He moved calculating eyes between us. "So keep working on the princess and Niadhir and get them to take you to different parts of the building so we can find it."

"So you can keep putting your lips to Nelyssae's ear while she giggles and touches your chest." I flicked my eyes to the ceiling and let out a dry chuckle.

"Yes. Same as you."

I huffed. "I haven't been doing anything like that."

"No?" Strange emotions blew across Shade's face. "Who was that clinging to his arm all evening, dancing and sipping sparkling wine? That wasn't you?"

"It's not the same thing!"

"It doesn't matter," Elaran cut in and heaved an exasperated sigh. "Enough with the squabbling. It's not getting us anywhere."

The assassin and I threw one last glare at each other before admitting that the elf was right and getting back on topic.

"Fine," I muttered. "We keep working on our targets. In whatever way we prefer," I added with a pointed look in Shade's direction.

He shook his head at me before filling in, "Until we find the end of the chute."

The mattress shifted under me as I placed my hands on it and pushed off. "Alright, plan settled. Now if you'll excuse me, I'm gonna go forget this day ever happened and pray to Nemanan that I never have to do anything like it ever again." Grabbing a hold of the window frame, I climbed back into the night while calling over my shoulder, "Good talk."

Cicadas sang far below me while I made my way back to my own room. Now all I had to do was keep playing nice and pour honeyed words into Niadhir's ear until he showed me around the castle. Getting people to do what I want would've been so much easier if I'd had my knives. A dull pang hit me when I thought about my trusted tools and clothes that were still missing. Without them, I felt even less like me. And I was forced to persuade people by other means. Like charming them. I blew out a breath and rolled my eyes. Sweet-talking. Oh joy. My specialty.

18.

Weeks dragged on without a single suspicious metal plate in sight. By feigning an interest in architecture, just as I had planned, I had gotten the unsuspecting Niadhir to show me a lot of strange rooms. Shade and Elaran had done the same and every night we'd met in the elf's room and filled in our map until we concluded that our combined efforts had combed this whole wing. And still no trace of a flower-stamped metal plate that would signify the end of the chute.

"What are you thinking about?"

How my escape plan has been entirely fruitless so far. But instead of voicing that out loud, I gave Niadhir a small smile. "Oh, nothing."

As I stabbed the embroidery needle into the white cloth again, I wondered briefly if anyone had ever actually answered that question honestly. If someone wanted to share what they were thinking, they'd already be speaking, wouldn't they?

The scholar smiled back at me before pushing a book out of the way to make room for another. I glanced at the half-empty library around us. Everyone else was occupied elsewhere and only the books in the white wooden shelves around us took note of our conversation. If I was going to make a move, it had to be now.

Since Elaran, Shade, and I had searched this entire wing more than once, we had come to the conclusion that the end of the chute had to be outside the castle. The only problem was of course getting out to check. I had tried hinting to Niadhir that I wanted to go outside but had been wholly unsuccessful. For all his intelligence, he was terrible at taking a hint. Now I had committed to redoubling my efforts which involved something truly horrible. Flirting.

Placing my ugly embroidery of a flower on the table, I leaned forward. "Actually, I was thinking about something."

Niadhir looked up from his book. "Oh?"

I had absolutely no idea how to be seductive so I just tried to copy the things I'd seen Nelyssae do to Shade at the numerous balls and banquets we had attended these past weeks. While twirling my hair with one hand, I placed the other on his arm and gave him what I hoped was a sultry smile.

"I would love to go outside and spend a day in town with you."

He blinked at me in surprise. "You would?"

The giggle I pressed out sounded fake even to my own ears. Stifling a cringe, I instead gave him a soft swat with the back of my hand. "Of course I would. Just you and me, strolling around your gorgeous city, looking at the architectural wonders and drinking in the sunlight."

"That does sound pleasant but we are not supposed to go outside." He tapped his chin. "But perhaps..." Putting his hand over mine, he gave me a smile. "Yes, perhaps it is time."

Ha! I wanted to jump up and pump a fist in the air. Take that, everyone who had ever doubted my sweet-talking skills. I was definitely telling Haela this when I got back.

Pain wrung my heart into a tight knot at the thought of the energetic twin I had left behind in Pernula. I missed her enthusiasm and optimism. She would've loved adventuring across the continent and if I'd asked her to come with me when I'd left, she would've said yes in a heartbeat. But I hadn't asked. I hadn't even said goodbye. Though, given our current predicament of being captives in the City of Glass, maybe that had been for the best.

"Yes, let us go outside." Niadhir snapped the book shut and placed it on the neat pile next to him. "Let me show you the splendor of my city."

Chairs scraped against the floor as we both rose and got ready to leave. The scholar held out his arm. In the weeks I'd spend with him–in the library, on architectural tours of the castle, in the rooftop garden, at balls and banquets–I'd almost gotten used to being escorted around in this fashion. Almost. I took his arm and let him lead me downstairs.

Guards in spotless white armor watched us intently as we descended the stairs. Yeah, there was definitely no slinking past them. We needed that chute. When we at last reached the ground floor, Niadhir steered me towards the grand double doors that marked the end of Starhaven. My heart pattered in my chest. I would finally get to go outside.

Bright sunlight and warm air filled with the scent of summer flowers and the sea met me. I drew a deep breath. Being confined inside in the same place for weeks on end without the possibility of moving freely was not ideal for a thief. Even if it was in a large castle. Just stepping outside those thick doors filled me with renewed energy, and a tiny green sprout of hope popped up inside my heart.

As we walked down the white steps, I scanned the area as discreetly as possible. Given where the start of the chute was located, if the end was here it had to be set into the outside wall on the left and fairly close to the door. Sun glinted off something shiny a bit further down. My heart leaped. That had to be it. However, there was no way to inspect it closer right now without raising suspicion so I had to settle for devising a plan for when we returned.

"I am so pleased you suggested this," Niadhir said as we began our walk along the stone street towards the city. "I have been wanting more time to talk."

More time to talk? I cast a confused glance at him. Wasn't that what we'd been doing constantly since I got here?

"About what?" I replied half-heartedly while continuing to map the area in my head for potential escape routes Elaran, Shade, and I could use once we got outside.

"About us. When you first arrived, you were a bit rough around the edges." He gave me a kind smile. "But I very much like the woman you have grown into."

Tearing my gaze from the smooth white walls that surrounded the castle grounds further down, I turned to meet his eyes. They looked so innocent and hopeful that I wasn't sure how to respond.

"Uhm... thanks," was apparently the best I could do.

The wrought silver gates at the end of the stone street had been left wide open but two guards in gleaming armor stood at attention on either side. They nodded at us as we passed. To get through them when we escaped, we'd need some kind of disguise.

"This is the City of Glass, capital of Tkeister," Niadhir announced and swept the arm not currently attached to mine in a wide arc.

A rather superfluous statement since I of course already knew that. However, I figured that he wanted to be dramatic so I reacted with an appropriate *ohh*. When he gave me a satisfied smile in return, I knew I'd read the situation correctly.

Even though my exclamation had been a calculated one, there was some truth to it. The city was stunning. Houses made from that strange white material that looked like frosted glass spread out around us in well-thought-out patterns. Awnings in white and silver rustled in the gentle breeze and the sound of rippling water drifted from somewhere up the street, mingling with the soft murmur of people strolling on the smooth stones.

"I can see a future for us here," Niadhir said.

Thankfully, a couple of star elves with long flowing hair stopped in front of a dressmaker's shop and pointed into the window, blocking our path. Weaving around them gave me time to think. When we had passed them, I had finally decided that an innocent question was the best response.

"What do you mean?"

He gave me a rueful shake of his head and waved a hand in front of his face as if to say that his comment had been silly. Since most of my attention went to finding ways for us to escape, I didn't press the matter and instead savored the silence that let me scheme in peace.

As we approached an intricate silver arch set into low white walls, the sound of rippling water grew louder. The polite scholar led us through it. On the other side, a manicured garden stretched out before us. Jasmine and white roses had been artfully placed alongside gleaming sculptures, benches, and a large glass fountain.

Joyful laughter rang out behind me. I stepped nimbly out of the way as two young star elf children raced past us on the footpath. They disappeared into the bushes on our right.

"You move with the grace of a cat," Niadhir said. His pale violet eyes drifted over my body, studying me. "I have rarely seen a human do that."

When you're a cat burglar, it kind of comes with the job description. But instead of informing him about my highly illegal choice of trade and the skills that come with such an occupation, I simply smiled and went back to filling in my mental map of the gardens.

Perhaps Niadhir could sense that my mind was otherwise occupied because he drew me to a bench nearby and sat us down. Placing an elegant hand on my cheek, he turned me towards him until I could see his earnest eyes roaming my face.

"I mean it," he said. "You are very beautiful."

Now that I didn't have to simultaneously keep a conversation going and map an ever-changing area in my head, what he said actually sank in. I blinked at him.

"You're serious?"

"Yes." He nodded at me. "Every time you dress up for a ball or a banquet, I see a born lady of the court. Has no one ever told you that before?"

I shook my head. "No."

How could he possibly find me beautiful? My looks were average, at best. If someone saw me in a crowd, they would've forgotten they'd ever seen me as soon as I'd left. A great attribute for a thief but not something that would inspire love songs. And that was among the humans. Here, not a single elf I'd come across could even be considered average. Everyone looked good. So to learn that he found me, of all people, beautiful was very hard to grasp.

Niadhir patted my hand and gave me a kind smile. "You have not been spending time with the right people, then."

"I've..." I trailed off when I noticed a figure across the garden.

Maesia was standing as still as the statue next to her. She fixed me with a hard stare. For a moment, she just stood there, silent and unmovable like a gravestone while her dark violet eyes bored into me. Then, she slowly shook her head. I frowned at her. Still holding my gaze, she raised a hand and drew her thumb across her throat.

What in Nemanan's name was wrong with that girl? I shot to my feet and turned back to Niadhir. Best not stay and find out. And besides, I still had a mission to complete.

"Let's get out of here."

His pale brows were furrowed in confusion and worry as he looked at me. "Is something the matter?"

"No, no, not at all." I cleared my throat and gestured vaguely at the scene around us. "I'm just excited to see more of the city, is all."

"Oh, of course." The scholar rose from the bench and held out an arm to me. "I have so much more to show you."

Sun continued beaming down on us as Niadhir escorted me through the city. Sometimes he would stop and launch into a lengthy explanation about some architectural feature or other. I only listened with half an ear when he talked because I was busy scheming. So far, I'd spotted a few potential safe houses but since we hadn't walked anywhere near the edge of town, I still hadn't figured out how to actually get out of the city.

After a while, my talkative escort had said something about the heat and the walk wearing me out and steered us back towards the castle. If he only knew the things I'd endured in my life, he wouldn't think a simple stroll under the sun was detrimental to my health.

"I am sorry," he said as we stepped onto the stone street leading to Starhaven.

"For what?"

"For whatever happened to you that invited this darkness inside you." He looked down at me with concerned eyes. "It must be such an awful burden knowing that you have sold your own soul to a demon."

Pretending to brush a speck of dust from my dress, I averted my gaze. "Yeah, I wasn't expecting that." My show of a carefree shrug fell kind of flat but I tried to make my voice light anyway. "I mean, I've always assumed that I'd been going to hell because of everything I've done. I just..." I drew a deep breath. "I just didn't expect that I was already doomed from the start."

Niadhir squeezed my arm tighter. "I cannot even imagine the crushing weight you must feel every day.

Honestly, between the devastating loss of identity and the rootlessness, I barely noticed the added load. I mean, what was one more boulder when you already had a whole mountain pressing down on your chest?

"I'll survive."

My concerned walking companion stopped and placed a hand on my cheek, forcing me to meet his eyes. "I hope so. The curse of dying by one's own hand hangs heavily over all Ashaana.

Please be careful. I do not think I could bear it if that happened to you."

"I have no plans on dying yet," I said and forced a light laugh.

Inside, however, strange feelings swirled. He cared whether I lived or died. People didn't usually do that and I wasn't sure what to do with those emotions. I shook my head. There was no time to deal with that right now because we neared the tall white walls of the castle and I had a plan to execute.

"Oh gods!" I exclaimed and pointed to a thick jasmine bush. "Look! A cat."

After expertly detaching myself from his arm, I rushed over to the bush and started moving branches aside.

"A cat?" Shoes thumped against stone as Niadhir followed me. "Are you sure?"

"Yes, a white one. I saw it slink in here."

I only had a few seconds before he reached me so while I pretended to look inside the bush, I flicked my eyes to the left and studied the metal plate set into the wall. A small stone path had been constructed between the bushes and it led straight to it. My eyes roamed over the flower etched into the metal. It was the same one. Casting my gaze up, I tried to estimate where this would be in the castle. This had to be it.

Slumping back on my heels, I transformed my face into that of a sad young girl. "Aw. There is no cat. I was so sure I saw one but it must've been the white flowers."

In my heart, I knew it had been a ridiculously flimsy excuse but I could think of no other way to suddenly rush over to a random part of the wall without drawing attention. I just hoped that his habit of seeing me as a clueless human and the fact that the metal plate was some distance away had kept him from realizing my true intent.

Bending down, he helped me to my feet. "I am sorry. Do you like pets?"

"I like cats."

That was true enough. I admired their stealth but I had never planned on keeping one as a pet. Niadhir didn't appear to see through my lies because he just patted me on the hand while leading me back to the front doors.

"They can indeed be a great comfort in times of distress." When we had stepped across the threshold and into the cool hall beyond, he motioned at the stairs. "Come. I will take you back to your room so that you can rest. I understand that it has been a trying day, walking so far in this heat and thinking about the awful curse placed on you."

The day I had been one second away from being hanged in Dead Men's Square, that had been a trying day. This one didn't even make my list of slightly uncomfortable days. I shook my head. People sure had differing views on what constituted a difficult life.

"Thank you, that would be nice," I said instead because I wanted to be left alone so that I could draw a map of the city while it was still fresh in my mind.

Now that I had finally found the end of the chute, we could start plotting our escape for real. Anticipation sparkled in my chest as we ascended the stairs. Soon, we would all be out of here for good.

19.

Murmuring filled the corridor. I met Shade's eyes from across the sea of star elves in white and silver. He bent down and whispered something in Nelyssae's ear. She glowered for a second but then accompanied him and moved towards me and Niadhir.

The polite scholar had come to collect me for dinner after he had given me a few hours of rest. Or so he thought. I had of course spent them all scheming.

"Ah, Lady Nelyssae and Shade," he said as the assassin and the lady reached us. "How are you this evening?"

"Very well, thank you," Nelyssae replied with a pleasant smile before turning to me. "Oh by the Stars, your skin looks a bit red."

Suppressing the urge to roll my eyes, I instead plastered an insincere smile on my face. "Yes, that's what happens when you finally go outside into the sun after spending weeks locked indoors."

She leaned her curves further into Shade's athletic body and placed a hand on his chest. "Maybe you and I should go outside too." Her pale violet eyes took on a wicked glint. "Perhaps we should go swimming."

"Swimming! What a great idea!" an excited voice called.

The chatting star elves shuffled aside to allow Princess Illeasia and Elaran to pass. Smiles appeared on the beautiful faces around us as the princess pulled the embarrassed-looking wood elf forward by the hand.

"We'd love to go swimming too," she said, breathless. "How about heading to the beach tomorrow?"

Nelyssae looked like she wanted to say no but couldn't because one doesn't refuse royalty. She forced a smile.

"Of course."

The princess gave her a vigorous nod before turning to me and Niadhir. "Are you coming too?"

"Oh, I am not sure if it is appropriate for men and women to bathe together in this fashion." He scrunched up his eyebrows. "But it might be nice to spend a day at the beach. Yes, I think we will accompany you."

Before I could comment on his strange sense of propriety, a commotion broke out by the doors to one of the smaller dining rooms that were used on days when there was no banquet. The crowd stirred and grumbled. I was just about to ask what was going on when a man in a white apron pushed forward and raised his voice.

"Ladies and gentlemen, I'm afraid dinner will be slightly delayed. There has been an unexpected accident in the kitchen. Thank you for your patience."

Princess Illeasia squinted at his retreating back. "We should see if we can do anything to help." Letting go of Elaran's hand, she turned to Niadhir. "If this is a mechanical problem, they might need your expertise. Please come with me."

The scholar glanced from me to Elaran to Shade. "But what about...?"

"I think they can survive fifteen minutes without us." She waved a graceful hand to the gorgeous elf next to her. "I'm sure Nely can keep them entertained."

Reluctantly detaching himself from the group, the scholar followed the princess towards where the cook had disappeared to. The otherwise confident lady looked uncharacteristically uncertain now that she was surrounded by nothing but foreigners. She clung tighter to Shade and was just about to open her mouth when panic flashed over her face. In a heartbeat, she had taken her hands off the assassin and stepped away from him.

Frowning, I twisted around so that I could follow her line of sight. Captain Hadraeth emerged from a room further down the corridor. I glanced between the anxious lady and the oblivious Guard Captain. After locking the door, he strode in our direction.

With her eyes still on the armor-clad elf, Nelyssae cleared her throat. "Excuse me, I will be right back."

Her sparkling dress swished against the floor as she disappeared further into the wide hallway. When she materialized in front of Hadraeth and pulled him towards the wall, an idea flashed through my mind.

"I have a plan," I whispered to my two friends. "Come on, I'll explain along the way."

Taking my word for it, they followed me through the mass of bodies without question. Polite conversation mingled with discontented muttering from the star elves about the delayed dinner as we made our way towards the door the captain had appeared from.

"I found the end of the chute," I said as we cleared a group of elves impatiently shuffling their feet.

"Where?" Shade demanded.

"Outside. I've also been scouting the city. I've got a couple of potential safe houses but if we can get inside Captain Hadraeth's room now while everyone is distracted, we might find important stuff like guard schedules or even a clear route out of the city."

"Unless you're carrying lockpicks somewhere inside that dress, we're not getting inside," Elaran hissed just as we arrived at the intended door.

I threw a scowl in his direction. "Have you met me? I always carry lockpicks." Placing a hand on each man, I pushed them into position. "Now, pretend that you're just standing here chatting casually. Make sure you block their view of me."

We were close enough to the rest of the dinner guests that we wouldn't look suspicious if someone noticed us but far enough away to enjoy some privacy. Kneeling down, I got to work on the lock. When that very satisfying click sounded, I edged the door open and slunk inside. I had assumed that this was his private room but when I stepped inside, panic shot up my spine. It was some kind of meeting room. If someone else was in here, I was screwed. Logic pushed through the dread and pointed out that if someone else had been here, Hadraeth wouldn't have locked the door behind him when he left.

Letting out a deep breath, I snuck further into the room. An array of gleaming swords, knives, bows, and armor decorated the walls but unfortunately, no sign of my blades. I darted over to the closest table and picked up a topmost sheet of paper. After perusing it, I snatched up another.

A sharp knock sounded on the door. Damn. I had barely even started looking and I was already out of time. Once I had replaced the documents, I sprinted back to the door and slipped out.

"Hurry!" Shade hissed at me before shoving Elaran forward. "Go distract her."

My heart slammed against my ribs as I relocked the door behind me. It clicked in place. I shot to my feet in time to see Princess Illeasia making her way towards us. Elaran was already moving to meet her but we still needed a reason to be all the way over here after she had left us in the middle of the crowd.

"We need an excuse for being here." My eyes flicked between the assassin and the approaching princess. "Something that would explain why we wanted privacy."

Shade pushed me up against the wall and placed one hand next to my head and the other on my cheek. His fingers caressed my jaw as he leaned forward and put his lips to my ear. His breath against my skin sent bolts of lightning through my body.

"How's this for an excuse?" he whispered.

"What are you doing all the way over here?" Illeasia's voice said from somewhere to my right. "I was... oh." Satisfied laughter bubbled from her chest. "I see."

Elaran cleared his throat. "Yeah, they... uhm..."

I couldn't see either of them because my vision was filled with intense black eyes staring at me barely a breath away but I was pretty sure Elaran was blushing.

"Let's leave them to it," the princess said. "Niadhir is helping them fix the machine. It should be ready in a few minutes."

Once we were sure they had left, Shade withdrew. Slumping back against the wall, I heaved a deep sigh as if I hadn't breathed at all in the last couple of minutes. That strange tingling sensation was back on my skin where his fingers had been. I shook my head to clear it.

"I only saw the guard positions for the wing next to ours," I said, trying to get my scrambled brain back on track. "There are almost no guards there but it doesn't help us because we have no way of getting there." Blowing out an annoyed breath, I clicked my tongue. "So, nothing useful."

Shade was silent for a moment before nodding. "We should move a bit further down so that we're not standing right outside this door."

We moved closer to the waiting star elves but didn't join them. Instead we both leaned back against the wall and watched them talk and grumble from a short distance away. I scanned the scene. Illeasia and Elaran had joined a distraught-looking Lady Nelyssae while Captain Hadraeth was nowhere to be seen.

"I'm thinking about getting rid of the darkness," I announced out of the blue. I wasn't even sure why I'd told him that.

The assassin next to me twisted his head to look at me, surprise evident in his dark eyes. "Why?"

"Because it will eventually kill me or make me kill someone I love." I let out a long exhale. "And I can't let that happen."

"You don't know that it will."

"It's happened to everyone else. Why would I be any different?" Flicking an impatient hand over my skirt, I blew out another sigh. "Besides, it's demonic powers from hell. Why would I want to have that inside me?"

"Because it's a part of you. Part of who you are." He held my gaze. "And having power doesn't make you evil."

"I sold my soul to a demon for it. How does that not make me evil?"

Giggling drifted from the group closest to us as a lady with dark silver hair gestured expressively about something. We watched them in silence for another few seconds before Shade broke it.

"How many times has it saved your life?"

Startled, I turned back to stare at him.

"Saved your friends' lives?" he pressed on. "I know it's saved my life more than once. You should see it as an asset."

Lost for words, I simply continued studying his face. Just for him to admit that he would be dead if it weren't for me was huge and that was what reined in my feelings of dread. Maybe he did have a point. The darkness had helped me through a lot of dangerous situations too.

"Ashaana have taken a lot more lives than they have saved," Captain Hadraeth cut in as he stepped in front of us. "I would recommend not listening to someone who knows absolutely nothing about the curse you suffer from. If you tally up the corpses you've left in your wake and compare it to the people you've saved, you will know it's the truth."

Irritation at him butting in on a conversation that was none of his business was dampened by the fact that he was right. I *had* left a rather long trail of bodies behind me.

Shade opened his mouth but before any sound made it out, the Guard Captain continued. "Lady Nelyssae is looking for you. You'd better go to her."

The Master Assassin gave me a long look before striding off into the crowd. Not wanting to be left alone with the strange captain, I wove through the sea of murmuring people as well.

Conflicting emotions battled for supremacy in my chest. On the one hand, I wanted desperately to cling to Shade's reasoning. The darkness had saved the people I loved more than once and it was definitely an asset when I found myself in a tough spot. But on the other hand, Captain Hadraeth was also right. I had used it to kill far more people than I had saved. And because of it, I had almost killed someone I cared about as well.

Was it a curse or an asset? I wasn't sure. As I neared our small group, I shoved out the annoying feelings digging holes in my chest and blew out a forceful breath. It didn't matter anyway. Tomorrow we would be one step closer to our escape and I couldn't afford to get distracted. Forcing a smile onto my face, I rejoined my companions. I had to stay focused. Otherwise, we were all doomed.

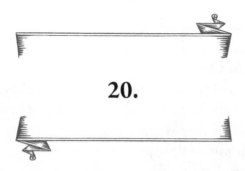

20.

Waves crashed against the shore. Closing my eyes, I drew a deep breath, inhaling the familiar scent of the sea. Each city might have its own signature scent—crisp and cold and pine needles for Keutunan, spices on a warm summer day for Pernula, and jasmine and roses for the City of Glass—but everywhere I went, the sea always smelled the same. Salt. Seaweed. And home.

"This was a great idea, Nely," Princess Illeasia chirped as she twirled around in the black sand. "I haven't gone swimming in ages."

Her eyes were as bright as the sun above us when she gazed at the glittering water. Undoing a knot on the side of her dress, she slipped out of the outer layer to reveal a much smaller dress. I squinted at it. The short skirt ended mid-thigh and straps across her shoulders held the whole thing up. Moving my eyes to Lady Nelyssae, I found her in something similar after she had dropped her long white dress on the sand.

Uncertainty filled me as I glanced down at my own body. I was wearing nothing of the sort. Instead, I had put on the simple white dress I usually wore when I didn't have to dress up for some formal dinner or other. Was I supposed to swim in that?

"Let's go!" Sand sprayed into the air as the princess raced to the shoreline. "What are you waiting for?"

While walking backwards towards the water, Lady Nelyssae curled a finger at Shade and Elaran, beckoning them to join her. "Come on then, boys."

The wood elf and the assassin exchanged a look before giving each other a synchronized shrug. Airy white shirts and pants hit the beach as they stripped out of their clothes until they only wore a pair of light pants that ended above the knee. I studied them. Lean muscles rippled as they straightened and started towards the sea.

Shade whirled around. A smirk played over his lips when he found my eyes roaming his body. "Coming?"

Startled, I cleared my throat and hoped the ridiculous blush that had flash over my cheeks was invisible in the bright sunlight. "I..."

"She is not wearing any bathing clothes," Niadhir cut in. He shook out a large blanket and placed it on the black sand. "And neither am I. We will remain ashore."

The Master Assassin turned hard eyes on the scholar, and for a moment it looked like he was about to say something, but then he just lifted his shoulders in another shrug and strode towards the water.

Niadhir lowered himself onto the blanket and started pulling books from a satchel. He patted the pale fabric on the ground. "Come sit down. I brought your embroidery."

Oh, hurray. Stifling a snarky remark and an eye roll, I plopped down next to him. White skirts billowed around me before settling over my legs. I blew out a sigh. Doing needlework wasn't exactly what I'd had in mind when they said we were going to the beach.

Out in the water, Elaran was standing at knee-depth glaring skeptically at the water. "It's a bit cold, isn't it?"

"Are you serious?" Shade arched his muscled back and dove under an approaching wave before popping up again. "It's a lot warmer than the sea back in Keutunan."

The grumpy elf crossed his arms. "We didn't swim in the sea. We swam in lakes in the forest. And they were much warmer."

While the cranky wood elf had been preoccupied informing Shade about the difference in water temperature, Princess Illeasia had swam around him and snuck up from behind. Just as the last syllable left his mouth, the princess drew her arms in a wide sweep and splashed a wave of water over him from behind.

A startled yelp leaped from his throat and he drew his arms up in shock at the sudden cold washing over his body. Joyous notes echoed across the beach as Princess Illeasia doubled over and laughed like there was no tomorrow. The grumpiness and shock melted from Elaran's features as he looked at her. His mouth drew into a smile as he placed his arms in the water and splashed twice that amount back on the princess. More laughter rang out.

Even I couldn't stop a wide smile from spreading across my face. Princess Illeasia was the perfect complement to Elaran. While he was always so full of duty and seriousness, she radiated excitement, playfulness, and a joy of living. He needed someone who brought light to his life. Looking at the expression on his face now as he joked around in the water made me forget for a moment that we were prisoners here.

"Are you not going to start your embroidery?" Niadhir asked.

I scrambled to my feet. "No, I..." Running my fingers through my hair, I cast my gaze around the area. "I'm just gonna walk around the beach a little. Need to clear my head."

Before he could respond, I strode off towards the dark gray cliffs boxing in this hidden beach. My head and my heart were getting all tangled up and I didn't like it. Elaran looked happy here. And from what I'd seen when I was out in town, so was everyone else who lived in the city. For a nation waging war and conquering others, they were a strangely peaceful people. I leaned back against the cool rocks. Maybe there was more to them than the villain stories I'd previously heard.

My eyes drifted to Shade. Droplets glinted off his skin as he emerged from the water. Lady Nelyssae swam forward and lifted a delicate hand to his head, pulling out a piece of a reed that had gotten stuck in his hair. She drew her fingers down his cheek as she removed it. I wondered if he was happy here too.

So as to not have to deal with the hurricane of emotions whirling through me, I tore my gaze from the assassin and pushed off the jagged cliff wall. A rowboat lay nestled in the black sand further down. I set course for it.

It was in surprisingly good state considering the fact that it had been lying out here in all kinds of weather. Placing my hands on the rough railing, I peered into it. Two oars, an empty bucket, and some coils of rope littered the bottom. I straightened and turned back to Niadhir.

"Hey, do you wanna go rowing instead of swimming?" I called.

The scholar looked up from his book with a befuddled expression on his face. "Rowing?"

"Yes. I wanna get out on the water too."

He looked about to refuse but when I put on my best sad face, he closed the book he'd been reading and got to his feet. "Yes, alright."

The keel of the rowboat left a rut in the sand as we pushed it to the waterline. It bobbed up and down on the waves once we got it out. At least it was too small to make me seasick. Niadhir rowed us closer to our swimming friends while I contemplated when to make my move. The sparkling blue waves hit the side and sprayed mist over the railing. I guessed this was as good a place as any.

A shocked gasp resounded as I stood up and pulled the dress over my head. Niadhir blabbered something incoherently before he finally pressed out a fully-formed sentence.

"Oh, by the Stars! Storm what are you doing?"

"Swimming." I dropped the white dress atop the coils of rope.

"In only your undergarments?" The distraught scholar averted his gaze so that he wouldn't have to see the two offending pieces of clothing. "This is not the proper way for a lady to behave."

Amusement blew past on Shade's face as he watched me from the water. I put one foot on the railing.

"Good thing I'm not a lady," I said before diving into the waiting sea.

Soft water enveloped my body as I disappeared below the surface. Relishing the refreshing coolness around me, I stayed below the waves for another few moments before kicking back towards the land of breathable air. Warm winds met my face when I broke through.

"Oh by the Stars, there you are," Niadhir's distressed voice rang out above me. "I thought you might have hit your head and fallen unconscious."

"Calm down." I executed a few long backstrokes. "If I can survive diving from a Pernish warship, I can survive diving from a rowboat." Swimming away even further, I called up at him, "I'll meet you back on the shore."

His disapproving comments fell on deaf ears as I let the waves carry me away. These star elves' strange sense of propriety was exhausting. Though, I suppose the nobles in Keutunan had a similar view of what ladies should and shouldn't do. Maybe the rest of the citizens here lived by less strict rules.

Lady Nelyssae pouted her lips and glared at me. "You should listen to him. This is not how a lady should behave."

In the water next to her, Shade flashed me a knowing grin that told me we were thinking the same thing. Doing as I was told had never been my strong suit.

"Oh don't be such a fuss, Nely," Princess Illeasia quipped. "You have to live a little."

After sending a quick smile in her direction, I swam back towards the beach before the nervous scholar dropped dead of indecency. As soon as the boat reached the sand, he scrambled out of it and raced back to the blanket. He snatched it up and shook it out before rushing towards me by the waterline. While twisting his head to the side, he held up the large cloth to protect my modesty. I chuckled at the embarrassed look on his face but took the offered cover anyway.

"I'm just gonna go grab my clothes and put them back on," I said as I wrapped the blanket around me and started towards the rowboat.

"Yes, yes, excellent idea," Niadhir said. "I shall wait over here."

Once I reached the boat, I scooped up the bundle at the bottom before moving to a more secluded part of the beach to get dressed.

Niadhir had pulled the rowboat back to its original position and our four swimming friends had gotten out of the water when I returned, wearing my white dress again. All five of them had squeezed together on the remaining blankets. I studied them.

Elaran and Illeasia were discussing something with their heads close together. The princess gestured wildly around her with an ecstatic look on her face, making the wood elf break into a smile as well. On their other side, Shade stretched his athletic body across the white fabric.

Most people would only appreciate his lean muscles, and though I did very much enjoy the view of them too, I also found myself staring at the pale scars decorating his skin. I say *decorating* and not *marring* because to me, they didn't diminish his looks. They added to them. As a person with a rather vast collection of scars myself, I understood what someone with marks like that had lived through. Surviving things like that took a lot of strength, mental and physical, and a great deal of cunning. And those were qualities I found very attractive.

Lady Nelyssae's eyes took on a malicious glint when she noticed my gaze. Propping herself up on one elbow, she placed her other hand on the assassin's chest in a possessive gesture and leaned down over him to whisper something in his ear. Narrowing my eyes, I shot her a dirty look but then glanced away because I didn't want Shade to catch me staring at him.

I might find the Master Assassin ever so slightly attractive but I'd never admit that to him. He received enough attention from women as it was. Women far more beautiful than me. Huffing, I crossed my arms. And feelings were still a bloody inconvenience.

We spent another hour so or drying off, chatting, and soaking up the sun. Niadhir pestered me about resuming my embroidery but I was content simply watching the waves and listening to everyone else talk. After a while, the dutiful scholar suggested that we should return to the castle, as too much sun might be bad for us, so we packed up and started the walk back.

"So is this like a private beach for royalty or something?" I motioned at the path cut into the cliffs around us.

"Not for only the royal family per se," Niadhir supplied. "But we are inside the castle grounds so only residents of Starhaven have access to it."

I already knew that, of course, since I had seen this path from my window but I still found it odd that no one else had been there today. In Keutunan, the harbor was usually packed with people trying to cool off during hot summer days. Maybe swimming wasn't a popular activity in this city.

Lady Nelyssae gave me a patronizing smile as we skirted around the castle. "Shouldn't that have been obvious?"

"What the hell is your problem?" I spat out.

The smug lady placed a hand on her chest in surprise. "My problem?"

"Yeah. All you ever do is try to make me feel like shit."

"Excuse me?" She harrumphed. "I only tell you as it is. It's not my fault that you're so ignorant."

Screeching to a halt a short distance from the main entrance, I yanked my arm from Niadhir's grasp and whirled on Nelyssae. "Ignorant? If you were dropped into my world, you wouldn't survive a day." A predatory grin crept across my mouth. "Even less if I was coming after you."

"Storm!" Niadhir said, aghast.

The arrogant lady jutted out her chin. "Resorting to threats is only the sign of a weak mind."

"Weak?" A laugh laced with madness dripped from my lips. "How about I show you just how weak I am?" I took a threatening step forward.

The horrified scholar made as if to intercept me but he had nothing on a trained thief. Darting to the side, I slipped right past him. Lady Nelyssae's beautiful face filled with terror when she saw me advance on her. Raising her hands, she took a step back. A body packed with hard muscles slammed into mine.

"That's enough," Shade's said in a voice brimming with authority. His strong hands restrained me before I could reach Nelyssae.

Thrashing against the assassin's grip, I spat curses at her over his shoulder. "If you ever make me feel like shit again, we're gonna finish this conversation. And that time, Shade won't be there to protect you."

Niadhir had gathered up the frightened lady in his arms and patted her on the back in order to calm her. Glancing towards the wall, I saw Elaran emerge from the bushes. He gave me a quick nod before taking up position next to the distracted princess as if nothing had happened.

Since he had his back to everyone else, no one but me saw the amused expression on Shade's face as he bent down towards me. "Don't you think that was a bit overkill?"

"Are you kidding?" I whispered back. "I considered punching her in the face but figured *that* was a bit overkill." Making a show of struggling against his arms, I hid the satisfied smile on my lips. "Elaran gave the all clear. We pulled it off. The latches are off the chute now."

The Master Assassin smirked at me. "Yeah, I saw. Should we keep at it for another minute? To really sell the bit."

I snorted. "I think we're alright."

Stopping my thrashing, I stared expectantly at him until he released me. Once he had, I transformed my face into an apologetic mask and looked to Niadhir and Nelyssae with the appropriate amount of shame in my eyes.

"I'm sorry," I lied. "I don't know what came over me. It must've been all that sun going to my head."

"Yes, well, I did warn you about the effects of too much sun." Niadhir cleared his throat. "Perhaps you should retire to your room and think about how you can avoid a situation like this in the future."

The sheer ridiculousness of that statement made me want to chuckle like a lunatic but I managed to suppress it and instead dropped my gaze. "Yeah, I think I'll go to bed early tonight."

Niadhir gave me a grave nod as he returned Lady Nelyssae to Shade's arm before leading me up the stairs. "That sounds wise."

I adjusted my dress to better hide the coils of rope currently wrapped around my body. Stealing them during that very calculated episode when I suddenly took my clothes off in a rowboat had been a piece of cake because Niadhir had barely dared look at me when I was indisposed. Thank Nemanan for his prudishness. I grinned as we moved towards my room. Now, I both had a way to climb up and down the chute and the end of it was unlocked. And I'd given Lady Nelyssae a piece of my mind. A most productive day indeed.

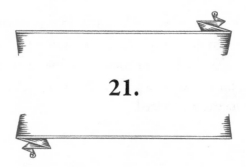

21.

The halls of the castle lay deserted around me, despite it only being a few hours after dinner. Opening the chute, I peered into the darkness. There was no way to know for sure if this would work. Apart from trying it. After tying the ropes together, I secured one end to the handle on the inside of the metal plate and let the other disappear down the hole.

"Come on, Lady Luck. Help a thief out."

Sending a prayer to Cadentia, I braced myself on the wall and climbed through the opening. With one hand on the rope, I pulled the plate shut behind me. The world turned pitch black.

"Man, it's dark in here," I muttered.

With the plate closed, I couldn't even see my own hands but it was the only way. If someone happened upon the open chute with a rope tied to it, I'd be in real trouble. Not to mention that I needed the support from the metal sheet bracing against the wall in order to lower myself down the rope. And then when climbing back up again, of course. After sending another prayer to the Goddess of Luck, I started down the square-shaped passage.

My breathing sounded unnaturally loud, but I knew it was just the confined space playing tricks on my ears so I tried to block it out and concentrate on the rope. Time crept by while I tried to imagine running free across the rooftops instead of crawling through a space so small it would make a tight-shelled crab claustrophobic. Eventually, I felt the knot tying one rope to the other under my hands. I continued downwards. The bottom had to be close now.

Empty air met my palm. My heart skipped a beat and I gripped the line tighter with my other hand before I could get them both back on it. Damn. I was out of rope. Stretching my legs as far down as I could, I tried to locate the bottom. They swung through the chute without finding purchase.

"Really, Cadentia?" I grumbled.

The end could be a finger's length below or it could be fifty strides and it was impossible to know which unless I let go of the rope. If it was too far, I might not be able to get back up. Blood pounded in my ears. Godsdamn it. I drew a deep breath and let go.

Fabric flapped around me as I slid down the chute. Panic welled up in my throat like bile when I kept gliding downwards. The end had to be here somewhere.

A jolt shot up my ankles as they slammed into something hard. It gave way and I tumbled out of the opening and onto the ground outside. Stones scraped against my legs. Ignoring the pain, I scrambled to my feet and ducked behind the nearest jasmine bush. My heart thumped in my chest.

No alarm rose. Putting a hand to a leaf-covered branch, I carefully bent it down and peered out. Moonlight bathed the courtyard in silver and cicadas played in the bushes but other than that, there was not a soul in sight. I let out a soft exhale while forcing my racing heart to slow down.

"Alright, so far so good," I whispered to myself. "Now, all we need is a way past the gate."

After sweeping my gaze over the area one more time, I snuck forward. There was another building next to the castle that I had never seen up close so I decided to start there. Gravel crunched under my feet as I darted across the stones.

When I got closer, I realized that it was actually multiple buildings clustered together. A gigantic white dome with a set of grand double doors far larger than the ones to the castle was flanked by two much smaller square-shaped structures. I squinted at it. What on earth was that used for?

The strange glass-like material was cool under my hand as I pressed my palm against one of the great doors. There was an odd atmosphere to this whole building. It felt ancient. Otherworldly. Whatever was in here had to be important. I bent down to study the lock on the doors and see if I could get them open.

Footfalls echoed across the courtyard. *Shit.* Making a split-second decision, I sprinted towards the square building on the right. If it had the same complicated lock as the dome, I was screwed. Praying fervently to Nemanan that it was an ordinary one, I skidded to a halt in front of it. The footsteps drew closer. I dropped to a knee and whipped out my picks.

Relief surged through me when I saw that it was a standard lock. It clicked open within seconds. Sending heartfelt prayers of thanks to Nemanan, I slid inside and closed it behind me.

Three large carriages met me on the other side. The smooth floor was silent under my feet as I tiptoed forward to examine them further. They looked familiar. Realization hit me like a basher's bat to the face as I traced my fingers over the metal wall. Prisoner carriages. This was what they'd used to bring us here.

The door was yanked open. Crap. My eyes darted across the room. Depending on how many people were about to enter this carriage storage, there might not be any place to hide. Except... I looked up. It would have to do.

Grabbing a hold of the window set into the side of the metal coach, I hauled myself up until I could reach the roof. The dress tangled around my legs. Silently cursing the thief-hating garment, I used my arms to draw myself over the edge and rolled to safety. I dared a quick glance down.

Captain Hadraeth stalked across the floor. I yanked my head back down and pressed myself as far into the carriage roof as was humanly possible. That treasonous heart of mine thumped so loudly in my chest I was afraid it would make the metal underneath me vibrate.

The Guard Captain's hunting footsteps echoed against the walls as he strode through the room. Straining my ears, I tried to follow his path around the carriages. They paused right below me. Blood pounded in my ears.

And then he moved again. His steps grew fainter until the sound of a door being pushed open finally cut through the pounding in my ears. I peeked over the top of the roof just in time to see the captain's white armor disappear into the night beyond. The lock clicked back in place.

Rolling over on my back, I let out a long exhale. I had barely dared breathe these last few minutes so I had a lot of missed oxygen to make up for. That had been close. Stroking the metal beneath me, I let a smile settle on my lips.

But now we had a way to get past the gate. I sat back up and started down the side of the carriage again. All we needed was a guard's armor for Elaran and we could ride right out of here in the very same thing that had brought us in. Ha! They would never see it coming.

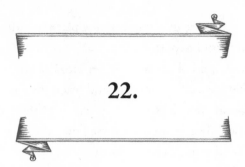

22.

Cold glass met my skin as I knelt on the floor. I cast another quick glance around the empty corridor before sliding my lockpicks into the waiting lock. A soft click sounded. Straightening, I pushed down the handle. Light from the hallway spilled into the darkness beyond. With my hand still on the cool metal, I waited. No sound or movement. I slid inside.

Strong hands grabbed me. I sucked in a sharp breath between my teeth. The door slammed shut next to me right before I was yanked to the side and spun around. My chest hit the wall with a slight thud. A muscled body pressed into mine from behind while an iron grip locked my arms behind my back.

"*That's* how you ambush an intruder breaking into your room," Shade whispered, his lips only a breath away from my ear.

"Show-off," I muttered into the wall. "And I already told you, you just got lucky I stumbled when you were breaking into mine."

The Master Assassin drew his fingers around my throat and then towards the back of my neck. "Is that right?"

His touch sent an involuntary shiver through my body. For some reason, I was having trouble thinking straight so I almost missed it when his grip on my wrists loosened. Instincts kicking in at the last moment, I yanked my arms apart and twisted away.

"And *that's* how you get out of an ambush." I smirked at him from a few strides away.

Shade let out a pleasant chuckle. "Only because I let you."

"Uh-huh. Keep telling yourself that."

Striding across the room, he made for the candle on the white wooden desk. Flames flickered to life, casting dancing shadows on the wall. The assassin turned back to me. His face got stuck somewhere between amusement and curiosity when he took in the state of my body.

"Been making trouble, have we?" He nodded at the red scrapes on my legs and the rumpled and stained dress I was wearing.

"Always." I grinned at him. "I've found our way out."

Genuine surprise filled his black eyes. "How?"

"I climbed down the chute and scouted the area. They store prisoner carriages in a building across the courtyard. If we steal a guard's uniform, we can have Elaran impersonate one of them and drive us right out of here."

"Impressive." He gave me an approving nod before confusion settled on his face. He tilted his head to the right. "How did you even climb the chute without rope?"

"Who says I did? I stole some rope from that rowboat today." I frowned at him. "What did you think I was doing when I just out of the blue decided to go swimming in my underwear?"

Surprised laughter rose from his chest. "I don't know. I thought you were just being your usual stubborn rebel self."

Tipping my head from side to side, I concluded that he had a point. I did have a certain flair for disregarding the rules that governed normal people's social interactions.

I nodded at the wall behind him. "Window or door?"

"How did everything look when you were sneaking around out there?"

"Empty."

Shade jerked his chin towards the designated entrance to his room. "Then let's go with the door."

After blowing out the candle, we slipped out the door and set course for Elaran's room.

The startled wood elf let out a sharp hiss and whirled around as a thief and an assassin snuck across the threshold. He released a huff and shook his head at us.

"I'll never get used to that," Elaran muttered. Abs and toned arms tensed and then disappeared under white fabric as he pulled on a shirt. "Can't you at least knock?"

"I don't knock." I gave him a light shrug before plopping down on top of his tidy bed. "But I have found a way out."

"What?"

Shade strode past him and dropped into the chair by the desk. "Apparently, that whole stunt with the rowboat wasn't just about being defiant."

Elaran frowned at the assassin before shifting his gaze to me. "It wasn't?"

"Seriously?" The mattress creaked as I threw my arms in the air in an exasperated gesture. "You make me sound like a three-year-old." I glared at the wood elf. "Do you want to hear about our way out or not?"

Matching my scowl, he just spun his hand in the air a couple of times, telling me to get on with it. I blew out an irritated breath but recounted the events of the evening anyway.

"How's anyone going to believe I'm a star elf?" Elaran challenged once I had finished. He drew his fingers through his auburn hair and flicked it over his shoulder. "I don't exactly look like them, do I?"

"We'll hide your hair under the helmet." I tapped a finger to my thigh. "And we're leaving when it's dark so they won't be able to see your eyes from atop the carriage."

He considered in silence for a moment before loosening his frown and giving me a nod. "When?"

"I think I have a way of liberating a set of armor," Shade cut in. "I can do it tomorrow."

We all exchanged a glance. Anticipation hung like a curtain of mist over the room.

"So, we're escaping tomorrow night then?" I asked.

Elaran and Shade looked at each other before turning to me. "Yeah."

A soft knock sounded. I shot up from the bed and whipped towards Elaran. On the other side of the room, the Master Assassin did the same.

"You expecting someone?" Shade pressed out in a hurried whisper.

Panic and confusion were mixed on Elaran's face as he shook his head. Another knock came. The elf shooed us towards the side of the room.

"In the closet," he hissed. "Hurry!"

Neither of us hesitated as Shade and I darted across the cool white floor and dove into the large piece of furniture against the wall. Wood groaned in protest as we landed and drew the closet door shut until only a small gap remained. Thuds echoed as we tried to disentangle our limbs in the cramped dark space. It was already a tight fit inside the closet and we both also wanted to see out the gap in the door, which made it even more difficult to find a comfortable position. Shade's muscles shifted against my body as he moved around me.

"Quiet," Elaran hissed again. "I'm opening the door now."

Hidden in an army of white garments, I spied through the slit in the closet door while the Master Assassin stood pressed against me from behind, peering out over my head. I could almost feel his heartbeat against my shoulder blades.

The handle clicked as Elaran pushed it down and opened the door to reveal the mystery visitor outside his room.

"Princess Illeasia," he blurted out and stumbled back a step.

"I'm sorry about just showing up at this hour unannounced." Her silver dress billowed behind her as the princess swept into the room and closed the door behind her. "I couldn't sleep and there's just something I wanted to tell you. Well, several things, actually. And some of them I can't say but I really want to and other things I..." She trailed off and let out a nervous laugh. "And now I'm just rambling. Sorry."

Elaran cast a quick glance at the closet. If I'd had more room to move, I would've facepalmed. Drawing attention to the thing you want to keep hidden by looking straight at it. Classic rookie mistake. When all this was over, I'd have to make a list of shady things I needed to teach Elaran.

"It's alright." The wood elf took a step towards the princess. "What was it that you wanted to talk about?"

Illeasia closed the distance between them even further. "My mother has brought a lot of visitors here over the years, and I've spent time with all of them, but this is the first time... I mean, I haven't felt like..." Gems clinked in her sparkling headdress as she raked her fingers through her glossy hair. "What I'm trying to say is that I've never met anyone like you before and I didn't expect that and during all these weeks we've been..." She let out a frustrated sigh. "I'm rambling again."

It took all my considerable self-control not to audibly gasp when the princess placed her elegant hands on Elaran and pulled him forwards. Her lips ravished his while she kept a tight grip on his shirt. The stunned wood elf tensed up at first but then leaned into her embrace and placed a hand on the back of her neck. I stared at them in utter shock. What in Nemanan's name was going on?

At long last, Princess Illeasia drew back slightly. A small sigh bordering on a moan escaped her lips as she leaned against Elaran's chest.

"That's what I wanted to tell you," she said.

Since Elaran had his back to us, I couldn't see the expression on his face but I figured he had to be pretty surprised as well. The wood elf let his hand drift from the back of her neck and down her arm. He must've been about to speak because the princess placed a finger over his lips.

"Before you say anything, I just need to know." She sucked in a shuddering breath. "Are you glad I told you?"

Placing a hand over hers, Elaran removed her finger from his lips. "Yes."

The nervous princess closed her eyes and let out a long sigh of relief. When she had opened them again, she drew him close and placed a kiss on his strong jaw.

"I have to go," she whispered in his ear.

Before Elaran had time to answer, she pulled back and escaped through the door in a swishing of silver skirts. The auburn-haired archer remained staring at the now closed door she had left by only seconds before. I blinked at the scene. What in the world had I just witnessed?

Shade put his hands on my waist. "As enjoyable as this position is, maybe we should rejoin our stunned friend?"

Trying to ignore the crackles that had shot through me when he placed his hands there, I shook my head to clear it of all the strange things that had happened these past few minutes. I pushed open the closet door and jumped out. Shade landed in the space I had just vacated while I made my way towards Elaran.

After skirting around his unmoving body, I frowned up at him. "You alright?"

He jerked back as if he'd been woken from a deep trance and blinked at me. "I..." Shaking his head violently, he strode to the bed and collapsed on it. With a hurricane of emotions whirling around in his eyes, he leaned forward and buried his face in his hands.

"What the hell is going on?" I demanded and threw out my arms. "Are you okay or what?"

Shade had resumed his previous seat and leaned back in the white chair. His face was filled with understanding as he watched the distraught wood elf. When Elaran finally looked up, the assassin held his gaze steady and gave him a lopsided smile.

"You're in love," he stated.

Pain, hope, and confusion drifted past on the elf's face. I stared at him. Elaran was in love? Was that even possible? I had always thought he was like Shade. A person who didn't fall in love. Someone who had a long list of important things to accomplish in life and no time for something as silly as feelings.

The ranger drew his fingers through his hair and heaved a sigh so deep I thought it would never end. "Yeah. Yeah, I think I am. But it doesn't matter."

"What do you mean it doesn't matter?" The assaulted cover sent a poof of air into my face as I dropped down on the bed next to Elaran. "Are you in love or not?"

"Yes, I'm in love," he snapped, the agony on his face so sharp it almost drew blood. "But it doesn't matter because I can't be. Not with her. My first duty is to protect my people and she's the princess of the nation threatening to eventually conquer my home. Whatever I feel is irrelevant. Duty comes first."

Loyalty, honor, duty. His cornerstones. My already battered heart bled for him even though I only partly understood his dilemma. I felt no particular loyalty to any city so sacrificing my own needs for the good of a country was as foreign to me as bowing to authority. But on the other hand, there was nothing I wouldn't do for the people I loved. Maybe it was the same concept. Only, his circle was a lot bigger than mine.

When Elaran noticed sympathetic looks on both our faces, he crossed his arms and drew his eyebrows down. His half-hearted attempt at a scowl fell flat due to the searing agony in his eyes but I pretended not to notice because I knew that if it had been me, I would've hated the sympathy too.

"This changes nothing," Elaran said. "We escape tomorrow as planned."

Shade studied him. "Are you sure?"

"Yes, I'm sure. Now get out." He flicked his hands at the door. "We all need to sleep because it might be a while before get the chance again. We'll do a final check in at dinner tomorrow."

The Master Assassin and I exchanged a glance. After unfurling my legs, I did as the elf told me and made for the door. I understood the desire to be alone when in pain and he was also right about needing sleep. If we were escaping tomorrow night, there wouldn't be much time to rest.

A soft click sounded as Shade relocked the door behind us. His intense black eyes met mine.

"One more day."

I gave him a slow nod. "One more day."

For a moment, it looked like he was about to say something else but then he just turned on his heel and strode back towards his room. After lifting my shoulders in a shrug, I did the same.

By this time tomorrow, it would all be over. No more dancing and formal dinners. No more conflicted feelings about getting rid of the darkness. I cast a quick glance over my shoulder at the closed door, behind which I knew a torn elf paced restlessly. No more laughter and smiles from Elaran. My head and my heart were both hopelessly tangled up as I reached my room. For better or worse, it would all end tomorrow.

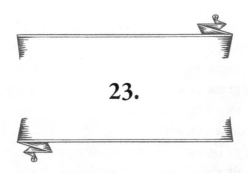

23.

Jasmine and roses filled the evening air. I traced my fingers over a gorgeous white flower as Niadhir and I strolled along the terrace while waiting for the banquet to start. When we reached a secluded corner, the scholar steered us towards a white bench. Once we were seated, he placed a hand over mine and turned to me with serious eyes.

"Have you thought about what you want?"

The unexpected question sent a flare of panic through me. My whole soul screamed, *I don't know!* However, instead of voicing that, I cleared my throat and tried to make my voice light.

"About what?"

Concerned violet eyes searched my face. "Freeing yourself from your demonic curse."

"Oh." I traced circles in the white fabric covering my thigh. "I don't know."

"Explain."

I frowned at him. "Explain what?"

"If you explain your reasoning behind each possible outcome, maybe I can help you come to a decision. What is it that makes you hesitate?"

A cool night wind swept through the jasmine bush in front of us. Listening to the soft rustling of leaves, I tried to put my scattered thoughts together.

"Well, I guess it's because it's part of me," I finally said. "One of the few parts of me that's still here."

"What do you mean?"

Normally, I wasn't one for sharing personal details but I needed to talk this through with someone who had a different perspective on things. For me. Even though I wouldn't get the chance to actually get rid of the darkness because we were escaping tonight, I wanted to discuss it. Or perhaps because of that. I needed to convince myself that I was making the right choice, because afterwards there would be no going back.

"It's just, I don't know who I am anymore." I let out a humorless laugh. "My whole life, my identity has always been based on who I am to someone else. A sister. A friend. A protector. But they don't really need me anymore. Everyone has their own life. Except for me. And I don't know what I'm supposed to be doing when I'm not living for someone else."

Niadhir looked down at me with even more concern swirling in his eyes. "That does not sound very healthy. You need to have a purpose in life. What do you want?"

"I don't know!" I snapped. At the startled expression on his face, I put a hand to my brow and massaged my forehead. "I'm sorry. It's just... that question. I don't have an answer to it."

He gave me a patient smile. "I understand. But what does this have to do with your curse?"

"Well, the darkness at least makes me feel like I have some sort of identity."

"Even if it is a toxic one?"

Blowing out a sigh, I leaned back on the bench. "I guess so."

The patient scholar gave my arm a light squeeze. "I understand. It is normal to cling to bad habits when faced with change. Change is difficult and old habits bring comfort in times of upheaval but the important thing is to have enough willpower to break free and courage to transform into something new. Something better."

"But the darkness isn't all bad," I said, desperately trying to throw up a flimsy shield to guard against his logic. "Shade pointed out that it has saved my life and also helped me save other people too. More than once. He said the darkness is an asset too. And I think he's right."

"Your friend Shade said this?" Niadhir pressed his mouth together in a disapproving line. "I must say, if he is supposed to be your friend, I am very disappointed in him. He knows that almost all Storm Casters die by their own hand and often kill their loved ones too, and he still encourages you to keep your curse. What kind of person would wish that upon anyone?" He shook his head. "If he truly was your friend, would he not want what was best for you? It sounds more like he wants you to keep it so that he can benefit from your power before it kills you."

Not sure what to say, I averted my eyes and went back to tracing figures on my dress.

"Do not worry," Niadhir went on. "I will never rush you. As I mentioned, this is a big decision. But I am afraid for you. I am afraid that you will be far past the point of no return and get yourself seriously hurt before you arrive at a decision. Please, do be careful." His mouth drew into a small smile. "I do not know what I would do if something happened to you."

Thankfully, my chance to reply was cut short by a voice from the glass doors announcing that the banquet was ready. All around us, well-dressed couples in white and silver rose and started weaving through the potted bushes in the direction of the banquet hall. Tipping my head up, I studied the glittering stars above for a moment.

As much I wanted to deny it, Niadhir had some pretty convincing arguments. Unfortunately, they were arguments for the wrong side. I had decided to discuss the matter honestly because I had wanted to be sure that I was doing the right thing leaving Starhaven without getting rid of the darkness but my conversation with the scholar had done the exact opposite. Now, I was even more uncertain whether I was making the right decision.

Tilting my head back down, I found my companion waiting for me with his arm offered. I blew out a deep sigh and took it. Persistent words jabbed into my mind as we made our way from the terrace and then through the banquet hall. *What do you want?* The question left a trail of echoes in its wake. I shoved it out. Getting distracted was dangerous and we couldn't afford mistakes right now. It was time to get to work.

A clatter rang out as I bumped into the table we were rounding, sending plates and utensils rattling against each other.

"Oh, by the Stars," Niadhir exclaimed. "Are you alright?"

Bending over the table, I righted the toppled glasses while a look of embarrassment flashed past on my face. "Yeah, uhm sorry, I wasn't paying attention. My mind was somewhere else."

"Ah, yes," the scholar said, "a preoccupied mind often makes one clumsy."

Clumsy? I was a cat burglar. And a damn good one at that. I never bumped into tables, sending silverware flying everywhere. Unless I wanted to, of course.

It took great effort to stop a satisfied grin from spreading across my face as I felt the knives I'd stolen disappear into my dress. Servants were already hurrying over to the table I'd ruined on purpose and in a few moments, it would all be returned to normal. No one would know that a thief had just lifted two deadly weapons from their banquet table.

"Ah, Captain Hadraeth," Niadhir said as we reached our seats. "How are you this evening?"

The Guard Captain was glowering at something further away but at the scholar's question, he tore his gaze from it. "Fine, thank you."

A moment later, Elaran and Princess Illeasia appeared from the crowd. The princess in her sparkling dress was so absorbed in her discussion with the wood elf that she didn't notice the rest of us until they had already arrived at the table. Surprise flashed past in her pale violet eyes when she found the three of us watching her.

"Oh, please forgive me!" Her embarrassed laughter bounced off the crystal and silver decorations around us. "I was somewhere else."

While Illeasia was busy apologizing for her distractedness and greeting her friends, another couple swaggered out of the mass of chatting star elves.

"Nely," Princess Illeasia said. "You look lovely as always. How was your day?"

The gorgeous lady ran a hand over the jewels gleaming above her cleavage. "Oh, it was wonderful. Shade showed me his sword fighting skills by sparring with a guard."

There was a slight pause as the Master Assassin looked to me and then Elaran with intense eyes. "Yes, a most productive day indeed."

It was on. He had succeeded in obtaining a set of armor for Elaran. My heart pattered in my chest. We were escaping tonight.

"He was excellent," Lady Nelyssae continued, completely oblivious to the secret message that had passed between us. She turned to Captain Hadraeth and gave him a hopeful smile. "Though not as good as you, of course. No one ever is. I would love to watch you spar some time."

Hadraeth scrunched up his eyebrows in a confused frown. "The sparring ground is no place for a lady of the court."

"No, of course not," Nelyssae amended. "I only meant..."

She trailed off and was spared further awkwardness by the arrival of Queen Nimlithil. The domed hall fell silent as the queen glided through the starlight spilling in from the glass ceiling and took up position by the high table. White gems rivalling the stars in beauty sparkled as she turned around.

"Welcome, my friends," the graceful queen said. "The stars have blessed us with another beautiful evening. Let us enjoy it." Glittering bracelets clinked as she swept out her arms. "Please be seated."

Excited murmuring resumed as the lords and ladies did as their queen bid and seated themselves on the cushioned chairs. Within a minute of the scraping furniture falling silent, servants in white appeared from the hidden doors with large silver trays in their hands. Wonderful aromas drifted up from the small plate filled with salad and fried cheese that was placed before me. I folded my hands in my lap without touching it.

By now, I had attended enough of these formal dinners to know that I should be waiting for everyone to receive their food before eating and which fork I should use when doing so. Knowing the rules didn't make them any less annoying, though. I hated being bound by social constraints in this way.

"Have you given any more thought to getting rid of your curse?" Lady Nelyssae called across the white tablecloth.

I blinked at her in surprise.

"Nely!" Princess Illeasia exclaimed.

"What?" The confused lady pushed her full lips into a pout. "It's why Queen Nimlithil brought her here in the first place. Everyone knows it." Her pale violet eyes turned back to me. "What I don't understand is why you haven't done it yet. Who would want to live with a demonic curse?"

Next to her, Shade's black eyes studied me intently before they shifted to his table companion. "It's not a curse. It's an asset."

"Forgive me," Niadhir interrupted. "I was going to remind you that this is a very personal decision for Storm, and one that we should not be discussing over dinner, but after your comment I simply cannot refrain from responding." The scholar met the assassin's gaze with a disapproving stare. "How can you say something like that and still call yourself her friend? You know full well that the curse will get her killed."

"It might not," I cut in before the Master Assassin could reply. I had no idea why white-hot fire suddenly burned behind his eyes, but I decided it was best not to find out. "Just because it happened to a lot of others doesn't mean it will happen to me."

The words rang false even to my ears but I didn't want Shade to do something rash that would screw up our escape plans so I had to say something to defuse the situation.

Niadhir whirled towards me, concern and outrage evident on his face. "What has it brought you before? Only death. How many people have you killed while lost in the darkness? How many friends have almost died because you could not control the curse?" He flicked a hand to Shade. "You almost killed him a few weeks ago. Then there was also that other friend who almost died in an ambush in Pernula when you failed to control it. How many others?"

Shade's face had become an unreadable mask but Elaran, who was much less adept at hiding things, whipped around and stared at me. I knew what they were thinking because the same thought spun in my mind. How in Nemanan's name did Niadhir know about that? I couldn't remember telling him about my fight with Shade in Travelers' Rest. Or about that time when Zaina had ambushed us when we first arrived in Pernula and she had almost slit Haemir's throat and shot the rest of them full of crossbow bolts because I attacked when the darkness ripped from my soul.

The most disconcerting part of all, however, was that he was right. I had brought death's cold breath to my friends' lives more than once. Not only the two occasions Niadhir knew about but also to Liam and Elaran. When we assassinated King Adrian, Liam had almost died and I had done nothing to save him because I had lost myself in the darkness and gone on a killing spree. Instead, Elaran had been the one to save him. He had sacrificed part of his own life to do it. If I hadn't been absorbed by darkness, maybe he wouldn't have had to.

"You know what, you're right," I said and blew out an irritated breath. "This is a personal decision. So how about we talk about something else?"

While the star elves around me had the decency to look abashed, Shade continued staring at me, eyes full of emotions I couldn't decipher. I averted my gaze and found Elaran watching me as well. He gave me a slow nod.

"Right, yes." Princess Illeasia cleared her throat. "I think everyone has received their food now." Her slender fingers gripped the glass goblet and hoisted it in the air. "Shall we?"

After a short pause, the rest of the table lifted theirs as well.

"To the beauty and grace of the stars," the princess said.

After everyone had echoed the phrase, they drank and then began eating. I remained staring at the glass in my hand. Everything had been so much easier when there hadn't been a choice. What Niadhir said made much more sense than I wanted to admit but I was still reluctant to give it up because the darkness was a part of me.

White wine swished against the edges as I returned the goblet to the decorated table. I didn't want to make a decision because what if I made the wrong one? At least, after tonight I wouldn't have to tie my brain in a knot trying to choose because there wouldn't be a choice left. I pushed all the worry out of my mind.

Tonight would be my last night here so I might as well enjoy the food. Especially this strange cheese dish that I had come to love. The texture was a bit odd but it tasted heavenly. Warm and salty. My mouth watered just at the thought of it so after picking up the correct fork, I stabbed the fried cheese. Cutting off a piece, I lifted it up. A wry smile settled on my lips. They might be a nation of conquerors but they sure knew how to cook.

Elaran, Shade, and I exchanged a glance over our raised forks. One more evening. Then we would all be out of here. Then we would all be free.

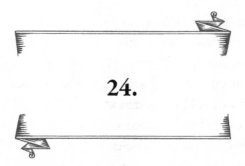

24.

The door clicked shut behind me. Shade and Elaran looked up from the stack of papers on the desk and nodded at me before returning to whatever last-minute task they were up to. I strode over to the usually tidy bed now littered with pieces of gleaming white armor and dropped even more stuff on it.

As usual, the banquet hadn't finished until well into the night and at that point, everyone was so exhausted that they made straight for their rooms. Tonight was no exception. I had already prepared everything before we left for the dinner, so when I returned, I only had to grab my things and then sneak straight over to Elaran's room. From the looks of it, Shade had done the same.

"Alright, once we get out there, I'll take care of the horse while you and Storm push the carriage out of the building," the Master Assassin said and moved his eyes from Elaran to me.

The wood elf nodded while I was trying to untangle everything from my voluminous skirts. We were all still wearing the elaborate clothes from the banquet because we would need every minute of preparation together. Once I'd finally gotten everything I'd been carrying loose and dropped the last of it on the bed, I nodded as well.

"You got any weapons?" I asked.

Shade magicked two knives from the sleeves of his formal jacket and twirled them in his hands while a satisfied smile spread across his lips. Of course he had. Our less shady elven friend, on the other hand, furrowed his brows at me.

"Where would I have gotten weapons?"

I smacked my lips. "Figured as much."

Moving with trained efficiency, I started producing one knife after the other from various parts of my clothes.

Elaran's eyebrows shot up as he stared at me. "What did you do? Hide a whole army in there?"

Shrugging, I waved a hand at the pile that had formed on his spotless white covers. "How many do you want?"

The auburn-haired archer blew out an amused breath through his nose and muttered something about sneaky underworlders but approached and picked up two silver knives that had been taken from their home in the banquet hall. When he was done, I met Shade's eyes and nodded at the pile again.

"Want some more?"

Amusement settled on his face as he sauntered over and grabbed two more blades. He gave me an impressed grin. "Much obliged."

"Anytime." I picked up a white breastplate and shifted my gaze to Elaran. "Should we get you into this armor then?"

Shade threw me a skeptical look. "Do you even know how to properly put on armor?"

"Uhm... no?"

"I didn't think so. I'll help him with the armor." The Master of the Assassins' Guild took the gleaming breastplate from my hands. "You should take your clothes off."

I jerked back. "What?"

His black eyes glittered as he no doubt saw the heat I could feel on my cheeks. A satisfied smirk spread across his lips. "I'm assuming you're not escaping in that sparkly thing so if you're planning on changing into other clothes, you should do that now."

"Oh." I cleared my throat.

All I wanted to do was throw a knife at his handsome smirking face but I decided that it would have to wait until after we had escaped. Narrowing my eyes at him, I had to settle for a glare before starting the arduous process of liberating myself from my formal outfit.

Jewelry from my hair and around my neck clinked as I dropped it into a neat pile on the bed. After pulling my hair back in a simple braid, I got to work on the dress. A deep sigh of relief escaped my throat as I finally got it off and placed it on the bed. These dresses weren't exactly built for breathing in. I threw a glance over my shoulder to see how Elaran and Shade were coming along.

The assassin snapped his head back to the elf in front of him when I found him looking at me. Frowning, I shook my head. What in Nemanan's name had that been about?

Once I had pulled on the plain dress I had chosen, I went about hiding knives and pieces of jewelry in there. If we were going to get all the way back to Pernula, we'd need money. And I'd bet my currently unavailable fortune that this stuff was worth more than enough for what we'd need.

"Hand me that helmet," Shade said and pointed at the one next to me on the bed.

"No one ever tell you that you should ask nicely?" I countered but picked up the helmet and walked over to him anyway.

"If you make sure his hair is inside, I'll put in on," the presumptuous assassin said as if I hadn't commented.

I rolled my eyes but did as he ordered regardless. Winding Elaran's auburn hair around my fingers, I twisted it up and put in on his head while Shade put the helmet in place. We both stepped back to study his handiwork.

"So, how about it?" Elaran demanded.

Shade glanced at me from the corner of his eye. "You think Cadentia is on our side tonight?"

"Lady Luck and I have a complicated relationship." I cocked my head and flicked my gaze over the wood elf. "But yeah, I think it's close enough to pass."

Elaran shifted uncomfortably in the shiny armor. "Good. Then let's get to it."

Since I had already finished getting ready, I just plopped down on the bed and waited. Shade had started unbuttoning his shirt but then stopped. He arched an eyebrow at me.

"You just going to sit there and watch me undress?"

I ran my eyes up and down his body before allowing my lips to curl into a smirk. "Yep."

If the damn assassin was going to deliberately make me blush, I was definitely going to get back at him. A baffled chuckle rose from his chest and he shook his head but he didn't turn away. Instead, his intense black eyes stared straight at me while he undid the buttons on his white shirt. I held his gaze. When Shade finally pulled off his shirt, I let my eyes roam across his body. Chiseled abs and toned arms flexed as he threw the white garment to the side. I grinned. And besides, it really was a nice view.

While I got my revenge on the Master Assassin, Elaran stomped back and forth across the room, swinging his arms, crouching and twisting to check the range of his movements in the well-fitting armor. He appeared satisfied because he gave the inanimate object a nod.

Looking down at the dress I was wearing, I tried to stave off a tidal wave of pain that threatened to sweep me out to sea and drown me in its merciless embrace. I would've done anything to get my clothes and, most of all, my knives back before we escaped. Leaving them behind felt like leaving a piece of my soul but there was no other choice. I had searched for them everywhere, hoping to catch just a glimpse of them, ever since I got here but to no avail. They were nowhere to be found.

With an irritated sigh, I scraped together all my inconvenient feelings and shoved them back behind the stone walls around my heart where they belonged. I had already lost so much of who I was so what was one more thing? The loss and heartbreak would have to wait.

"Ready?" Shade asked and moved his gaze between us.

Elaran and I nodded in unison.

"Alright, let's leave this place forever then."

I wasn't sure if Elaran had managed to say goodbye to Princess Illeasia without tipping her off about our escape since his face betrayed nothing as he stalked to the door. Another person who had decided that loss and heartbreak would have to wait. It made mine seem silly in comparison but his suffering did nothing to dull my own pain. Grabbing the coils of rope from the bed, I slammed the walls up around my heart again and followed the elf and the assassin out the door.

The gleaming corridor lay empty around us as we snuck towards the chute. Shade opened it and I fastened the rope to the handle on the inside. Soft thudding came from the square-shaped duct as I let the line fall down into the darkness.

"Okay, remember that the rope doesn't reach all the way to the bottom," I said. "So when you're out, you've gotta let go and slide down the rest of the way."

Elaran elbowed past me. "I'll go first. If I fall down on top of you in this armor, it won't end well."

Seeing as he had a point, I didn't argue and instead let him climb into the hole first. Shade followed right after. As soon as the assassin had taken up position next to the elf, I joined them. With my back pressed against Shade's chest, I drew the metal plate shut.

"Alright, you can start climbing now," I whispered to Elaran in the oppressive darkness.

The rope snapped taut next to me as he began his descent. When Shade's body heat disappeared from my shoulder blades, I knew he had started downwards as well. I waited another few seconds before following.

Only our strained breathing echoed against the metal walls as we made our way towards the bottom. I spent my time once again imagining running free across the Thieves' Highway in Keutunan instead of the awfully confined space I was in.

"This is the end of the rope," Elaran announced somewhere below.

"Alright, let go and then brace yourself for a rough landing."

Scraping sounds drifted upwards as his armor slid against metal. Rustling clothes followed it as Shade let go of the rope as well. After sending a quick prayer to Nemanan, I did too.

Since the end of the chute was already down, thanks to Elaran, there was nothing to break my speed so I flew right out the opening. Something softer than stones caught me on the other side and let out a cough. I turned my head to find Shade's body underneath me.

"Sorry," I mumbled as I disentangled our limbs and scrambled off him.

Dusting ourselves off, the three of us straightened and took in the scene. The courtyard lay deserted in front us, just as we had expected. Without another word, we snuck towards the carriage storage. So far, everything had gone according to plan but I couldn't prevent my heart from thumping in my chest. The hardest part still remained. Fooling the guards at the gate.

Insects of the night sang in the bushes as I knelt in front of the door and drew out my lockpicks. Once it clicked open, I rose and pushed down the handle.

The door flew up and banged against the wall as it bounced off it. All three of us stumbled back a step as a horde of elves in white armor streamed out and formed a semi-circle in front of us. Their gleaming swords were pointed straight at us. I whipped out two knives just as the row of armed star elves parted to allow one more to pass.

"Did you really think I wouldn't notice you stealing a set of armor?" Captain Hadraeth demanded. "What kind of Guard Captain do you think I am?"

Blood pounded in my ears. Godsdamn it. I shifted my weight while gripping the knives tighter. How were we supposed to get out of this?

"Now," he continued, "put those silly utensils down and let's go back inside."

Moonlight glinted off the blades as the guards raised their swords further in warning. I risked a glance at my companions. Both of them gave an almost imperceptible shake of their head. So, we weren't backing down then. Good. I'd been itching for a fight.

Steel flashed through the air as I threw the knife in my right hand. All hell broke loose around me as the assassin and the wood elf attacked as well. Unfortunately, it quickly became obvious that these knives had been made to eat with and not to throw at armed attackers because the one I'd hurled at the guard sailed hopelessly off course. He batted it away easily with his blade. Drawing another one, I crouched into an attack position.

The star elf guard sprang forward and swung his long sword at me. Fighting in this damn dress was a nightmare. Fabric flapped around me like sails, slowing down my movements and betraying my directions. I twisted out from the sword strike and stabbed at my assailant. He slammed his blade down in defense, making the flimsy piece of cutlery in my hand fly from my grip.

An armored elbow connected with my jaw. My head snapped to the side and for a moment, I was afraid something was broken. Blinking black spots from my vision and trying to ignore the throbbing spreading across my face, I cast a quick look at my friends.

Our ridiculous kitchenware weapons had us at a severe disadvantage. Shade was engaged in a losing battle with two star elves while Elaran looked to be only a few seconds away from being defeated by Captain Hadraeth.

Rage surged through me. After everything we had done, after all the scheming and sneaking and those damn balls I'd endured, it couldn't end with this miserable failed escape attempt. The darkness screamed in my soul. I wouldn't let it end this way.

Black clouds exploded from my body. Lightning crackled around me as I flexed my fingers and turned to my friends. The fighting had screeched to a halt as the star elves around us stared at me with apprehension drifting across their faces. I leveled black eyes roaring with fury on Shade and Elaran.

"Run," I ordered in a voice hard as steel.

I only had time to see them spin around before the whole squad of star elves advanced on me. A laugh laced with madness dripped from my lips. *Come try it.* I threw my arms to the sides.

A deafening boom echoed across the courtyard as thunder and hurricane winds blasted from my hands. Shards of glass whirled past me as the building behind me cracked. The dark haze pressed in on my vision. Another ear-splitting crash rang out. Screams pierced the fog around me and bodies flew in every direction. The last thing I saw before I lost myself in the darkness was a huge chunk of frosted glass toppling from the wall.

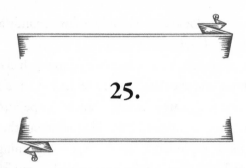

25.

My eyes shot open. I flew up and scrambled away. Heart hammering in my chest, I tried to make sense of my surroundings and piece together a spotty recollection of what had happened before I blacked out.

The smooth white walls of my room betrayed nothing as they stared mutely back at me. What was I doing back in my room? Hadn't we tried to escape? Memories came flooding back. The squad of star elves. The fight. Me screaming at Shade and Elaran to run. Storm winds and thunder as a building broke apart.

Right. We had tried to escape and I had stayed behind to make sure that Elaran and Shade got out. A contented feeling mixed with the dread in my chest. If my friends had made it out, it would all have been worth it.

I snuck across the floor and pressed an ear to the door. Cold glass cooled the panic that had flushed my cheeks. No sound came from outside. Placing a hand on the handle, I tentatively pushed it down. It opened without issue. Huh. I wasn't locked in.

Captain Hadraeth's serious face appeared in the crack. The door slammed as I drew it shut again. Damn. If he was standing guard outside the door, there was no point in climbing out the window. Elaran and Shade's room was most likely also under guard. If they were there. I desperately hoped they weren't.

Drumming my fingers on my thigh, I paced back and forth across the room while trying to figure out what my next move would be. After a few minutes, the door opened again. I watched with growing dread as Queen Nimlithil swept into the room in a flurry of silver skirts.

The queen met my gaze with sad eyes. "Come with me."

Suspicion flared up my spine but seeing as I couldn't exactly refuse, I followed her billowing dress when she turned and strode out the door. My heart thumped in my chest as we neared Elaran's room. When the silver-haired queen didn't slow down, I allowed a brief spark of hope into my chest.

As we drew closer, I realized that the door was open. Casting a quick glance inside, I found Elaran's former room empty. When we passed Shade's door and I made a similar discovery, relief exploded like fireworks in my chest. They made it out. My mouth drew into a smile. Elaran and Shade were free.

While Queen Nimlithil led me through corridors, down stairs and then up other ones, suspicion crept back into my mind. We had just pulled off a semi-successful escape. Why wasn't I locked in a dungeon?

"Wait..." I stopped and stared out the window to my right. Another tower stood right outside it. Tilting my head, I squinted at the opposite windows. "Isn't that the library?"

"It is the floor above it," the queen replied and waved me forward.

"So, we're in a different wing." I frowned at her. "What are we doing here?"

She didn't reply and instead continued leading me down the hall until we at last stopped in front of a plain white door. "I do not think there is a way to prepare someone for something like this so I will not try." After one last sad look at me, she pushed down the handle. "This will be hard for you."

A strange bedroom met me on the other side. I frowned at the star elf in the long white coat. He looked almost like a doctor. My gaze moved from his grave face to the person sleeping on the bed. Shade. My heart sank. He hadn't made it out. In my head, I still tried to process the scene. What was he doing all the way over here? And why was he sleeping?

Queen Nimlithil placed a light hand on my back and steered me towards him. "When you tried to escape and you summoned that storm, some terrible things happened. You killed half of my guards in that squad and your friend Shade... he was either struck by a lightning bolt or blasted away by winds. Or hit by the collapsing building. Possibly all three."

My mouth suddenly felt very dry. I worked my tongue around it before managing to produce any sound. "What are you saying?"

"He has not woken up since." Her sad eyes turned to me. "The doctors are not sure if he ever will."

"No." I shook my head vigorously. "No. This is some kind of trick."

"I wish it were." She guided me forward until I was standing right next to his bed. "We have tried everything but I am afraid that he still has not woken up."

Dropping to my knees next to the bed, I placed a hand on Shade's chest. It rose and fell slowly.

"Hey," I said and shook his body. "It's me. You can stop pretending now."

The assassin's body moved in time with my hands but then remained still once I stopped shaking him. Pure terror clawed into my chest and placed its cold hands around my throat.

"Shade, it's time to come back now," I pressed out through a constricted throat. Tears welled up in my eyes. "Shade!" I shook him violently again but his beautiful eyes still didn't flutter open.

Whirling back towards the queen, I stared at her, desperation dancing in my eyes. "What's wrong with him?"

"We are not sure," she said in a soft voice. "We think he might have suffered some form of head trauma in the blast."

The blast that I created. My shallow breath came in fits and starts. This couldn't be happening. It couldn't be real. But I could see him, touch him, and I knew that it was happening. Was real. I shook his body again with renewed strength. It rolled limply back and forth but produced no other response.

My breath wheezed in and out of my constricted throat with increasing speed. He had to wake up. He had to.

Soft hands wrapped around my shoulders and pulled me to my feet.

"I am afraid there is more," the queen said.

"Where's Elaran?" I blurted out between bursts of air barely bringing oxygen to my lungs.

Queen Nimlithil said nothing as she led me across the room and towards another part of it hidden behind a sheet. Blood rushed in my ears. I worked my tongue around my parched mouth again while my heart continued slamming into my ribcage. The queen pulled the fabric aside and my world shattered.

There on a table lay Elaran. His eyes were closed and his body was completely still. No soft breaths raised his chest. I tried to take a step towards him but my legs refused to obey so I stumbled forwards and tumbled to the floor. Elaran's arm fell down and swung in front of my eyes. My hand trembled as I reached out to touch his wrist.

Cold skin met me as I put my fingers where his pulse should have been. Nothing. I let out a wail so raw it almost broke every window in the room. My whole reality crashed down around me like a smashed glass tower. Another howl ripped from my throat. My trembling hand that had confirmed my worst nightmare collapsed to the floor along with the rest of me. An unending flood of tears streamed down my face.

I felt hands around my arms and heard distraught voices call out but they might as well have been on another continent. Thrashing against their hands, I tried to claw my way back to Elaran but it was like trying to fight the tide.

The white corridor appeared briefly in front of my drowning vision again before I was dumped in another room. Someone said something but I couldn't hear past the deafening ringing in my ears. As soon as the hands left my shoulders, I collapsed on the floor.

It was as if a bottomless pit had opened up inside me and I just kept falling further down into the darkness. Shade was in a coma and Elaran... Searing pain ripped my heart to shreds as my mind tried to finish the thought. Elaran was dead.

He was dead! I slammed my fists into the smooth floor with enough force to shatter bones. He would never again draw his eyebrows down and cross his arms with a scowl on his face. Never again call me a pregnant moose or a cockroach. Sharp rocks ground my heart into dust. He would never again back me up without question. Never again smile at a stupid joke. Never fight to protect the ones he loved. Never love. Never live.

The tightly wound cord that had kept my sanity in check snapped. I shot to my feet and grabbed the first object I could reach. Glass shattered and white flowers sailed through the air as I hurled the vase into the wall. A feral cry tore from my throat. I snatched up the bedside table and smashed it into the wall. Chips of wood flew across the room as it crashed into the unyielding wall of frosted glass. The chair was next. And after that the desk. Then the bed. Broken boards and glass whirled across the room as I destroyed everything I could get my hands on.

Strength drained from me like life from a corpse and I collapsed to the floor again. I didn't even bother pushing the fragments of ruined furniture out of the way as I curled into a ball and pulled my knees up to my chest. Wrapping my arms around my legs as if it was the only thing tethering me to this world, I broke into hopeless sobs.

Elaran was dead. I had killed him. A pitiful cry like that from a wounded animal made it past the choked moans spilling from my throat. How could I have let this happen? I pounded a hand to the floor until it throbbed. By all the gods, I had created a blast strong enough to destroy a building. Of course people would get hurt by it! How could I have been so careless?

Water gathered in a pool underneath my cheek. I squeezed my eyes shut. The door must have opened because strong arms suddenly lifted me from the floor. I was only vaguely aware of the white armor against my body as someone carried me through the halls. My mind was too far gone to care about what was happening.

I had played with forces beyond my control and my friends had paid the price. A choked sob bubbled from my chest. The armor disappeared from underneath me and a soft mattress took its place. Elaran dead. Shade in a coma. I buried my face in the pillow. How could I go on living after this?

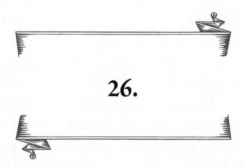

26.

Decades might have passed for all I cared. Lying on my side with my knees pulled up to my chest, I watched the light against the wall dim and then return again. Light to darkness. Darkness to light.

Servants brought in food. I wasn't sure if they did it once a day or several times a day but it sat untouched on my desk until they came and removed it again. After all, I didn't really need the sustenance. All I did was lie in that bed, staring unseeing at the light and darkness that rose and fell across the wall. But the star elves seemed to disagree because after a while, they started forcing me to eat. Everything tasted like ash but I chewed and swallowed anyway.

Sometimes, I would roll off the bed and curl up on the floor instead. The mattress was too soft and too high up. I needed the grounding feeling that the cool hard floor provided to stop my sanity from blowing out the damn window they kept opening. Whenever they found me there, they returned me to the bed.

Every day was the same. An endless sea of pain drowning me in glass shards and black despair. I wanted to shove a hand in my chest and rip my heart out so I wouldn't have to feel anything ever again.

Time blurred together but did nothing to heal the abyss inside me. Instead, one life-draining monster fed off the other until all the pain I had experienced in my life ate at me from all sides. Everything I touched died. It really was true that the only things I was good at were to hurt and destroy and burn things to the ground. And memories of it haunted me day and night.

Blood bubbles popping and light disappearing from vivid brown eyes in an alley where I had gotten Rain killed.

A red stain spreading across Liam's chest when I had left him to die alone after he got shot in King Adrian's tent.

Elaran giving up years of his life to undo that mistake.

Queen Charlotte dying in the Silver Keep because I hadn't warned them in time.

The torrent of pain in Shade's eyes as his little brother was forced to banish him because I had made an enemy of the Fahr brothers.

Liam leaving me and the Underworld behind because all I ever did was bring violence and bloodshed to the people around me.

Shade's unresponsive body in that awful white room.

The cold skin of Elaran's limp hand swinging from the table.

Everything that had happened, everything I had been through, had chipped away at me for years. A caring bit here. An understanding bit there. Cutting off pieces of my soul and snuffing out the lingering specks of light until there was nothing left but cracked stone walls splattered with blood from the death of my heart.

But time kept moving on, indifferent to the hollow husk I had become. A new dawn still rose every day. Even though the world had already ended.

I wasn't sure when it started, but at some point Niadhir appeared in the chair by the desk. His talking was just background noise to me because I couldn't bring myself to care about what he said, but he kept coming back anyway.

"I don't care about what kind of food they're bringing tomorrow," I muttered one day.

"Oh by the Stars!" Niadhir shot up from the chair. "You responded."

Heaving a deep sigh, I rolled over on my back. The scholar dragged over the chair and sat down right next to my bed. I could feel his concerned gaze looking for eye contact but I didn't want to meet it.

He placed a hand on my arm. "How do you feel?"

How do you feel? That had to have been the most superfluous question of the century. How did he think I felt? I blew out an irritated sigh.

"It is only, you have been unresponsive for weeks." He gave my arm a gentle squeeze. "I was worried."

Weeks? So that was how long I had been lost to the never-ending nightmare. But then maybe…? A brief glimmer of hope flickered to life.

"Shade?" I asked.

"Still no change. I am sorry."

And just like that, the tiny spark suffocated under the oppressive darkness that came rushing back. I flipped over on my side and turned my back on the concerned scholar.

He was back in that chair the next day anyway. Sometimes he read, but mostly he talked. In the beginning, it was just light subjects like what he was currently reading or something that had happened in the castle. I only replied occasionally. As the days passed and I started responding more often, he brought up more serious topics.

"There is something I have to warn you about," Niadhir said one day. "Or rather, someone."

Lately, I had managed to sit up when he visited so I drew my knees up and leaned back against the headboard. "Who?"

The scholar snapped his book shut and placed it on the bedside table between us before turning to me with grave eyes. "Princess Illeasia. Apparently, she was..." He cleared his throat as if he was too embarrassed to continue. "Apparently, Princess Illeasia was in love with Elaran."

Simply hearing that name sent a wave of pain crashing over me but at least my mind didn't shut down again. "I know."

"Ah, I see." He coughed again. "Well, I fear I have to warn you to stay away from her. The princess is beside herself with grief and... rage. She blames you for Elaran's death—"

"As she should," I stated in a flat voice while guilt ripped its claws into my chest.

"Unfortunately," Niadhir continued as if I hadn't interrupted, "it has gone so far that she wants you dead."

"As she should," I repeated.

"Queen Nimlithil has been trying to change her mind and has kept her from you but..." The concerned scholar trailed off when I sank into the mattress and turned my back on him again.

Whatever else he wanted to say, I didn't want to hear it. This conversation was over. Princess Illeasia was right: I was responsible for Elaran's death and she should want me dead. Hell, *I* had wanted me dead too. It had even gone so far one time that I had stared out that open window for hours, contemplating jumping out. But I hadn't done it because I didn't deserve a quick death. I deserved to live in this unending agonizing existence.

The door opened and Niadhir strode through. I squinted at the light playing in his silvery white hair. He must have left some time yesterday after I retreated into myself again because the birds mockingly chirping outside the window announced that another damn dawn had broken.

"Storm," he said and dropped into the chair. The lines on his forehead betrayed that he was irritated. "Enough is enough."

Drawing myself up against the headboard, I frowned at him.

"It has been weeks. You cannot keep doing this. This is not living!" He blew out a frustrated breath. "Are you really going to disrespect Elaran's memory by spending the rest of your life as a braindead vegetable?"

I blinked at him as if he had slapped me. "What do you mean? I'm not disrespecting Elaran."

"Yes, you are. He has been denied life but you still have it. Yet, you choose to spend every day in bed waiting for time to pass." The chair creaked as he shifted his weight. "That is disrespectful."

"But how can I continue living after..." My throat constricted and refused to speak the words. "After what I did."

His pale violet eyes softened and he leaned forward to place a hand on my arm. "It is never too late to turn your life around. No matter what villainous deeds you have done in the past, you can always start anew today. You can always leave the darkness behind and embrace the light." Placing graceful fingers on my cheek, he turned my head towards him. "And, if you wish, you will always have to option to free yourself from your demonic curse so that you can truly walk unhindered in the light."

"I... uhm..." I began but then trailed off because I didn't know how to respond.

A gust of warm summer winds blew in through the window and ruffled the white curtains. Niadhir stood up and ran his hands down the already immaculate shirt to straighten it.

"Now, two ladies will arrive shortly to help you bathe and get dressed." He gave me a brisk nod. "After that, we are going for a walk."

Only sputtered protests made it out of my mouth as the scholar turned on his heel and strode out the door. I didn't want to go for a walk where other people might see me but it appeared as though I had no choice so I tumbled out of bed.

Usually, my body was made up of lean muscles thanks to all the fighting and climbing that came with my job, but those had wasted away after weeks of bedrest and barely eating. Now as I looked in the mirror for the first time in weeks, I found a skinny thing with lifeless eyes staring back at me. I wanted to throw something at the awful reflection.

Though, it forced me to admit that perhaps Niadhir was right. Maybe I had to start using my muscles again before I wasted away into nothingness. And he was right about something else too. If I just remained there in bed, waiting to die, I was disrespecting Elaran's memory. Pain lashed through my body. And insulting him was the last thing I wanted.

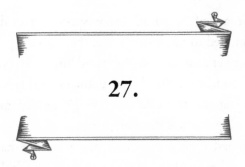

27.

People were staring. A lot. Gripping a fistful of my white dress tightly, I tried to ignore their looks but it was impossible. Their whispers and long glances behind me made my back itch. Niadhir didn't seem to notice because he just kept leading me downstairs while chatting lightly about his research.

When we at last reached the ground floor, my legs shook with exertion. Man, I really was out of shape.

"Oh," the scholar said abruptly.

Following his gaze, I saw what had produced the strange reaction in the middle of his lecture on last century's building practices. *Oh, indeed.* Queen Nimlithil and Princess Illeasia were standing further into the hall. Based on the jerky way in which the princess threw out her arms and snapped her head back and forth, she was furious.

"Do you remember what I told you about Princess Illeasia's state of mind at the moment?" Niadhir said and took a step back.

I retreated a step as well. "Yeah."

The angry princess threw up her arms and flicked her head to the side. She drew back. *Shit.* We had been spotted. Illeasia didn't hesitate a second. Taking a long step forward, she advanced on us. Behind her, the queen snapped her fingers which made an elf in white armor spring forward. Captain Hadraeth skidded to a halt in front of the charging princess and motioned for her to stay back. She stared him down but when he didn't move aside, she stalked away in the other direction.

"Could you hear what she was saying?" I asked, my eyes still on the billowing skirts of the mad princess.

We watched Queen Nimlithil put a delicate hand to her brows and rub her forehead in silence before the scholar replied.

"Yes. She was once again trying to convince her mother that she should have you executed." He flinched as if he had just realized what he had said. "I apologize. Perhaps I should not have answered that honestly."

"It's alright." I waved a hand in front of my face. "I wanted to know."

Niadhir readjusted his position on my arm and turned us around. "We should go."

Nodding at his statement, I followed him down the corridor in the other direction. We moved through hallways I had never been in before. The only room I had been in here on the ground floor was the large domed one that was used as a banquet hall and ballroom so I had no idea where we were going.

At last, we stopped in front of a big white arch. I peered into the room beyond. Starhaven's signature scent of jasmine and roses drifted out on humid air. Rippling water echoed from inside.

"What is this?" I asked.

Sad violet eyes met me. "We burn our dead and cast the ashes to the wind so that our loved ones can join the stars. That means there are no graves to visit." He motioned at the entrance. "This is where we come to talk to the spirits of our deceased."

Cold hands squeezed my heart. They had burned Elaran's body? Was that even what he would have wanted? A flood of tears pressed against my eyelids. Loyal, strong, and brave Elaran had been laid to rest surrounded by strangers in a funeral rite I wasn't even sure his culture shared. Unsuccessfully, I tried to ward off the guilt stabbing into my chest.

"I thought perhaps it would help you in your loss," he finished.

Not being able to get my voice working again, I simply stared through the opening until Niadhir took the lead and walked us across the threshold.

Green plants mingled with ponds, brooks, and tiny waterfalls which gave the fragrant air a touch of humidity. My guide steered me towards a white bench in a corner. The sofa was flanked by jasmine bushes and a smooth pond stretched out before it.

"The spirits of our loves ones can hear us here so if you want, you could talk to Elaran," he said and motioned at the bench. "You can sit here. I will wait outside until you are finished."

When his arm left mine, I almost collapsed on the floor. Stumbling forward, I slumped down on the white sofa and gazed around the domed room. The pond in front of me was like a mirror. Every leaf and flower around its rim was reflected in the water. A thin curtain of mist drifted over the area and enveloped me. It really was beautiful. If there was anywhere the dead might hear me, it was here.

"But you're probably not even here," I whispered to the empty room. "If I know anything about you, your spirit is back in Tkeideru. Stalking through the forest." A choked sob bubbled from my chest. "Looking after your people."

Only the soft rippling of water answered me.

"And they're waiting for you." I tried to swallow past the lump in my throat. "Keya. Faye and the twins. Faelar." A flood of tears spilled over my cheeks. "But you won't ever come back." I pressed my hands to my face. "Oh, Elaran. I'm so sorry. I'm so, so sorry."

Convulsions racked my body as I sat there in the mist by the pond, repeating useless words that would never be enough to express the soul-crushing regret and guilt I truly felt. I drew a shuddering breath and straightened.

Niadhir was right. If I just quit and lay down to die, Elaran would be mad at me. He'd give me some great speech about honor or something and tell me to stop being useless and pull myself together. I managed a shaky smile. Yeah, that was exactly what he would do.

So I gathered all my bright memories of Elaran and filled my torn heart with them. Then, I picked up the life-sucking monster that was my grief and shoved it in there too before slamming up walls so thick no one would ever get through them again. I would carry my friend with me. Always. And once a day I would come here and let him out. The rest of the time, he would remain behind those walls because otherwise, I wouldn't be able to function. If I left that bottomless chasm of grief open, I would never stop crying.

After sucking in a deep breath, I stood up and made my way back out. Niadhir was waiting for me in the corridor when I emerged from the room full of souls. His concerned eyes searched my face.

"Are you alright?" he asked.

I didn't think I would ever be alright again, but I nodded anyway.

He studied me for a few seconds before speaking again. "Would you like to go and see Shade?"

Pain stabbed into my heart and I didn't trust my voice so I only nodded again.

"Very well." Niadhir held out his arm. "Come with me."

My breathing grew increasingly labored as we made our way towards the other wing and up the stairs. Only my pride prevented me from asking him to stop so that I could catch my breath. When we at last arrived at the plain white door, my heart was racing. Though, it wasn't only because of the walking.

My guide pushed down the handle and opened the door for me. "I shall wait out here."

Giving him a slow nod, I took a few halting steps across the threshold. Shade was still lying in that bed, breathing but unmoving. All those awful feelings that I had locked away threatened to break through the barricades so I slammed up another set of stone walls around my heart.

Soft thuds sounded as I stumbled over to his bedside and sank down on my knees next to him. "You have to wake up. You have so much left to live for. So much to do. All the plans and schemes swirling in that head of yours."

Shade's chest only continued rising and falling in a slow rhythmic motion.

"Do you hear me?" I yelled and shook him violently. "You godsdamn arrogant manipulative bastard! You're not done yet. Do you hear me? Pernula needs you. Your guild needs you. Your little brother needs you! I..." I trailed off.

Slumping forward, I placed my forehead against the mattress. I didn't beg. Sure, I had pleaded for someone else's life before but ever since I was a little kid, I had never done it for myself. Never. Except today.

"Please," I whispered. "Everyone is leaving me. Don't you dare do it too. You have to come back. Please, I'm begging you."

He would've loved that. Getting me to kneel and beg him for something. A strained chuckle bubbled from my chest. Damn assassin. But I would've gladly sacrificed my pride to see that stupid face of his smirk at me again.

When he didn't wake up and give me a smug grin, I pushed to my feet. Swaying a little from standing up too fast, I looked down at his unresponsive body. My locked-up feelings were about to smash through the second layer of walls so I averted my gaze and stumbled back towards the door before they broke through completely.

If I was going to survive this, I had to keep my emotions stored away. At least my heart was already cold and black. Not to mention dead. I closed the door to my friend in the room behind me. Where did I go from here?

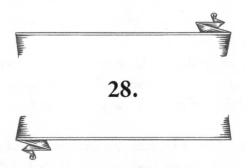

28.

A deafening scream echoed around me. I sat bolt upright. My drenched clothes clung to me like a second skin. Untangling from the sheets, I stumbled to the window and threw it open. Cool night air rushed in. I closed my eyes and let the gentle winds calm my racing heart.

It had been more than a week since I was yanked out of my living death state. Every night since, I had been plagued by nightmares. Elaran and Shade were often in them, dying, bleeding, being crushed by buildings. And there was a lot of screaming. Only, I never knew if I just did it in my dreams or if I actually screamed out loud in my sleep.

Placing my hands on the chilled material, I climbed up on the windowsill. After drawing my knees up to my chest, I leaned back against window frame and gazed into the night. Stars glittered in the dark water behind the cliffs.

Niadhir had told me that having a routine every day would help, so most days looked the same now. The first thing I did was ask about Shade, even though there still wasn't any change, and then after breakfast I went to the Spirit Garden to talk to Elaran. Though, mostly I didn't actually talk. I just sat there and thought about him while trying not to drown in sorrow. But I didn't cry.

I couldn't. If I allowed myself to start crying again, I would never be able to stop.

The rest of the day would be spent in the library and then in the afternoon we would take a walk outside before heading to dinner. And then of course it was time to sleep and revisit my nightmares.

There had been a banquet last week but I had refused to attend. Too many people. Nothing to celebrate. But this week, I hadn't been given a choice. Niadhir had simply declared that we were going to the ball tomorrow because it was time for me to rejoin society. I didn't want to but I felt even less like fighting so I hadn't protested.

A gust smelling of seaweed and saltwater made the curtains around me flutter. I hopped down from the windowsill. If I was going to survive getting dressed up tomorrow and dancing in a room filled with people, I would need a few more hours of sleep.

Climbing into bed, I buried my cheek in the soft pillow and squeezed my eyes shut to stave off the dripping pain that never left me. It was time for some more nightmares.

29.

Hauntingly beautiful notes from violins tried to break my heart. Little did they know that it was already dead. I stared at the scene around me with the detachment of someone looking in through a window even though I was actually in the middle of it all.

Twisting sculptures of crystal and silver sparkled in the moonlight spilling in from the clear dome. The decorations matched the elaborate garments and gleaming jewelry adorned with white gems that the dancers wore and created an ever-changing sea of glittering snow and ice.

"I am glad you decided to come," Niadhir said.

I hadn't exactly had a choice but instead of pointing that out, I simply nodded. The scholar gave me a smile and held out his hand.

"Would you care to dance?"

In the weeks we had spent here before our disastrous escape attempt, we had attended numerous balls so now I actually knew how to move in step with everyone else during those synchronized dances. During all that time, I had never grown to like it, though. All of these formal events were bound by so many rules, and having to follow rules made me feel like I couldn't breathe.

"Storm?" he asked again.

Lifting my shoulders in a slight shrug, I took his offered hand. He led me into the crowd while a satisfied smile spread across his lips as we joined the dancefloor sparkling with glass and stars.

The dancers were forming two long lines, one with men and one with women, so Niadhir and I took up position in our respective places. Since I had already memorized the steps, I let my mind wander as the row of ladies moved forward.

Everyone looked so happy. They danced and celebrated like there was no tomorrow and then they did it all again the next week. Dining and laughing and spending time with their friends while not a care in the world marred their gorgeous features. Maybe I had judged these events too quickly.

As I twirled around in my white dress and rejoined Niadhir and two other star elves I let the corners of my mouth twitch upwards ever so slightly. My dance partner beamed at me from above our interlocked hands.

A dark shadow flashed past the edge of my vision. While being careful not to miss a step, I twisted my head to find the source but only rows of dancers met me. Just as I was about to give up, a familiar face stared at me from between two elves in silver suits. I drew in a sharp breath between my teeth. What the hell was he doing here?

Rogue's blue eyes were locked on me from across the floor. I blinked repeatedly at him. When I stopped, his blond head had disappeared again. Shaking my head, I tried to catch up with the dance I had fallen out of sync with. Niadhir looked at me with concern in his eyes as I rejoined him.

"Are you alright?" he whispered as we touched hands before drawing back again.

"I'm fine," I replied while we once again moved towards each other.

Gray eyes met mine over the scholar's shoulder. I jerked back.

"Queen Charlotte?" I breathed.

Her light brown hair hung limply over a gray dress that didn't appear to move at all as she glided into the sea of spectators. I squinted at where her form had disappeared before another turn in the dance took me in a different direction. The Fahr brothers glared at me. Next to a long table overlaid with silver trays and glasses filled with sparkling wine, they watched me with death in their eyes.

My step faltered and I stumbled out of the line. When I raised my gaze again, they were gone. Sucking in a desperate breath, I pushed my way past the glittering dancers and made a run for the doors to the terrace. The voluminous dress I was wearing got caught in star elves and furniture alike but I didn't care. I continued my headlong dash until I finally made it outside.

That flowery scent of jasmine and roses was so cloying and sickly sweet that it made me gag. Longing for some crisp sea air, I set course for the far side of the terrace. Elves stared at me but I ignored them. The white railing was cold under my arms when finally made it. Leaning against it, I heaved deep breaths.

"It's not real, it's not real," I repeated over and over again while I desperately clung to the frosted glass for support. "It's just my mind playing tricks on me because it's not used to being around this many people."

"Storm!" Niadhir called as he wove through the potted bushes and strolling star elves. "By the Stars, what is the matter?"

Tearing my gaze from the dark cliffs beyond, I turned to face him. "I thought I saw..." I trailed off. How was I supposed to explain that I had seen dead people among the dancers? I waved a hand in front of my face. "Never mind."

Creases appeared in his forehead as he furrowed his brows. "Are you sure?"

"Yeah." I nodded at the music drifting in from the glass doors. "Let's go back inside."

After one last curious look, Niadhir held out his arm and escorted me inside.

The flower-scented air hadn't helped clear my head much but at least the cooler temperature slowed my thumping heart and brought some logic back. Dead people don't get up and travel across a sea and an entire continent to lurk in a ballroom. It had just been my brain's way of telling me that the sudden onslaught of sensory impressions was difficult to process after weeks of solitude.

"Oh, Niadhir," Lady Nelyssae said as she and her posse stopped right in front of us. She looked me up and down, distaste evident on her face. "And Storm. So you're the reason Princess Illeasia and Captain Hadraeth aren't here tonight. Instead of their wonderful company we get... you." She flicked her eyes over my body again while her luscious lips curled in disgust. "Great."

"Yeah, sorry," I mumbled.

Niadhir raised his eyebrows in surprise while the glamorous lady and her friends simply elbowed past me and disappeared into the crowd. I didn't know how they had expected me to react but I was all out of snarky comebacks.

"Would you like to resume dancing?" the scholar asked and motioned at the floor to our right.

The synchronized dance had broken up and instead, the couples swayed to the slow string tunes in pairs of two. I shrugged. My companion took that as a yes and led me towards the open space at the middle of the room. He placed one hand in mine and the other on my waist.

"I am so proud of you," he said as we moved in rhythm with the violins and harps. "You have grown so much. When you arrived, you were aggressive and unyielding but now you have transformed into a proper lady with grace and composure." His pale violet eyes roamed my body. "And beauty."

How he found me beautiful was beyond my comprehension. Same with the transformation. I had always been athletic but not moving and barely eating had made my lean muscles all but disappear. Now, I was just skinny. And the lady with grace and composure he talked about was just as foreign. I didn't feel beautiful and composed. I felt weak.

But the sincerity in his eyes when he had said it made me pause. Maybe it was my own values that were off? I had always had a clear view on what kind of person I should be but lately, I had started to doubt that image.

Niadhir smiled as he spun me in a circle before placing his hand on my waist again. All around us, flowing skirts in white and silver twirled in the air as the other dancers did the same. I let my gaze drift over their happy faces.

Last year when we'd been manipulating the election in Pernula, Liam had said some things that were starting to make more and more sense. Not everyone's life was filled with violence and bloodshed. These people's lives certainly weren't. Liam's half-unspoken theory that I was the reason behind the messy life of blood and screams had rang true then already – and even more so now. Maybe I was the one who needed to change?

"I have wanted to say this before but I have not yet found the right moment," Niadhir said as he continued leading me through the dance. He looked deep into my eyes. "I see a future for us here. You and I getting married, buying a house in the city, having children."

My breath hitched and I stumbled a step. He tightened his hand on my waist to steady me while hopeful eyes searched my face.

"What do you think?" he asked.

What did I think? I didn't know. Marrying, buying a house, and having kids had never even crossed my mind. That was the kind of things upperworlders did, not thieves from the Keutunian Underworld. Liam's excited face on his first day at work selling hats drifted across my memory. But then again, just because I was an underworlder now didn't mean I had to keep being one.

That persistent question echoed through my mind again. *What do you want?*

I watched the safe and contented star elves around me. Living like this, I wouldn't be a danger to my friends. Instead, life would settle into a comfortable pattern that didn't include stealing from lethal people, getting blackmailed by powerful nobles, or fighting and killing relentless attackers. My grip on my old self wavered. Liam had left the Underworld behind. Maybe it was time I did too.

"That sounds like something worth considering," I answered at last.

My dance partner beamed at me. All these questions and life decisions had made my head spin so when there was a slight pause in the music, I excused myself and fled to the drinks table. Picking up a glass flute, I emptied its contents in a few quick gulps before reaching for another. Niadhir was closing in but I just needed a moment to myself so that I could think, so I turned my back on him.

Dark violet eyes bored into me. I jerked back from the shock of finding someone standing straight in front of me when I turned around.

"The weak do not survive here," Maesia said in a voice of steel.

"I..." Footsteps sounded behind me so I cast a glance over my shoulder at the approaching scholar. When I returned my gaze to the silver-haired elf in the white dress, she was gone. "What the...?"

"Who were you talking to?" Niadhir said as he sidled up next to me and placed an arm around my back.

"I... uhm... I don't know." I lifted my shoulders in a shrug. "No one, I guess."

With a firm hand on my lower back, Niadhir steered me back to the dancefloor. I barely managed to drain my drink and place the empty glass on the table before I was out of reach. The delicate crystal thing wobbled as I pushed it onto the edge of the white tablecloth.

I didn't want to dance but I followed him anyway. What I really wanted to do was be alone for a while and think about all the confusing things swirling around my brain. It felt as though something monumental was about to happen, something that would change my life forever, and I wanted to make sure that I made the right decision.

My mind churned as I trailed behind Niadhir. Maybe it was time to leave the Underworld and become a better person. I drew a deep breath. Maybe it was time to get rid of the darkness.

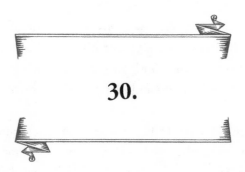

30.

White mist swirled around me. The smooth material was cold underneath my legs as I sat in front of the pond in the Sprit Garden and watched the reflections of the dark green leaves in the water. I wanted to talk. Wanted to tell Elaran about my thoughts but I couldn't get my mouth to work. Knowing that he wouldn't be able to answer threatened to bring a tidal wave of grief down over my head so I kept silent.

Water rippled from behind a wall of jasmine bushes. I inhaled deeply and closed my eyes. If he was here, what would he say? Would he advise me to get rid of the darkness and become an upstanding citizen? Honor was a big thing with him, so probably. Oh, how I wished he could answer. I opened my eyes.

A young girl with brown hair sat cross-legged on the other side of the pond. She watched me with big brown eyes. Cold hands strangled my heart. *Rain?*

The girl who had been my sister in all but blood before I had gotten her killed just continued looking at me curiously. I desperately wanted to go over to her but my body might as well have been made of stone. It refused to move. Rain cast a glance over her shoulder as another figure emerged from the mist.

Sharp blades ripped my heart to bloody shreds. Across the water, Elaran approached until he was standing right next to

Rain. I forced a few shallow gasps in and out of my throat. The auburn-haired ranger held out his hand. Rain took it and climbed to her feet. They both looked at me for a long moment before they turned around and Elaran led Rain by the hand into the mist.

I toppled forward. Dampness from the pond and the mist seeped into my clothes as I curled up on the floor and drew my knees up to my chest. With one hand pressed against the hard floor, I forced my lungs to continue drawing air. My jagged breaths created a thin coat of fog on the smooth white floor.

Elaran and Rain had been here. Both of them had died because of my actions and now the only time I would ever be able to see them again was as spirits in a place of mourning. Talons gripped my heart and yanked it apart. It was all my fault.

A sob bubbled from my throat but I stifled it before it could turn into a flood. At least they were together now. I could see them in my mind's eye. Elaran grumpily crossing his arms while looking after the energetic Rain who bounced around the place in search of mischief. Letting that image comfort me, I tried to ward off the grief that threatened to swallow me in its dark abyss.

After a few minutes, my breathing finally started working on its own again without me having to consciously force oxygen in and out of my lungs. I stayed on the floor a while longer before pushing myself up. The room swayed before me.

When I at last stumbled out of the room and into the corridor beyond, I found Niadhir staring at me. I placed a hand on the wall to steady myself and then cut him off before he could say anything.

"I want to see Shade," I stated.

The scholar put a hand to my shoulder and gave it a short squeeze. "If that is what you wish, I will get in touch with the doctors and arrange for you to visit him today."

"Yes."

He nodded and then held out his arm. My previous feelings about being escorted aside, I was grateful for his arm now because without it I was pretty sure I would've collapsed. Confusion whirled around inside my mind as we moved away from the Sprit Garden. I had to talk to Shade.

AFTERNOON SUNLIGHT filtered in through the windows and fell across Shade's pale face. I remained staring at him for another moment before I could convince my disobedient legs to move. Wood scraped against the floor as I dragged over a chair and dropped into it.

After my visit to the Spirit Garden, I had spent the rest of the day in a daze before Niadhir had at last escorted me to the wing opposite the library. I had waited the whole day for this but now that I was here, I suddenly didn't know where to start. Casting a glance over my shoulder and out the open door, I made sure that the scholar had kept his word and waited a bit further down the hall. When I found the doorway empty, I turned back to Shade and sucked in a deep breath.

"I think I'm gonna get rid of the darkness," I blurted out.

The assassin, of course, couldn't answer but it was easier to pretend that he could because at least he was right there in front of me. As opposed to Elaran. Tears welled up in my eyes but I pushed them down and got back on topic.

"I haven't done it yet because..." I let out a long exhale and raked my fingers through my hair. "Well, because I felt like it was the only thing I had left of who I was. Of the things that made me, me." Placing a hand on his chest, I gave him a sad smile. "You said it was an asset but you're wrong. It is a curse."

His muscled chest rose and fell slowly under my hand. I could almost convince myself that he was only sleeping. Almost.

"I mean, look where it's gotten me." I threw out an arm in a desperate gesture. "Where it's gotten you." My throat closed up and I had to forcibly push out the next two words. "And Elaran."

While I was keeping the tears at bay by sheer force of will, the birds outside the window had the gall to chirp. I shot up from the chair and stalked across the room.

"Why do you keep singing?" I bellowed out the window. "Don't you know there's nothing left to sing for?"

The startled blue birds dove for cover at my shouting and raced away from the building.

"Damn feather flappers," I muttered.

For a moment, I just continued watching the windowless floor that housed the library in the opposite wing until my irritation had dissipated. With my eyes still on the library that Niadhir and I had spent so much time in, I opened my mouth again.

"Niadhir was right. He warned me that Storm Casters often end up killing people they care about by mistake." I slammed a hand into the windowsill. "Why didn't I listen?" Warm afternoon air filled my lungs as I drew a bracing breath. "But maybe it's time now. Maybe it's time that I got rid of this demonic curse."

"Princess Illeasia!" Niadhir called from somewhere outside in the corridor. "What are you doing here?"

I whirled around. Not sure if I could bear the pain of a heartbroken princess attacking me, I darted across the room and dove behind the door before she had a chance to see me. Smattering footsteps sounded in the hallway.

"Princess, you need to come with me," Captain Hadraeth said.

"No! Is she here?" the princess demanded. Niadhir must've shaken his head in response to her question because she pressed on. "I'm not stupid, I know she's here somewhere. I heard her talking. I'm not going anywhere until you tell me where she is."

Shuffling feet echoed from outside. Illeasia must've looked inside the room and found it empty while the Guard Captain had followed her. Behind the door, my heart pattered in my chest. She sounded furious.

"Don't touch me!" she snapped. "My mother wouldn't take kindly to you touching me without my permission."

Hadraeth sounded weary as he replied, "Queen Nimlithil is the one who ordered me to do this, remember? Now, please, come with me."

When she had at last stalked down the hall, I slipped out from behind the door. I didn't usually hide from a fight but if I was going to get rid of the darkness and become an upperworlder, I had to change my ways. And besides, I was pretty sure that beating up the princess of my new host country wouldn't make me very popular.

"She has left," Niadhir said from outside the door. "Are you finished?"

"Almost."

With a heavy weight settling over my chest again, I returned to Shade's unresponsive body. I stroked gentle fingers along his cheek. Though I wasn't sure why I had done it, it felt right.

"Next time I come here, I promise you that I will have once and for all made a decision about all this." I studied his handsome face. "And in return, you'll promise that you've woken up next time I walk through that door. Deal?"

The Master Assassin didn't reply but I took it as a sealed deal anyway. Burying the pain under layers of stone, I turned my back on him and walked out of that awful white room. Thankfully, Niadhir didn't ask me what I'd talked to Shade about. I was trying to make a life-changing decision and I didn't want to tell any of the star elves about it until I had made up my mind. I wanted it to be my decision.

But I had also meant what I'd said to Shade. I had to make a decision soon. As we made our way down the stairs, my mind drifted back to the heartbroken princess roaming the halls. Before I hurt someone else.

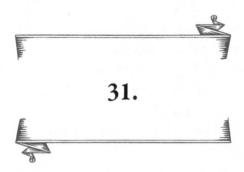

31.

Soft sounds came from outside my door. I sat bolt upright. With my heart thumping in my chest, I scrambled out of bed in a mess of tangled sheets. Moonlight spilled in from the windows, casting the room in a pale silver shimmer. In the light coming from under the door, shadows from two feet were visible. Someone was breaking into my room.

A tiny voice filled with hope pushed to the front of my mind. *It's Shade!* He had kept his promise and woken up after my visit yesterday. It had to be him. Who else would be picking the lock on my door in the middle of the night? Relief and joy bounced around inside me like an excited three-year-old. Shade was back.

Metal clinked on the other side of the door just as I made it there. It was the sound keys made when clanking against each other. I paused. A voice of reason elbowed past the giddy hopefulness. *What if it's not him?*

Of course it was him. Who else would it be? But the suspicious part of my mind refused to be shoved aside. Taking a quick step, I slunk in behind the wall. Better sure than dead. Or however the saying went.

The lock clicked. Blood rushed in my ears as I watched the handle being pushed down. In only a few seconds, I would find out if it really was that arrogant assassin that I so desperately wanted to see smirk at me again. A shard of light appeared on the white floor as the door was edged open.

The light spilling in from the corridor grew until it illuminated my bed on the other side of the room. My heart slammed against my ribs. Any second now.

"Empty?" a voice whispered. "This doesn't make any sense. Where is she?"

Disappointment washed over me like a cold dark wave and snuffed out the tiny spark of hope that had dared to flicker in my heart. It wasn't Shade. White fabric billowed as Princess Illeasia strode into the room.

"After everything it took to get here, she isn't even here," she hissed.

Melting into the shadows, I snuck along the wall so that she wouldn't see me if she turned around. Sudden realization shot up my spine and pushed the crushing disappointment aside. The princess had broken into my room alone at night. She was more of a danger than I'd initially thought. If she'd found me sleeping soundly in that bed, she could've just stuck a knife in my heart and then slipped out again without anyone being the wiser.

Illeasia turned my room upside down in a mad search for me while I shadowed her like a wraith. My heartbeat pulsed in my ears. She threw open the closet and ripped the dresses aside. I hadn't seen her a lot since I'd been yanked out of my living death state but the few times I'd seen her, she had been very different. Before Elaran's death, she had seemed so full of life and joy but now, she just looked so angry all the time.

Heavy footsteps rushed through the corridor. Shit. If she had an accomplice coming, I couldn't remain out in the open like this. Whipping around, I dropped to the floor and rolled in under my bed just as the second person stomped across the threshold.

"Princess Illeasia!" Captain Hadraeth exclaimed. "What in the world are you doing?"

From under the mass of tangled sheets hanging down from the bed, I watched him advance on the princess. She stomped a foot on the floor.

"How did you find me this quickly?"

Ignoring her question, the captain ushered her towards the door. "Where's Storm?"

"I don't know. But as you can see, she's not here."

"I will have some guards look for her but now, we are going back to your room."

Illeasia scoffed. "Always following my mother's orders." Her voice grew fainter as she and Hadraeth disappeared into the hallway. "There will come a time when you have to pick a side. Hers or mine."

Footfalls leading away from my room mingled with more rushed ones approaching.

"Find the girl," Captain Hadraeth ordered what I assumed to be the other guards.

Figuring it was best not to cause an incident by remaining hidden, I rolled out and climbed to my feet just as two guards in shining white armor barreled into the room. They jerked back in surprise and blinked at me.

I flicked an impatient hand at the rumpled covers next to me. "She didn't check under the bed."

After giving each other a sideways glance, the two guards nodded and backed out. Keys clanked and then the lock clicked shut again. I slumped down on the bed and massaged my forehead.

That had been close. If I hadn't been such a light sleeper, I would most likely be dead by now. Drumming my fingers on my thigh, I tried to shake the strange feeling that had taken over me. It was all so backwards. I didn't hide under my bed while someone broke into my room. I was the one breaking into the room. But not anymore, apparently.

Was this what my life would be like as an upperworlder? Uncertainty flashed through me while that incessant question banged against my skull again. *What do you want?*

Since I still didn't have a clear-cut answer to that question, I just toppled to the side and curled up in my bed again. Pulling the covers over my head, I sent a prayer to Nemanan. Tomorrow would be better.

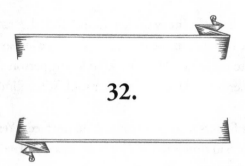

32.

"Princess Illeasia tried to kill me last night," I stated flatly.

Niadhir looked up from his books and blinked at me. "I beg your pardon?"

"Yeah, she broke into my room while I was sleeping but I heard her coming so I hid before she could do anything."

A couple of star elves shuffled past our table with stacks of books so tall I was convinced they would topple any second. They disappeared behind the white bookshelf with their precarious piles still intact.

"That is very troubling," the scholar next to me said. "You must be terribly shaken."

Considering all the creative ways in which people had tried to kill me before, last night's event wasn't much to be frightened about so I just shrugged in reply. Creases appeared in his forehead as he looked at me, worry written on his face.

"Are you sure you are alright?" he asked. "You do know that Princess Illeasia will keep coming after you? She is in a lot of pain."

I picked at a thread in the half-finished embroidery in front of me. "I know. I know she's in a lot of pain." Shoving the fabric away, I let out a frustrated sigh. "She was a bright happy person who spread light everywhere and now I've hurt her so bad she's trying to kill me." The wooden frame and the embroidered flower came to a halt in the middle of the table just as I dropped my head into my hands. "I took a kind loving person and I broke her. Made her bring darkness into her soul. What kind of person am I?"

Elegant fingers pried my hands from my face. "Yes, you have done a lot of bad things in the past but you are still worth saving. You can still become a better person but you are the one who has to choose it." Niadhir squeezed my arm. "I could not help overhearing what you said when you visited Shade."

"You eavesdropped on me?"

The scholar gave me a patient smile. "No, not eavesdropping per se. We elves have very good hearing and you were speaking rather loudly. I even think you screamed at times."

"Oh." I cleared my throat. "Right."

"I heard you saying that it might be time to rid yourself of your demonic curse. That is a great first step towards the light. Have you made a final decision?"

Picking up a needle, I started flicking it between my fingers. "I don't know."

"Did you talk to Elaran about it when you visited the Spirit Garden this morning?"

I shook my head.

"Perhaps you should. The spirits of our loved ones can offer more guidance than we think."

Talking to Elaran when I knew he wasn't really there made that gaping black hole in my chest widen so I was reluctant to do it. But maybe I had to in order to make a decision. I dropped the needles back on the pile and got to my feet.

"I need to think." The chair scraped as I pushed it back in while waving a hand towards the back of the room. "Those book towers at the back, I'll be there sorting books. I need to be alone but still do something to keep my hands busy."

Niadhir frowned at me for a second but then nodded. "If that is what you need."

"It is."

"Very well. I will be here when you are done."

Without bothering to reply, I strode along the aisle of packed white bookcases and towards the other side of the room. I couldn't think with his concerned eyes watching me, and sorting books gave me an excuse to be alone for a while.

Muted conversations drifted to my ears as I passed a table of scholars engaged in a discussion about something or other. I drew my fingers along the spines as I passed another bookshelf. At last, the gigantic towers of stacked books appeared. The spare door that had misled me when I first got here was still tucked in behind the furthest piles. Hiking my skirt up, I waded into the sea of literature.

Soft thuds echoed as I picked apart a pile and reorganized it. The monotonous task helped clear my mind while I tried to make a decision about my future. Or at least work up the courage to go back to the Spirit Garden and ask for Elaran's advice.

Placing my hands on the biggest stack, one that made it all the way to the ceiling, I tried to shift it so that I would have some more room to move. It swayed precariously but edged a little to the side. Not wanting to have hundreds of books crash down on top of my head, I decided not to push my luck and instead be satisfied with the small extra space it had already provided me.

What was the worst that could happen if I went back to the Spirit Garden? I would tell an empty room how I felt and Elaran wouldn't be there to answer. But he was already gone so that didn't change anything. Tilting my head up, I let out an exasperated breath. I squinted at the ceiling. Huh. With brows furrowed, I tipped my head back down.

Inside my brain, reason won out at last. The only thing that would happen if I went down there was to reconfirm that my friend was already gone. And it was time I accepted that.

A small pile of books toppled over as I climbed back out. It was time to face the empty silence of the Spirit Garden.

WATER DRIPPED BEHIND the flower-covered bushes and white mist swirled in the air. I drew a deep breath. How did I even start?

"Hi, Elaran," I mumbled awkwardly. "I don't even know if you can hear me but I need your help." A humorless laugh escaped my throat. "Pretty rich coming from the one who got you killed, right?"

A dark green leaf fell into the pond, creating ripples on the surface. I drew another deep shuddering inhale.

"I'm thinking about giving up the last bit of my old self. The darkness." Placing my hands on the damp material, I braced myself on the couch. "What do you think I should do?"

No grumpy archer with his furrowed brows and crossed arms broke the stillness. Only the soft dripping of water echoed throughout the room. That gaping maw in my chest split wide open.

"Of course you're not answering." I barked another bitter laugh. "You're gone. Just like everyone else. One more corpse in the vast trail of bodies I've left in my wake. Hurt and destroy and burn things to the ground. That's all I ever do. The Oncoming Storm, indeed."

My vision blurred and I shook my head to clear it. That infernal calming sound of rippling water made me want to break something. I shot to my feet.

"You're dead!" I screamed at the empty room. "You're all dead!"

Blue eyes stared at me from across the pond. I jerked back as Rogue grinned at me and started around the water. On the other side, the well-oiled blond hair of Eric and William Fahr appeared. They glared at me while advancing in the same direction.

"You're dead," I repeated. "You're not really here."

"You butchered my son," Eric Fahr whispered in a voice filled with poison.

Rogue's grin turned malicious. "Yes, you did kill me. Even after I begged for my life. You didn't have to kill me but you did it anyway. Just because you wanted to."

Shaking my head, I took a step back just as two more figures appeared from the mist. A muscular man in workman's clothes and a gangly one with messy hair and glasses strode towards me.

"I was a scholar," Keutunan's late Master of the Scribes' Guild said. "I never hurt anyone. Never. And you killed me. Poisoned my beloved tea and watched me die."

"I..." I stammered before giving my head a violent shake to clear it. "This isn't real."

The previous Master of the Builders' Guild crossed his powerful arm and shot me a look of such devastation that I thought I would crumble to dust right there.

"I had a son," he stated. "A wife and a son who needed me to provide for them. And you killed me. What do you think happened to them afterwards? Did you think they lived happily ever after? No. Without me to support them, they fell into poverty."

"No." I shook my head. "I checked on them afterwards and they were fine."

The white mist parted around them as they drew closer. "How long has it been since you were back in Keutunan? They are *not* fine anymore."

The three Fahr men had almost rounded the pond, so I backed away further. While the Guild Masters I had killed last year to save Liam continued advancing on me, a whole horde of men appeared. King Adrian cocked his head to the right and stared at me with steel in his black eyes while the soldiers around him started forward.

"You butchered my men," the late king declared. "They were only doing their job and you killed them for it. They were going to stand down there in my tent after you had slit my throat but you flew into a dark rage and killed them anyway." He threw his arms wide. "They had families, you godsdamn street rat!"

My hand shook as I raised an arm and held up a finger. "They were gonna kill me. They almost killed Liam."

"Not only did you conspire to kill my husband, you are the reason I am dead as well." Queen Charlotte materialized in the mist like a gray statue. "If you had not been so late with your warning, and had not been fighting with my son, I would not have had to take a bullet for him."

I stumbled backwards, almost tripping over the couch. They were closing in on me from every direction now but I continued backing away while panic and dread spread like cold poison through my body, weighing down my limbs.

"I never meant for you to die," I mumbled at the gray queen.

"What about me?" A man with brown hair and thin lips had appeared to my left and was quickly rounding the pond as well. "Me, you meant to kill."

"You deserved it." I drew a shaky breath and pointed a finger at Makar. "You deserved what you got."

"Did I?" Lord Makar waved a hand at the Fahr brothers. "They pressured me into doing it. I couldn't refuse a member of the Council of Lords." He moved his arm to indicate Rogue. "And just like Eric's son, I begged you not to kill me but you did it anyway. You cold-blooded killer. You really are rotten all the way through."

"Even when you don't do it on purpose, you bring death to everyone around you." A young girl with brown hair stepped out from behind a blooming jasmine bush. "I told you I didn't want to get involved but you just had to show off your skills. And then when you had the chance to stop a guy from stabbing me, what did you do? You hesitated. And I bled out in a filthy dark alley."

"Rain," I gasped. Tears welled up in my eyes. "I'm sorry, I didn't mean to. You know I didn't mean to."

"Yes, but that's the problem, Storm," a man's voice said. Auburn hair billowed in the air as Elaran strode forward. "Bad things always happen when you're near. You blasted me with hurricane winds, shocked me with lightning, and then dropped part of a building on top of me." My friend shook his head. "You don't think. You just do whatever you want and it's everyone else who pays the price."

"Please don't say that, Elaran. I never meant for..." I trailed off.

Damp leaves brushed against my arm as I retreated further into the room. Rogue was only a few paces away and his dad and uncle weren't far behind. The Masters of the Builders' and Scribes' Guild closed in from the other side while King Adrian, Queen Charlotte, and all the soldiers cut off the escape route to the door. Lord Makar leered at me from behind their blockade. The worst sight of all, however, was the disappointed eyes of Elaran and Rain as they approached me from the other side of the still water.

My foot slipped on some wet leaves and I stumbled into another couch. Fabric ripped as I stepped on my dress in a desperate move to remain on my feet. Hatred and displeasure burned in the eyes around me. Cold glass met me as my back slammed into the wall at the back of the room. I whipped my head in every direction. People I had killed closed in from all sides. I was trapped.

"You killed me in my sleep," the Master of the Builders' Guild said. "Right next to my wife and while my son was sleeping in the next room. What kind of monster are you?"

I held up my hands in a silent plea to stop their advance. "Please."

"You got us involved in a fight I didn't want to be in and then you let me die in it." Rain shook her head at me. "You should've had my back. Why didn't you have my back?"

"I did! I had your back." Tears streamed down my face. "I just made a mistake. A mistake."

Elaran pushed through the crowd of corpses and stopped right in front of me. "You killed me. I thought you were supposed to be my friend."

Yellow eyes gazed at me from only a stride away. Eyes that would never again see the light of day. My heart twisted into a tight knot until pain dripped from it. Eyes that I had shut forever. Air refused to fill my lungs. I slid down the wall and braced myself on my hands and knees. Choked sobs burst past my closed throat while tears full of regret and guilt formed a pool on the floor. Above me, accusing voices continued raining down blame while the ring of dead bodies closed in, bending down and stabbing condemning fingers at me.

"You murdered my son."

"My wife had to sleep with her dead husband in her bed for hours."

"I begged you to spare me."

"You killed me because you wanted to."

"All you ever do is bring violence and bloodshed to the people around you. You should've stayed away. Everyone is much happier without you."

"Monster."

"Bringer of death."

"Villain."

The agony inside me was so sharp I thought I was going to shatter into a million pieces that could never be made whole again. Slumping down on my side, I cradled my head in my arms and rocked back and forth. My breath came in fits and starts. The descent into madness is a slow one indeed. But when you finally reach the bottom, the whole tower crashes down on top of you all at once.

"Please stop, please stop, please stop," I begged the people I had killed and whose sympathy I did not deserve.

Everything I was, everything I had been, fell away from me like shards of a shattered mirror until all that was left was the guilt and pain and the massacred heart inside my hollow chest.

A voice tried to break through my sobbing and labored breathing but I couldn't hear what it said. I was long lost in my own personal hell. Physical pain stung my cheek as someone gave me a hard slap. My eyes fluttered open to find dark violet eyes staring at me.

"You have to fight!" Maesia growled at me.

I couldn't even muster enough energy to be surprised that she was there. Instead, I simply looked back at her with dark green eyes that had lost every single spark they had ever held.

"I don't want to fight," I whispered. Sobs racked my exhausted chest. "I'm tired of fighting."

Not sure whether the strange star elf was actually there or if she was just another figure sent to torture me, I closed my eyes again and went back to crying my shattered heart out on the cold hard floor.

They were right, all of them. I had killed them, either by choice or by carelessness, and I had broken the hearts of the loved ones they left behind. No wonder. What else could a cursed girl who had sold her soul to a demon do? I poisoned everything I touched. Hopelessness washed over me. How was I ever supposed to make up for all the awful things I had done?

33.

"**S**torm," a soft voice said. "Come back. Follow my voice."
Still lying on the damp floor and forcing gasps in and
out of my lungs, I opened my eyes. The mist had parted and the
people I had killed were gone. Instead, Queen Nimlithil and
Niadhir crouched beside me. The queen placed a graceful hand
on my cheek.

"Come back to us."

"There is nothing to come back to," I whispered. "I can never
make up for all the hurt I've caused."

"No one is beyond saving," the queen said while Niadhir
picked me up and drew me to my feet. "And there is always
something you can do."

The concerned scholar looped an arm around my back to
keep me from falling over. He bent down and leaned his
forehead again my temple. "I was so worried."

"Niadhir," the queen in her gem-decorated headdress began,
"I think perhaps it is time to share our secret with Storm. She
needs to know that there is still hope."

"I agree."

Since I was too drained to question or argue, I simply
allowed them to lead me out of the Spirit Garden and to
whatever destination this secret was located. I blinked against

the warm afternoon sun when we unexpectedly stepped outside the castle doors. The fresh air helped clear my head but I was still in shock.

"Can we just stop here for a moment?" I said and dug my heels into the stone. "I need to breathe."

Arriving anywhere unprepared and without my wits was causing panic to flare up my spine. Whatever they wanted to show me, I had to be in control of myself before we got there. The queen and the scholar looked at me with curious eyes but came to a halt in the middle of the courtyard. I withdrew from Niadhir's grip and turned to face the sun. Closing my eyes, I inhaled deeply while the golden afternoon rays warmed my face.

Those ridiculous birds were back, chirping happily from the trees, but despite my irritation at their undue joy, their song helped ground me in the present. For those precious few seconds, there were no ghosts from my past haunting me, no searing agony or blinding regret. Only me, the birds, and the warm sun.

Though I still felt exhausted and drained like a hollow husk, those few moments of peace allowed my brain to calm down and move from pure survival mode into some kind of normalcy. When I opened my eyes again, I could once more process what was happening around me.

We were outside, standing in the courtyard about halfway to the carriage storage. The late afternoon sun painted the brilliant white castle to my left in golden swirls. Leaves rustled in the breeze. I drew another deep breath of fresh air. Now. Whatever they wanted to show me, I was ready now.

"Okay," I said.

Queen Nimlithil nodded at Niadhir, who resumed his place beside me. They led me towards the building where they stored prisoner carriages. Just when I was about to ask why we were going there, they adjusted their course and aimed for the grand double doors set into the gigantic white dome next to it. That strange otherworldly atmosphere vibrated inside me again as we stopped outside the doors. I wondered what was in there.

Metal clanked as the queen produced a large and complicated-looking key. It was unlike anything I had ever seen. I squinted at it while she used it to unlock the doors. A thud sounded. Niadhir grabbed a hold of the handle on the left and pulled. It swung open on soundless hinges.

"There is no way to prepare you for what you will see inside, so I will not even try." Queen Nimlithil motioned for me to enter. "Please go ahead."

The inside of the enormous dome was like a world in itself. Lush green grass stretched out before me while sunlight streamed in from the open ceiling high above. A waterfall tumbled down from gray cliffs and pooled into a lake. I stared uncomprehending at the humongous white creature lounging by the side of the water. Light glinted off its shiny scales as it raised its head to stare back at me.

I sucked in a sharp breath between my teeth. Stumbling backwards, I flattened myself again the wall.

"That's a dragon!" I stabbed a shaking finger towards it. "That's an actual dragon!"

"Yes, it is." Queen Nimlithil put a gentle hand on my back and pushed me forward. "This is Aldeor the White. He and I have been friends for many centuries. I promise, he will not harm you."

The rows of sharp teeth gleaming in the sunlight would suggest otherwise but after an initial moment of resistance, I let the queen guide me forward. Getting eaten by a dragon would at least make for an interesting death.

"I don't understand," I said. "People say all the dragons are gone. That they disappeared around the same time as magic did."

"They are correct," Niadhir said as he sidled up to me and placed an arm around my back. "More or less, at least."

The scholar and I stopped at the edge of the water while the queen continued along its edge. When she reached the dragon's hulking shape, she placed a hand on his jaw. Leaning forward, she whispered something that I was too far away to hear. Aldeor the White closed his silver-colored eyes in an affectionate gesture before opening them again.

Huh. Queen Nimlithil was telling the truth. The two of them were indeed friends.

"Aldeor approached me centuries ago with a growing concern." The queen stroked the dragon's hard scales as she returned to us. "A concern that I share."

I could barely take my eyes off the majestic dragon. His white scales shimmered in the sunlight and cast glittering reflections in the water. Wisdom seemed to drift from his whole being. Never had I imagined that I, of all people, would one day get to witness such a spectacular sight.

Finally tearing my gaze from the extraordinary wonder in front of me, I turned to Queen Nimlithil. "What concern was that?"

Sadness washed over her beautiful features. "First of all, the endless struggle for technological development is destroying nature and creating lethal weapons. But most importantly, there is too much hurt and pain in the world. Every day, people fight and kill each other, leaving devastating grief behind. Do you remember my reason for outlawing firearms?"

"Yeah."

"It is for the same reason. Without pistols, the death and destruction is less prominent. Fewer people are killed in needless acts of anger."

Scrunching up my eyebrows, I studied her. "But people still die. Even without guns. They die of swords, arrows, knives." I shrugged. "Old age."

"That is correct. Declaring pistols illegal was only a small part in a much greater plan." Queen Nimlithil spread her arms in a hopeless gesture. "The main problem is that there is so much pain across all of Weraldi. The world should be a peaceful and beautiful place. Not marred by death and violence and scars."

Agony from what had happened in the Spirit Garden echoed through me. I gave her a slow nod. The world could definitely use a little less pain. "Alright, yeah, I can see where you're coming from but there's no way to actually get rid of pain."

Silence spread across the green grass as the queen and the scholar paused and looked at me with eyes full of conviction.

"Yes, there is," Nimlithil said at last. "Do you remember when I told you that my husband was assassinated?"

I nodded.

"It was centuries ago now. We were involved in a conflict with a neighboring country. The assassin was there for me but my dear husband was the one who died. Afterwards, I was devastated." A cloud passed over her beautiful face. "And furious. I brought my army and I wiped them out. The whole country."

Staring at her with wide eyes, I tried to think of something suitable to say. I came up blank.

"It was only after I had laid waste to everything and razed their whole nation to the ground that I noticed all the suffering." Tears gleamed in the queen's eyes. "Weeping widows and orphaned children were what was left after the dust had settled. I shall forever regret the decision I made in anger the day my beloved was taken from me."

Niadhir tightened his grip around my waist.

"Afterwards, I dedicated my life to finding a way to free people from their suffering," Queen Nimlithil continued. "Life, no matter how long or short, should be filled with love and happiness. Aldeor and I both share this philosophy. That is why he brought his proposal to me."

Water crashed onto the rocks on my left while I waited for the queen to continue. I couldn't help being nervous. Whatever she was about to tell me, I was pretty sure that not a lot of others knew it. And yet, a thief from Keutunan was about to learn the truth about the world.

"There is a spell," she began. "Or a ritual, rather, that can free people from pain. You still experience all the wonderful emotions like love and happiness. All it does is block the awful emotions like grief and pain. That way, you experience life the way it was meant to be experienced. In joy."

Frowning, I shook my head. "How is that even possible?"

"All magic comes with a price, and as you can imagine, the cost for a spell of this magnitude is quite high."

"The price is actually the rarest currency of all," Niadhir broke in. "Magic itself."

"Quite right." Queen Nimlithil motioned at the white dragon. "Aldeor draws the magic from all of dragonkind and he is the one who channels all that magic into the spell."

My mouth dropped open. "So that's why all the other dragons have disappeared."

"Yes." The star elf queen gave me a sad smile. "It is an unfortunate side effect of the spell. Since dragons are the usual conduit between magic and the rest of us, their place in this world became superfluous when they could no longer share magic with us in the same way. That is why they have all but disappeared."

"So... they're all dead?"

"No!" Queen Nimlithil exclaimed, aghast. "Killing all the dragons? That would have been a terrible crime. No, the other dragons have simply left for another continent. They do not need magic for their own purposes and when they could no longer share it with anyone else, they saw no reason to keep living here with us. But Aldeor assures me that they are happy in their new home."

"Wow." I pressed a hand to my forehead in an effort to process these mind-bending claims. "But then what happened to everyone who already had magic? People say there used to be these great mages or something."

Nimlithil and Niadhir exchanged a glance. I shifted my weight on the soft grass while looking from one to the other.

"What?" I asked.

"Now we come to the part why we are even sharing this with you in the first place," Niadhir said. He cleared his throat. "You see, adding more magic, in addition to the dragons' contribution, makes it even stronger and sees to it that it can encompass more people."

"Okay...?"

The scholar knitted his hands behind his back. "There are no more great mages because they all selflessly agreed to sacrifice their magic to feed the spell."

Skepticism must've flared like a torch on my face because Niadhir pressed on before I could voice my doubt that people would just willingly give up their magic.

"I know what you are thinking," he said. "But magic cannot be forcibly taken from someone. It can only be given freely."

"We did not want to burden you with this," Queen Nimlithil looked at me with a face full of compassion. "But you were hurting so much and looked desperate for a way to make up for all the pain and suffering you have caused so we simply wanted to tell you that there is hope."

Niadhir placed a hand on my arm. "Your curse, even though it is demonic in origins, is also a form of magic. If you decide to rid yourself of the curse, you could also decide to give it to Aldeor so that he can make the spell even stronger." His slender fingers squeezed my forearm. "If you wish, you could also complete the ritual and rid yourself of all your own pain. You do not have to carry the pain of Rain's death any longer. Or Elaran's death. Or any of the other deaths you have caused."

Grief and anguish so strong I almost doubled over bubbled to life in my chest again. Was there really a way to stop all this hurt? I desperately hoped they were telling the truth because I would do just about anything to never have to experience the events of the Spirit Garden again. If I did, I was certain I would die of agony.

"Is it really true?" I moved pleading eyes between them.

"Yes." Niadhir gave me an encouraging nod. "You can once and for all be free from your demonic curse and all the awful pain and guilt you are carrying and then you can start anew. You can make up for all the misery you have caused by giving others the option to free themselves from their pain too."

High up, above the open ceiling, a pair of seagulls squawked. I tipped my head up to the stretch of blue sky visible there. A world free of pain and suffering. Wouldn't that be something?

"This is why you wanted Shade and Elaran to stay," I stated as sudden understanding clicked in place. "Even though they're not Storm Casters."

The queen nodded. "Shade is the General of Pernula and Elaran was the Head Ranger of Tkeideru."

Her use of the past tense almost had me breaking into sobs again but I managed to keep it together. "You wanted them to spread the word about the spell."

"Yes. You see, the ritual cannot be completed on someone who does not agree to it of their own free will. That is why I tried to explain to you that we do not conquer any lands. We never force anything on anyone. We simply give them the choice. But because of the misconception of our true purpose, no countries are willing to listen unless we go there ourselves."

"But we do not conquer," Niadhir repeated. "Every nation under Queen Nimlithil's protection has agreed willingly to join. If Shade and Elaran had brought word to their respective countries, it would have saved us the trip."

Pressing the heels of my hands to my temples, I tried not to become overwhelmed by the sheer magnitude of what I was suddenly involved in. I didn't make decisions for cities and nations. I made them for me. All the politics aside, what it all really came down to was two things. Did I want to make up for all the hurt I had caused, by giving the darkness to the white dragon? And, did I want to complete the ritual so that I could never hurt like this again? After today, I already knew in which direction I was leaning but I didn't want to rush a decision like this.

"I need to think," I said.

"Of course," Queen Nimlithil said. "Take all the time you need. All we wanted to do was show you that there is hope. There is a life full of love and happiness waiting for you, if you want it. So please, do not fall into despair."

"Thanks, yeah, I'll try."

While the queen glided over the grass to bid Aldeor farewell, Niadhir led me back up the gentle slope. My mind was completely scrambled. Too many voices saying too many things were muddling up my brain so I pushed them all back. Once I was alone, I would deal with them one at a time.

Winds ruffled my hair as we stepped outside and started back towards the castle. I drew a deep breath. The information I had learned today was far too important to rush through but one question refused to be silenced. *What do you want?*

34.

That night, I didn't sleep at all. Countless questions, scenarios, and explanations flitted around my brain like restless dragonflies. I threw open the window and climbed onto the windowsill. My nightgown fluttered in the jasmine-scented air as I leaned back against the frame and watched the stars glitter in the dark water.

All my previous assumptions about the star elves had been wrong. They weren't heartless monsters laying waste to the rest of the continent. They really were trying to make the world a better place. The true villain was actually me. And other people like me, spreading violence and death everywhere.

Now, they had given me a chance to start over. To become someone else. Someone better. I could get rid of my demonic powers and get my soul back and then free myself from the terrible pain I had been carrying with me ever since I had gotten Rain killed eleven years ago. Eleven years. That was a very long time. And I wasn't sure I could cope with another decade of those feelings combined with the even stronger agony from Elaran's death.

Maybe it really was time to let go of everything I had ever been and become a completely new person. A person who fit in. Someone that others liked and wanted to have in their lives.

Tracing circles on the cool frosted glass, I listened to the cicadas play far below. I spent another hour staring into the night in silence before finally returning to bed when the rising sun cast its pale rays across the horizon. Tomorrow was another day. Maybe I would at last make my final decision then.

THE SMELL OF NEWLY baked bread drifted in the air. I picked up a silver fork and used it to move fresh fruit onto my plate, making room next to the still warm loaf and the slices of cheese. After weaving through the tables in the small dining room, I plopped down on the chair opposite Niadhir.

"A full plate for breakfast? I am glad to see that you have regained your appetite," he said and gave me smile. "You barely ate anything at dinner."

"Yeah, I had a lot on my mind." I reached for the pitcher of water between us. When I lifted it, I noticed that it had left a ring on the white tablecloth. Not wanting to make our table for two even messier, I took care not to spill as I filled my glass. "But now I'm starving."

"I can imagine. We gave you a lot to think about yesterday."

Using my knife, I cut the round bread in two and placed a slice of cheese on one side. I knew that they were supposed to be eaten separately, but I liked them together. The warm airy bread and the compact salty cheese complemented each other nicely. And then of course some fresh fruit after that.

Gazing around the room we ate breakfast in every morning, I felt like I saw it for the first time. Really saw it. Couples in beautiful dresses and crisp suits were sharing the first meal of the day together while chatting pleasantly about the day's coming events.

"Are you meeting your sewing circle today?" a star elf in a white suit asked by the table to my right.

"Yes, dear," a beautiful elf in a silver dress replied. "You know we meet every day. But we also have a tailor coming to show us the new dresses for the banquet."

"Oh, that's right!" He patted her on the hand. "What an exciting addition to the day."

I let my eyes drift over the other couples having similar conversations. This was what my life would be like. Safe. Comfortable. A peaceful and calm existence with a set routine and no more surprise blackmails and fights. I would never again think about Rain and Elaran and feel the pain of grief. Clarity and certainty like nothing I had ever felt before pushed through all the hurt and pain and everything I had gone through. *What do you want?* I finally knew the answer to that question.

"I wanna do the ritual," I declared. "Both of them, actually. Getting rid of the darkness and giving it to Aldeor and then also getting rid of the pain."

An excited smile tempered by cautiousness spread across Niadhir's face. "Are you quite sure? There is no rush."

"I'm sure." I gave him a firm nod. "I don't think I've ever been this sure about anything in my whole life."

It's funny, you'd think that making a huge life decision like this would require some sort of dramatic setting. Like, standing atop sharp cliffs gazing towards the horizon and listening to the powerful waves crash against the rocks. Not sitting at the breakfast table eating a piece of cheese. But I've often found that it's the small things, the everyday things, that turn out to be the most important in the end.

"I am so glad to hear that." He reached out and squeezed my hand. "We have such a wonderful life ahead of us. A life in the light." Another giddy smile quirked his lips. "When would you like to perform the first ritual? Right before the banquet this week?" He tapped a slender finger to his lips. "Or perhaps something more significant. The ball the week after?"

I scrunched up my eyebrows and chewed the inside of my cheek. "What about the full moon?"

"Yes, yes." He nodded. "It is only a few weeks away and it is a day of great symbolism. Starting a new life in the light when the moon is at its brightest. Yes. I shall inform Queen Nimlithil at once."

Plates and utensils clinked as Niadhir shot up from his chair in a burst of excitement. I reached out to steady the swaying glasses before standing up as well. He held out his arm with the enthusiasm of a schoolboy and then proceeded to lead me out the room on feet that practically skipped. Smiles followed us from the other tables.

"Would you like to remain in the library with your embroidery while I inform Her Majesty?" the scholar asked as we reached the hallway outside.

"Actually, I quite liked sorting books." I lifted my shoulders in an embarrassed shrug. "The physical movement helps keep the pain in my heart away."

"I understand. Then that is what you must do until you are finally free of it."

Our footsteps echoed against the smooth walls as we ascended the stairs.

"Is it possible to send a letter to someone?" I asked as we made our way up another flight of stairs.

"Why do you ask?"

"Well, it's just..." A fist squeezed my heart. "Liam. He's probably worried sick not knowing what happened to me. I kinda left without saying goodbye."

"Oh."

"Yeah, so I just wanted to tell him that I'm okay now and that I've finally found where I belong." More pain bled from my heart and I choked back a sob. "And I need to tell them about Elaran."

"I see." He gave my arm a reassuring pat. "And you are right, it is an important part in leaving your old life behind. I shall have pen and paper delivered to you in the library while I speak with Queen Nimlithil and then when I return, I will take you to the roof."

"The roof?"

"Yes, that is where the carrier doves are kept."

Chatting conversations were replaced by quiet murmuring as we reached the library. The scholar brought us to our usual table and rearranged some scrolls while talking to another elf. I waited patiently next to him. When he at last told me that pen and paper were on their way, I nodded and then set course for the book stacks at the back.

Just thinking about Elaran had made the chasm in my chest crack open again and I really needed to do something with my hands to keep my mind off it. The time until Niadhir returned was spent writing and then methodically moving books from one pile to another.

"How are you faring?"

I jerked up and whirled around to find Niadhir watching me with an amused expression on his face. "Oh, I lost track of time." Scratching the back of my neck, I blinked at the scene around me. "You're back already?"

"Yes. Queen Nimlithil is happy that you have found your way back to the light and she has agreed that the full moon is an excellent day for it." He moved his gaze around the clutter. "Have you written the letter?"

"Yeah." I nodded before climbing back out again. "We're going now?"

"I think that would be wise. Afterwards, I would like to resume my research and I would prefer not to take another break until our next meal."

"Alright." I smoothed my skirt as I reached him. "Lead the way."

Holding out his arm, he escorted me through another series of hallways and up several flights of stairs until we reached the rooftop garden we had visited the first time I had met him. We followed a path of artfully placed bushes and trees in silver pots towards the middle of the roof.

"Wow." I stopped briefly and stared at the white tower that had appeared before us. "Never seen anything like this before."

The tall round construction was filled with holes and in them, pure white doves cooed. One of them took flight, stretching shining feathers towards the clear blue sky. Something made of metal gleamed on its back.

"Meet Starhaven's carrier doves," Niadhir said with a proud smile.

Holding up my hand to shield my eyes from the sun, I studied the birds. "What makes carrier doves different from, you know, regular doves?"

"Magic."

"But I thought–"

"The spell, yes." He waved a light hand at the tower. "Since they only have mere trace amounts of magic in their blood, it would not make a difference to the spell. Besides, this is a highly valuable way of communicating. One only needs to whisper the name of the desired recipient and the dove will find them."

I gave the strange birds an impressed nod. "Very valuable indeed."

The scholar motioned for me to approach the tower so I took a step forward and held out a hand next to the closest hole. Short claws grazed my skin as a dove fluttered out and landed on a peg next to me. Furrowing my brows, I studied the small tube secured on its back by straps.

"You place the letter in there," Niadhir explained. When I began rolling up the sheet of paper, he lifted his hand. "May I? It is only to make sure that the dove will be able to carry the weight."

I had a feeling that it was actually to check what I had written in it, which annoyed me quite a bit, but I had nothing to hide and I didn't feel like fighting so I handed it over without protesting. Pale violet eyes skimmed the page while he pretended to weigh it in his hand.

"Yes, the dove will be able to carry this," he announced as he handed it back to me.

Unscrewing the top of the tube with one hand, I stuffed my letter inside with the other. The dove flapped over to my empty palm. After telling it where to go, I launched the bird into the air.

"Good luck," I said as it flew into the bright sky.

"You do not need to wish it luck." Niadhir took my arm and gave it a small pat. "It will arrive at its destination regardless."

With my eyes still on the disappearing white dot, I nodded. "I hope so."

Watching the dove take flight felt like screaming my decision to the sky. It was a nice feeling after all this time of uncertainty and doubt. There was no going back now. After this, everything would change.

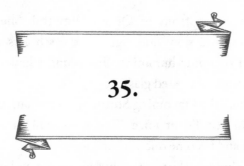

35.

A procession of scholars in white suits stood in two rows at the entrance to the library. Queen Nimlithil in her sparkling silver and gem-covered headdress waited in front of the open doors. I wiped my hands on my dress as Niadhir led me towards her. The plain one I had opted for today once again fit my frame well.

In the weeks since I had informed everyone about my decision, I had made a few changes. I had stopped going to the Spirit Garden. There was nothing more to say to the dead so there was no point in going there. I had also started eating regularly and exercising again. Both by sorting books in the library but also at night. The sunken eyes and the withering body was gone and my lean muscles were finally back again.

My mind was doing better too. Ever since I made my decision, the nightmares had stopped. And so had the ghostly visits from people I had killed. If that wasn't a sign that I was making the right decision, I didn't know what was.

"Do not be nervous." Niadhir gathered up my arm and gave it a squeeze. "You are making the right decision," he confirmed as if he had heard my thoughts.

I drew a deep breath. "I know I am."

We stopped in front of Queen Nimlithil. She bent her graceful neck in a slow nod right as the scholars around us started up a rhythmic humming. The sound vibrated between the smooth walls of frosted glass.

"Welcome, the Oncoming Storm of Keutunan," the elegant queen said in a confident voice. "Today, you will leave your dark past behind and become one with the light."

In a swishing of skirts, she whirled around and glided into the library. Captain Hadraeth stepped out of the shadows inside and followed her while Niadhir guided me across the threshold. The chanting scholars trailed behind us as we moved through the empty library towards a large space in the middle. An old and incredibly thick book waited on a small side table.

Niadhir had talked me through the ritual earlier, so I knew what to expect, but my heart still thumped in my chest. It would soon be over.

The star elves in their white suits formed a ring around me while Niadhir took up position behind the heavy book. Hadraeth's eyes flashed with displeasure when he was forced to stand further away but he kept his mouth shut as his queen stepped into the circle. She raised her hands.

"Stars, we ask you to bring this wayward soul into your kind embrace." Bracelets clinked as Queen Nimlithil drew her arms in a sweeping pattern. "Show her the way into the light."

Around us, the rhythmic chanting grew louder. Niadhir cleared his throat and began reading a passage from the book but it was in a language I didn't understand so I had no idea what he was saying.

The other scholars raised and lowered their voices in tune with the ritual reading. Clothes rustled as they started tracing symbols in the air. Nimlithil threw her arms up and joined in with the sacred words being spoken. Blood pounded in my ears. I drew my hands over the white sleeves on my forearms. With her arms still raised towards the ceiling, Queen Nimlithil closed the distance between us.

"Stars, show her the light." She turned in a slow circle in front of me. "Let her forever leave the violence behind."

Old texts, long forgotten by the rest of the world, echoed against the library walls. Slender hands swished through the air as the scholars drew the air patterns faster and faster. When the queen opened her mouth, a commanding voice crackling with ancient strength and wisdom rose. The air was thick with thrumming power. My heart slammed against my ribs in time with the vibrations that bounced off every surface when the deafening chorus approached the climax.

Nimlithil whirled around to face Niadhir. My muscles tensed as I stood up on my toes and raised my arms.

The chanting stopped. Violet eyes stared at me from every direction as dead silence descended on the library. I pushed the knife tighter against Queen Nimlithil's throat.

"Now, you will do exactly as I say or your beloved queen dies."

Niadhir stared at me with such a dumbfounded look on his face that, for a moment, I thought his brain had frozen completely. The other scholars appeared to be in similar states of shock.

With my hand on her silver dress, I tipped the tall elf a little further back to get my blade in a better position. "You know who I am so you know I'm not bluffing."

"Storm!" Niadhir finally pressed out. His distraught voice echoed through the utter silence that had fallen. "By the Stars, what are you doing?"

"That would be a mistake." Ignoring the distressed scholar, I moved my eyes to the seething Guard Captain outside the ring. "Do you really think you can draw that sword and get all the way over here before I can slit her throat?"

Captain Hadraeth's handsome features were twisted in rage. "That's an empty threat because as soon as you kill her, I will kill you."

"I bet you will." Shrugging was difficult in the awkward position my body was in so I only managed a slight lopsided one. "You might get to kill me but that won't change the fact that your queen will also be dead. So, go put your sword on that table over there before I run out of patience."

Anger darkened his eyes but my gamble on his unwillingness to see his queen murdered just to get revenge on me proved well-founded when he stalked over to the table and surrendered his weapon.

"Good choice." I nodded towards the entrance. "Now, take all these fine scholars and lock them up in the room to the left of the library. Then get back here and close the library doors on your way in." I shot him an iron stare. "I'll be watching. If you try anything, she dies."

"Storm!" Niadhir called as the captain herded him and the others towards the doors. "What is the meaning of this?"

"I thought it was obvious." Frowning at him, I gave him the same look of an exasperated teacher explaining something to a particularly slow child that he had so often given me. "This is me rejecting your offer to get rid of the darkness and become an upperworlder." A grin spread across my mouth. "I look so much better in black anyway."

"Storm!" he called again, alarm present in his pale violet eyes. "It is not too late. You can still renounce the darkness. Storm!"

With a firm grip on the queen, I moved us sideways so that I could see all the way down the corridor and into the hallway beyond the library doors.

"I do not understand," Queen Nimlithil said in a sad voice. "I thought you understood that giving up your curse will help others live a happier life. Why would you deny the world a chance to be free of pain?"

"Because you're going about it all wrong! I understand what you're trying to do but this isn't the way."

Between the rows of bookcases, the group of confused scholars shuffled forward with an impatient Guard Captain behind. Hadraeth cast a quick look at me over his shoulder before flicking his hands at the other star elves, telling them to hurry.

"Getting rid of pain isn't the answer." I let out a long exhale and shook my head even though the queen couldn't see it. "Pain and grief are a part of life. It's how you know it was real."

Queen Nimlithil clicked her tongue. "You are not making any sense. Hurting when thinking about someone you loved is not a good thing."

"Yeah, it is. Yes, every time I think about Rain or Elaran, my heart will break." Just speaking those words proved the statement true because a flash of agony shot through me. "But that's not a bad thing. My heart breaks because I loved them. The pain you feel when they die is the price you have to pay for all the years of love they gave you. It's what makes the connections we form real. And precious."

Captain Hadraeth glared at me from outside the library as he locked the door behind the scholars. For a moment it looked like he contemplated leaving to get backup but then he gave his head a violent shake and stalked back towards us. Queen Nimlithil shifted awkwardly in front of me as I pulled us both away from the main corridor. The library doors rattled as the captain slammed them shut.

"You are wrong," she said. "Pain is never a good thing."

Deciding not to argue my point further, I just continued moving us towards the side of the room in silence. To never again think about Rain or Elaran and feel sad was not what I wanted. The pain of their passing was how I honored their memory and remembered my love for them. Removing people's ability to feel pain and grief wouldn't make the world a better place. It would only give everyone a half-life. Maybe in time, she would realize that I was right. I tipped my head from side to side. Though she had already lived for centuries and not figured it out, so probably not.

"There, I've locked them in," Captain Hadraeth said as he appeared between the rows of white bookshelves.

"If the door isn't locked, you'll regret it." I moved the kitchen knife I had stolen at dinner yesterday higher up under the queen's chin to really drive the point home.

"It's locked," he snapped. Silver-decorated armor shifted as he crossed his arms. "Now, let her go."

Nodding at a metal pipe set into the wall, I flashed him a quick smile. "Yeah, I'm not giving up my leverage just yet. See that pipe over there?"

Captain Hadraeth followed my gaze before turning back and giving me a curt nod.

"Good. Take out your handcuffs."

"I don't have any handcuffs on me."

Grabbing the back of the queen's neckline, I bent her further back and pressed the blade tighter against her throat. "You really wanna play this game?"

Violet eyes so cold I almost got frostbite bored into me. For a second, everything was still. Only the soft popping of the candles in their glass containers broke the silence as the Guard Captain and I stared each other down. Then, he averted his gaze and yanked out a pair of manacles from the back of his armor.

"Yeah, I thought not." I nodded at the sturdy metal cylinder again. "Go stand next to that pipe."

The delicate glass candle holders on the tables clinked as he stomped over.

"Lock one side of the handcuffs around one of your wrists and then throw me the key," I instructed.

Metal clicked into place as he pushed it shut around his left wrist. After another icy glare, he lobbed the key in my direction. It slid over the smooth floor and came to a halt next to my feet. Leaving it there, I pulled the queen with me and moved towards the fuming guard.

"One wrong move and she dies," I warned as we closed in.

Hadraeth didn't respond but he didn't move either so I stepped closer until we were standing on the other side of the pipe.

"Hold out your arm," I told the queen. When she did, I turned to the captain. "Draw the handcuffs around the back of the pipe and then lock her wrist in the empty one."

Outrage flashed in his eyes but he complied with my orders. When the final click signaled that both Captain Hadraeth and Queen Nimlithil were locked together with one arm behind the sturdy metal tube, I whipped my knife from the queen's throat and darted away.

While lifting a hand to my brow in a mock salute, I shot them a satisfied smile. "This is goodbye, then."

"As soon as you try to get down the stairs, the other guards will catch you," the Guard Captain said. "And then you're mine."

My smile turned into a smirk. "They can try." I whirled around.

"Wait!" the confused queen called right as I was about to stride away. "Why are you doing this? I do not understand at all. No one forced you to agree to this ritual. Even if you did not want to do it, you could have lived here with us. Why would you want to leave?"

I stopped. Tapping a finger against my thigh, I considered whether I owed them an explanation or not. A small chuckle escaped my throat. I didn't. But they were going to get one anyway because *I* wanted to finally tell them how I really felt.

After swinging back around, I lifted my shoulders in a light shrug. "I don't want this."

"A safe and comfortable life in a palace, free of pain and struggle." She furrowed her manicured eyebrows. "How could anyone say no to that?"

"Because I hate it here!" An exasperated laugh bubbled out from my chest. "I have since day one. I'm not an upperworlder." Shaking my head, I pulled at the white fabric of my skirt. "The ridiculous dresses and being escorted around like some weak defenseless child! The formal dinners, the five hundred different forks, the polite small talk about stuff you don't even mean, the synchronized dances. I hate it all."

"Those are lovely parts of our culture," Queen Nimlithil protested.

"There are too many rules!" I threw my arms to the sides in a frustrated gesture. "I'm not allowed to wear what I want, eat when or how I want, do what I want! Women here sew and do embroidery and the most exciting part of their week is trying on dresses. Dresses. *That's* the most exciting thing that happens to them!" Disbelief dripped from my whole body as I shook my head. "How can anyone want that kind of life?"

The queen shook her head as well. "I do not understand you at all. It is a wonderful life."

"No. It's not. Not for me."

"If not that, then what is it that you want?"

"Freedom! I want to do whatever I want, whenever I want, and however I want." A wide grin spread across my mouth. "I'm an underworlder. Always have been. Always will be."

Queen Nimlithil stared at me, uncomprehending. "How could anyone desire such a complicated life full of death and disappointment?"

"Yeah, my life is violent and complicated and messy." I gave them another shrug. "But it's *my* life. I decide what to do with it."

Memories of Liam, the twins, and all my other friends rose to the front of my mind. They all had their own lives now but that didn't mean there wasn't a place in it for me too.

"And I will always steal, cheat, and kill to protect the people I love." I flicked my hand in a nonchalant gesture. "If that makes me a villain, then fine, I'm a villain."

The beautiful queen stared at me in complete befuddlement while the captain's stern eyes flashed from anger to uncertainty to confusion. An insane chuckle slipped my lips. I whirled around and set course towards the entrance to the library.

"I'm a villain!" I shouted, still laughing like a crazy person.

As soon as I was out of sight, I veered right. I wanted them to think that I was leaving by the front doors and that I would be trying to get down the stairs. My mouth drew into a smile as I snuck further into the library instead. It was time to head to my real exit point.

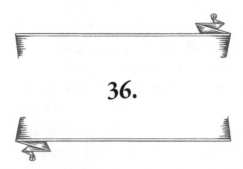

36.

Towers made of books rose before me. I hiked up my skirt and launched myself from the ground. Leather creaked beneath me as I raced up the staircase of books I had secretly built in the back of the library these past weeks. Bracing myself on the smooth ceiling, I put a hand to the wooden trapdoor and pushed.

That day in the library, before I had my complete breakdown in the Spirit Garden, when I had come here to sort books in order to clear my head and work up the courage to talk to Elaran, I had pushed the tallest stack of books a little to the side. That was when I had discovered the edge of a trapdoor. Since the library was on a different floor, I couldn't go back and check it out at night. But I had managed to sneak up there and see where it led one day when Niadhir had been occupied.

Having an escape route was always good, even if I hadn't planned on using it at first. However, after that day in the dining room when we ate breakfast and the reality of what life here would be like had hit me like a brick to the face, I knew what I had to do. And by then, I already had a plan in mind.

I climbed up the hole in the ceiling and then rolled over on my stomach. Leaning back down, I grabbed a hold of the spare door I had found on my first visit to the library. It was a very tall door but it wasn't long enough to reach all the way from the floor to the ceiling so I had secretly propped it up on a stack of books. Wood creaked as I hauled it up.

Once it was through the hatch, I placed it carefully on the ground and closed the trapdoor behind me. Hopefully, they would never realize that this had been my exit point. Or if they did, I banked on it being after I was already gone.

The full moon painted the empty room in silvery light. There were no windows in the library but here, a whole row of wide windows provided an excellent view of the adjacent wing. I threw open both sides of the clear glass panes.

Jasmine and roses drifted in on the cool night wind. Hoisting the spare door, I carried it over and braced one side on the windowsill. This was the one thing I hadn't been able to actually test beforehand since I would never have managed it before Niadhir discovered I was missing. Instead, I'd had to rely on my eyes. Praying to Nemanan that I had accurately judged the distance, I pushed the door forwards.

It scraped against the frosted glass. The further out I pushed it, the harder it was to keep it level. My heart skipped a beat when the door dropped a good arm's length. With blood rushing in my ears, I threw my weight on the back of the door. The assaulted slab of wood groaned but rose to a more horizontal level again. I barely dared breathe as I continued pushing.

Only a little further. My arms shook as I moved the door forwards. *Please let it be enough*. A soft thud sounded. I released a long exhale as the front of the door lodged itself in place on the opposite windowsill. It was only by about a hand's length, but the tall spare door had been long enough to reach between the towers. Just as I had predicted. Or hoped.

The frosted glass was cold underneath my palms and knees as I climbed up on the windowsill.

"Alright, Cadentia," I said to the Goddess of Luck, "I know we have a complicated relationship but if you've got any good fortune to share with me, I could really use it right now."

Lady Luck didn't answer but I placed a hand on the white door and started forward anyway. Wood creaked beneath me. I tried to slow my racing heart but it refused to obey and continued slamming against my ribs while I crawled onto the flimsy bridge I had built between the wings.

My dress fluttered in the air as the night wind snatched at the fabric. I knew I should keep my focus on the next building but my morbid curiosity won out and I risked a peek down. Silver light from the moon radiated off the white castle but the ground was so far below that it was completely shrouded in darkness.

I let out a long exhale. "Yeah okay, so if this door breaks, I'm definitely gonna die."

As if it had heard me, the wood groaned dangerously under my knees. I sucked in a breath and crawled faster. My heart dropped into my stomach when the jerkier motion made the door wobble underneath me. Forcing myself to slow down, I tried to ignore my hammering heart and the creaking wood.

When I at last reached the other side, I pressed myself against the glass and closed my eyes for a second. Well, that was one more thing to add to the list of stupid dangerous shit I'd survived in my life. Opening my eyes, I drew out a needle-turned-lockpick and slid it through the crack in the window. After lifting the latch, I climbed inside.

My feet hit the floor soundlessly. I didn't want to waste time drawing the spare door inside so I just left it there and snuck through the darkened hall. This was the other part of my plan that I hadn't been able to check thoroughly beforehand. I only had my previous visits to go by and they might have been less than ordinary but there was nothing I could do about it now. If unexpected trouble arose, I would just have to deal with it.

The plain door that was my target appeared further down the corridor. *Huh. No guard.* Not trusting my luck, I kept to the shadows by the wall as I slunk forward. When I reached it and no army of star elves jumped out of hidden corners, I closed the final distance. Suspicion crept into my mind as I studied the door. *No lock.* Could it really be that easy?

Placing a tentative hand on the door, I waited for some unseen trap to smite me down. Nothing happened. I pushed down the handle. Light flickering from inside spilled into the dark hallway. Drawing a deep breath, I slid inside but left a tiny crack in the door open behind me just in case it was a trap.

A surprised gasp ripped from my throat. "Shade?"

On the floor of the room where I had visited the unconscious assassin, that same assassin stood staring at me. Surprise flashed over his handsome face. His very much conscious face.

"You're awake?" I pressed out through a quickly closing throat.

His mouth drew into a smile.

"Storm?"

I froze. That voice. It couldn't be. Throwing out a hand, I braced myself on the doorframe. My mind was threatening to shut down. It simply couldn't be.

Auburn hair swung in the air as Elaran stuck his head through the opening to the side of the room. The side where his lifeless body had lain on a table. Where my whole world had been broken beyond repair when his cold limp hand had hung from the table.

My knees buckled. I crashed to the floor with enough force to jar my bones. Sobs racked my body. I pressed one hand against my mouth and the other to the floor to steady myself.

Elaran was alive. I hadn't killed him. All this time, he had been here somewhere in another wing of the castle. Alive. My arm wasn't enough to support me anymore and I slumped forward. With one hand still covering my mouth, I doubled over and rested my forehead on the cool floor while I cried with unrestrained relief and shock. He was alive.

A light hand touched my shoulder blade. "Storm?"

I sucked in another desperate breath at feeling his touch and hearing his voice again. Relief and boundless joy flooded my chest but my battered heart was afraid of me opening my eyes again. If I did, he might be gone again. Gathering all the courage I had left, I pushed off the floor and stared straight into the space where I feared he would no longer be.

Concerned yellow eyes stared back at me. I pressed my hand harder against my mouth while tears spilled down my cheeks like a spring flood. It was real. He was real. Elaran, fully alive, crouched in front of me. I grabbed a fistful of his shirt and yanked him towards me.

Pulled off balance, his knees hit the floor right in front of mine. I wrapped my arms around his chest and hugged him so tightly I wasn't sure I'd ever be able to let go. He stiffened in surprise but then leaned into my embrace. Toned arms encircled my body.

"It's you," I croaked. "It's really you. You're not dead."

"I'm not dead," he said.

Another string of sobs racked my body. For a long moment, we stayed like that. Only when I was certain that it was not some cruel trick and that my friend wouldn't disappear if I let him go did I let my arms fall to my sides again.

"How are you alive?" I pressed out in a hoarse whisper.

Elaran drew back slightly and then pushed off the ground. I remained kneeling on the floor because I didn't think my legs would support me just yet. When I didn't move, Shade and Elaran exchanged a look. While the elf lifted me to my feet and plopped me down on the bed, the assassin pulled over a chair. The soft mattress bounced underneath me as Elaran sat down.

"He was never dead," Shade said and nodded at the wood elf. "And I was never in a coma."

Not being able to believe that the thing I had prayed for every day for weeks on end had actually come true, I shook my head. "How?"

"You remember that purple mist they used to knock us out when they brought us here?" the Master Assassin asked. "The one that kept us unconscious for most of the trip?"

"Yeah."

"That's what they used."

The bed creaked as Elaran shifted his weight. "Princess Illeasia explained that they dosed me with enough of it to make it look like I was dead." He shrugged. "Apparently, they wanted to do the same with Shade but couldn't because he's human."

"They didn't know how much to dose me with so that I'd look dead without risking actually killing me." The black-eyed assassin rolled his eyes. "Ironic, right?"

"So they just used the same dose as last time and knocked him out so you'd think he was in a coma," Elaran filled in.

Of course. These star elves were skilled with chemicals. A sudden realization flashed through my mind.

"Wait. Princess Illeasia told you this?" I tried to put the spinning pieces of the puzzle together in my mind. "Then she knew you weren't really dead. Then she wasn't actually trying to kill me. But why was she so angry then?" I shook my head and shot up from the bed. Shock and relief still rolled off me like tidal waves but we didn't have time for any lengthy explanations right now. "But now isn't the time."

Elaran cast a quick look at Shade. "Yeah, that brings us to our question. What's going on? What are you doing here?"

Renewed energy from finding Elaran alive and Shade awake made my whole soul sparkle. I flashed them a satisfied grin.

"I'm rescuing you, of course." Furrowing my brows, I studied them. "But why haven't you left already? There's no guard and the door was unlocked. You could've just walked out."

The assassin nodded at the door. "Notice anything strange?"

Squinting at it, I realized that there was no lock on the inside. Or a door handle, for that matter.

"You don't need a guard or a lock if the door can't be opened from the inside." He gave me a sad smile. "And now you're stuck here too."

"What kind of amateur do you take me for?" I smirked at him and strode towards the door. One slight push and it swung outwards. "I suspected it was some kind of trap when it was unlocked and no one was guarding it." Still grinning, I clicked my tongue. "As if I'd close a door like that behind me."

"Suspicious and distrusting as always." Shade chuckled.

I jerked my head at the door. "Come on then, let's go."

The ranger and the assassin exchanged another look.

"We should probably..." Shade began.

"Yeah," Elaran filled in before motioning for me to follow him into the other side of the room.

I trailed after the two of them as they moved to a closet at the back. An army of white garments swung slightly as Shade pulled the doors open. Shoving them to the sides, he stuck his whole torso inside.

"What are you doing?" I asked, completely bewildered.

"I thought you might like these back." He withdrew from the wardrobe and held up a very familiar pile of soft and sharp objects.

"Is that...?" I ran over to him and grabbed the whole pile. "It is! Where did you get them?"

All of my trusted knives lay neatly piled on top of my black and gray clothes. Happiness lit up my whole being. The final missing piece had been returned.

"Princess Illeasia brought all our stuff some weeks back," Shade said as he pulled out his own black clothes and twin swords. "She said she was getting us all out that night and that she was just getting you. But she never returned so we assumed she failed."

Realization snapped into place. Oh. That night when she broke into my room. It hadn't been to kill me. It had been to bring me to Shade and Elaran and help us escape. By Nemanan, I really had been a fool.

After placing his own things on the table nearby, the Master Assassin withdrew a pile of green and brown clothes followed by two more swords. "We kept our stuff hidden for when we'd get another chance to escape." He flashed me a smile as he put Elaran's stuff next to his own while the elf retrieved his huge back bow. "Like tonight."

"Well, thank you, Princess Illeasia," I said as I pulled the white dress over my head.

With every knife and every piece of clothing I put on, I felt the real me return bit by bit. Shade's black eyes kept wandering in my direction as I dressed. I returned the favor when he unbuttoned his own white clothes and showed off that athletic body. His lips drew into a satisfied smirk before he put on his tight-fitting black shirt again. Elaran shook his head and said something under his breath while securing his bow to his back.

A sense of completeness, of finally being whole again, filled me when I stuck the last throwing knife back in place behind my shoulder. I let out a contented sigh. I was myself again.

Amusement glittered in the assassin's eyes as he watched me. "Ready?"

"Of course I'm ready." I grinned at the both of them. "I'm the one rescuing *you*, remember?" Jerking my head towards the door once more, I motioned for them to follow. "Let's go."

Flickering candlelight spilled into the hallway when I opened the door again. I paused. Silence still reigned outside. Pushing it all the way open, the three of us snuck outside and into the dark halls of the castle. It was time for the second part of my escape plan.

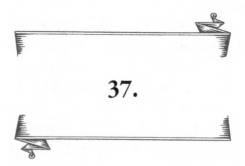

37.

Raised voices echoed from the stairwell. I froze. Shoving my two friends back, I darted up the stairs behind them and into the empty hallway again.

"Let's try the one on the other side," I whispered and nodded down the hall.

Elaran took the lead and skulked through the corridor on silent feet. Analytical black eyes met me as Shade turned to me while we moved side by side. He cocked his head to the right.

"You were surprised to see me awake," he stated. "What was your original plan? You were going to carry me through the whole castle?"

"Well, yeah," I muttered. "It's not the first time I've hauled your unconscious ass to safety, remember?"

A soft chuckle escaped his lips. "Point taken."

The opening to the other stairwell became visible in the distance. We slowed down. Straining my ears, I listened for any sound of the guards. Distressed murmuring drifted upwards. Followed by shuffling feet.

"Shit," I hissed. "They're coming."

We sprinted back the way we had come until another disconcerting sound reached our ears. As one, we froze. Thumping feet closed in from the other side of the corridor as well. *Shit.* I flicked my hands in a hurried gesture, motioning for them to start down another passage. They obeyed without question. Our feet produced soft thuds as we ran down another darkened hall. A solid wall of frosted glass appeared in front of us.

"Damn," I swore. "It's a dead end."

"What's the plan?" Elaran whispered.

"The stairs was the plan!" I threw out my arms in exasperation. "Apparently the guard positions I found in Captain Hadraeth's room are no longer accurate. They must've doubled the guards after I ruined the ritual."

"What ritual?" Shade asked.

As I waved them forwards, we started back up the corridor again. "I'll explain everything later but I kinda put a knife to the queen's throat and locked her and Captain Hadraeth in the library."

"You did what?" Elaran exclaimed.

"Shh!" Veering left at the next turn, I led them into another hallway. "Like I said, it's kinda complicated but I'll explain everything when we're safe."

Dark violet eyes stared at us as we rounded the corner. Oh, crap. Elaran and Shade bumped into me as I skidded to a halt in front of a stern-looking star elf. Pursuing feet thundered behind us.

"Come with me," Maesia ordered. When no one moved, she threw us an irritated scowl. "Do you want to live or not?"

Somewhere behind, the group of guards was closing in. The three of us exchanged a hurried glance but when the strange star elf whirled around and started down the corridor, we all followed her. The sharp lines of her dress remained almost static as she strode forwards with confident steps.

This was the woman who had done nothing but threaten me from the day I arrived. I had a very hard time believing that she was here to help us. But following her might at least buy us some time to get away from the guards.

Silver moonlight streamed through the window at another dead end. Maesia turned around. The hard lines of her face were illuminated by the pale light.

She pointed to a metal plate set into the wall. "Get in."

Suspicion crept into my mind. I narrowed my eyes at her. "Why should we trust you?"

"Because I'm your only chance."

"Not good enough." I shook my head at her. "All you've ever done is threaten me. Why should we believe you want to help us now?" Pointing to the metal plate, I arched an eyebrow at her. "For all we know, that leads straight into a dungeon. Saving the guards from having to fight us."

As if on cue, the smattering of feet behind us grew louder. Maesia spat out a frustrated groan and threw her arms out. Her violet eyes turned black as death and dark smoke twisted around her pale arms. I stared at her in utter shock.

"Y-you... you're a Storm Caster," I stammered.

"Yes, I am." The black clouds spun around her for another second before they pulled back and her eyes returned to their usual dark violet color. "Trust me now?"

"Yeah."

"Good," she snapped and stabbed a finger at the metal plate. "Now get in. It'll take you to the ground floor."

While Elaran and Shade started forward and pulled open the top of the chute, I just continued staring at Maesia, completely stunned.

"Why didn't you say anything?" I finally managed to press out.

"I didn't know if I could trust you. Queen Nimlithil has brought other Storm Casters here before and I always try to get them to leave but almost all of them end up going through with the ritual." She lifted her shoulder in an unapologetic shrug. "If you'd gone through with it, you'd have ratted me out. I couldn't risk it."

Elaran had made it into the hole in the wall. "There's no rope."

"I know," Maesia said. "Just slide all the way down. You won't need to get back up anyway."

The wood elf gave her a nod and then pushed off. A rustling of clothes combined with a slight scraping sound rose as he disappeared into the chute. The star elf Storm Caster waved me forward just as Shade climbed into the mouth of the tube as well.

"Here." She pressed a folded piece of paper into my hand. "This is where you'll find the rest of our people."

The thumping feet drew closer. Stuffing the paper inside my vest, I cast a panicked glance over my shoulder while Shade slid down the chute. We were out of time.

"I have so many questions!" I said in a desperate voice.

"I know." Maesia pulled me forward and shoved me towards the hole in the wall. "But you have to go so make this one count."

Folding up my limbs, I climbed into the top of the tube as well. "Did I really sell my soul to a demon to get my powers?"

"No."

Profound relief flooded through me. That oppressive weight that had been crushing my chest for weeks lifted and I felt like I could breathe again.

"I still have my soul?" I mumbled.

"Yes. That was two questions. Now go." She pushed me into the chute.

Darkness enveloped me as Maesia closed the metal plate while I slid further down the tube. I hadn't sold my soul to a demon! It had just been a lie. An awful, awful lie.

My stomach lurched as the metal suddenly disappeared beneath me and I flew out of another hole in the wall. Shade let out a surprised groan as I landed right on top of him. His muscles shifted against my body as he pulled me towards him before lifting me up and setting me down on the floor next to him. Utterly failing to keep a ridiculous blush from my cheeks at his touch, I scrambled to my feet in a hurry before he could see it.

Candlelight flickered in an unadorned hallway. I squinted at the scene. For some reason, I felt like I had been here before.

"Isn't this the servants' corridor by the ballroom that we checked out all those weeks ago?" Elaran asked.

The memory clicked into place. "Yeah, it is."

This was where we had confirmed that the star elves used a network of these chutes for something and that if we could find the end of the one on our floor, we could get out. That is, before the Queen of Tkeister had interrupted our scheming.

After getting to his feet as well, Shade dusted himself off and nodded in the direction of the banquet hall. "Let's get going then."

The three of us sprinted through the empty corridor until we reached the plain door that separated the servants' space from the glamorous ballroom.

Pressing an ear against the white wood, the Master Assassin listened for trouble on the other side. After a quick nod in our direction, he pushed down the handle.

There was no grand event tonight so the vast room lay deserted. None of the candles had been lit but the bright full moon cast its silver rays through the clear glass dome and illuminated the scene.

We darted through the empty tables towards the main doors. With their long limbs, Elaran and Shade arrived first, with me skidding to a halt behind them a few seconds later.

"It's gonna be swarming with guards out there," I panted.

Shade cracked the door open and peeked out. "It's empty right now."

"Then let's make a run for it," Elaran said.

"We're not even..." I began but the assassin and the elf had already slipped out the door.

Silently muttering curses at their inability to stop and listen, I followed them. Out was out, after all.

Raised voices came from down the hall and running feet closed in at an alarming rate. Shade whirled around and shoved us both back.

"Go back!" he hissed.

We sprinted towards the ballroom again but it was with growing dread I realized that we wouldn't make it in time. The guards would round the corner before we got through the door and as soon as they saw us, it would be over.

Panic seeped through my chest like ice. It couldn't end like this after everything it had taken to get here. My heart thumped in my chest. It couldn't.

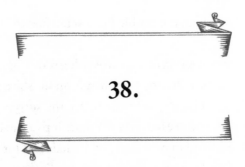

38.

One more second and they'd see us. I threw a panicked glance over my shoulder and got ready to draw my knives. This was it.

"Hey! What are you doing here?"

The racing footfalls fell silent just on the other side of the corner, allowing another pair of moving feet to be heard. Silver skirts billowed in the corridor as the owner of the voice stepped forward from the other side. Princess Illeasia cast a quick look at us before turning back to the waiting soldiers that we couldn't see.

"They were spotted two floors up. Mother said to hurry." She made a shooing motion with her arms. "Go!"

"Yes, Princess Illeasia!"

Smattering resumed as the guards ran back the way they'd come. Elaran, Shade, and I stared at the princess as she swung around and started towards us. She arched an eyebrow.

"That goes for you too. Hurry up and get inside the ballroom!"

Finally snapping out of our stupor, we darted the last bit to the door. Shade yanked it open and held it up for us. When the princess had made it through as well, he drew it shut. Silence blanketed the room.

"Thank you," Elaran mumbled and scratched the back of his neck.

Illeasia continued striding across the room until she was right in front of him. Placing both hands on his shirt, she pulled him towards her. I barely had time to see the surprise flicker in his eyes before the princess drew the ranger into a passionate kiss. Elaran nestled a hand in her silvery white hair and for the two of them, the rest of the world seemed to have disappeared. A wide smile spread across my mouth.

After a few moments, reality trickled back into the minds of the two elves and they broke apart. Both of them had a deep red color on their cheeks. Stifling a chuckle, Shade and I exchanged a glance.

Princess Illeasia cleared her throat while Elaran spent another second gathering his wits.

"I'm sorry I didn't get you out earlier," she said.

Elaran ran a hand through his ruffled auburn hair to smoothen it. "You did try."

"No, I mean before..." Illeasia turned apologetic eyes on me. "Before everything happened."

Guards stampeded past in the corridor outside. We had to keep moving. The others appeared to be thinking the same thing because, without speaking, we all started towards the glass doors on the other side.

Nimbly skirting around a cluster of chairs, I studied the princess. "Why didn't you?"

"Because she's my mother. And my queen. I couldn't go against her orders."

"But you did it anyway, in the end," Shade observed. "Why?"

Glass decorations clinked as Illeasia accidentally bumped into a table. Her hands shot out to steady them. Once she was certain they wouldn't fall, she returned her focus to the path ahead while answering the assassin's question.

"This time, she took it too far." The princess wove around a long table. "The other Storm Casters she's brought in usually agree to give up their powers after she tells them that they sold their soul for it."

Since I didn't want to bring unwanted attention to Maesia, I decided not to mention that I now knew it was a lie.

"But not you," she continued. "You're probably one of the most resilient people I've ever met. And stubborn."

Elaran snorted. I rolled my eyes at him but didn't interrupt.

"My mother recognized it too. She has never gone to this length before. Never tried to break someone like this before. Making you think you killed your friend." She shook her head, anger and disgust evident on her beautiful face. "It's unforgivable. That's why she kept us apart. I wanted to tell you that he was alive but she wouldn't let me."

A dark blue sky glittering with stars appeared above us as we followed Illeasia onto the terrace. Jasmine and roses filled the air as we moved through the paths between the bushes.

"And she's wrong about the ritual for getting rid of your pain too," the princess said as we drew closer to the railing. "Life is worth living. Every feeling you have is worth experiencing. That's what life is about. Living. In every possible way."

I placed a hand on the cold railing as we finally reached the far end. "If you really think that, then why haven't you done anything about it?"

"Storm!" Elaran protested.

Illeasia held up a hand. "No, it's alright. She's right." Silver hair fluttered in the breeze as she turned to me. "I have let my mother do what she wants for far too long. I might not be able to do much to stop it because she's still my mother and still my queen, but from now on, I'm at least going to try my very best."

Sincerity burned in her eyes so I gave her a nod in acknowledgement.

"But now you have to go." She motioned between the dark cliffs and the ballroom. "Before they figure out that I tricked them."

Pain flashed over Elaran's features. Illeasia drew him into another long kiss that could've melted an ice cap. I glanced away and instead started climbing up on the railing.

"This is what I mean," the princess said. "The pain on your face now tells me that what we have is real."

Elaran cupped her cheek in a gentle gesture. "Of course it's real.

Illeasia placed her hand over his. "If only we had met under different circumstances."

"Yes." Agony was evident on his face as the wood elf let his hand drop. "Is this it, then? Is this all we get? A few short weeks of stolen moments while our respective nations get ready for war against each other?"

Tears dripped from Illeasia's eyes. "Maybe it won't come to that."

"You don't believe that."

She swallowed back a sob and pressed her lips together but didn't reply. Elaran drew her against his chest. Sitting on the cold white railing, I watched the normally so grumpy archer stroke a hand over Illeasia's flowing hair while fighting back tears.

My heart bled for him. For them. To find each other only to be forced into opposite sides of a battle that neither of them had chosen. Life. Such a cruel thing.

Love and hurt mingled on their beautiful faces as they wrapped their bodies together and shared one final kiss. Afterwards, Elaran ran his fingers down her cheek one last time before turning around and jumping over the railing without looking back. A choked sob bubbled from her throat.

Shade and I nodded at the princess in unison before following our elven friend into the darkness below.

Tucking and rolling with the motion, I rose from the drop unharmed. There was no point in asking Elaran how he felt because the answer was obvious and the question would only cause the wound inside him to open up again so I kept silent. Shade appeared to be of similar mind because he said nothing either. Instead, the three of us took off across the dark gray rocks.

"Head for the beach," I instructed.

We veered right and aimed for the path leading through the cliffs to the water below. Running out here on the rocks in this darkness was dangerous. One wrong step and either one of us could end up with a broken ankle. Using the path was a risk since it was more likely to be patrolled by guards but we were better equipped to deal with fights than broken limbs.

Shouts rose in the air. A squad of star elves in white armor slammed straight into us from behind an outcropping. I drew my hunting knives.

While ducking under a fist, I twisted out from the sword coming for my chest. The star elf guard who had swung the fist was engaged by Shade while the one with the sword recovered and swiped at me again. I threw up my blade to block the strike while aiming a kick at the side of his knee.

He saw it coming and jumped out of the way at the last moment. An elbow connected with my side. Air exploded from my lungs and I stumbled sideways.

With barely a second to spare, I threw up one arm to protect myself from another fist while the guard in front of me lunged again. I slammed up my other arm and managed to deflect the blow just as it struck. Steel ground against steel.

I was only vaguely aware of Shade and Elaran also fighting two or three guards each while the two surrounding me renewed their attacks.

Steel whizzed through the air. Bending all the way backwards, I brace myself on the ground and evaded the swiping sword. So as to not waste the motion, I followed through and kicked a leg upwards. My boot connected with a wrist and the sword flew from the guard's grip.

A hand shot out. I yanked my leg back and rolled to the side, barely managing to avoid getting caught by a strong fist. Metal dinged against the stones I had previously occupied.

Whirling around, I sprang to my feet just in time to see a sword coming for my face. I threw up both hunting knives.

Grinding steel rang out as the sword crashed into my intersecting blades. A boot hit my stomach. Gasping in air, I stumbled backwards and dropped my arms. Jagged rocks cut into my body as I slammed back first into the stone outcropping behind.

Two swords sped for my throat. I threw up my arms to block them but I wasn't fast enough.

Metallic dings sounded as the blades reached the stone beside me, forming a cross and trapping my neck against the rocks. My heart hammered in my chest as hard violet eyes stared at me from the other side of the swords. It was over. I had lost.

39.

"Stop!"

My eyes darted around the area to find the source of the voice. Shade and Elaran were still engaged in fights with their opponents but the battle staggered to a halt as the star elves lowered their weapons. Captain Hadraeth stood straight-backed in his white armor, staring at something in the distance. Following his gaze, I found what he was looking at.

Up on the terrace, Princess Illeasia stood watching the scene. The sparkling dress gleamed in the bright moonlight and her long silver hair fluttered in the wind. For a moment, everything was still as the princess and the captain looked at each other. Then, Hadraeth tore his eyes from the beautiful princess and turned back to his men.

"Let them go," he said in a tired voice. "Let them go."

Dumbfounded, I stared at him while my mouth dropped open. Had he just ordered them to...? However, before I could ask what in Nemanan's name was going on, another figure appeared out of the darkness.

"Captain Hadraeth!" Lady Nelyssae called. Her elaborate dress billowed behind her as she rushed down the slope. "I saw you leave earlier. I knew you would find them."

Still trying to catch her breath, the elegant lady placed a hand on the captain's white armor. Irritation flitted like flies over Hadraeth's face.

"Lady Nelyssae, you shouldn't be here," he said.

"Of course, you're right." She drew a hand through her straight hair and cleared her throat. "I just wanted to make sure that you were alright. I will go inform Queen Nimlithil at once that you have caught them."

My heart sank. Behind the two guards keeping me cornered against the stone wall, Elaran and Shade gripped their swords tighter and began raising them again.

"No," the captain said.

Nelyssae jerked back in surprise. "No? What do you mean *no?*"

"You're going to go back to the castle like nothing has happened." Hadraeth waved a hand in the direction of the gleaming jewel that was Starhaven. "You never saw us or them." His dark violet eyes flashed with displeasure as he turned them on his men. "I said let them go! Don't make me repeat myself a third time."

Steel whooshed through the air as the two swords disappeared from my neck. Instinctively, I ran a hand over my throat. No blood.

"The same goes for everyone here," the captain continued. "None of this happened. The area was clear when we swept it. Understood?"

"Yes, captain."

"I understand." Lady Nelyssae cast a longing look in Hadraeth's direction before shuffling back up towards the castle.

The stern Guard Captain jerked his chin at us. "Go."

Not wanting to give him a chance to change his mind, the three of us sheathed our weapons and sprinted into the darkness without another word. Only when we were halfway to the beach did I dare a peek over my shoulder. The dark rocks were empty. Captain Hadraeth had taken all his men and returned to the castle.

"What the hell happened back there?" I blurted out as we reached the final passageway cut into the steep cliffs. On the other side, a hill waited. And then the sea. "Lady Nelyssae hates me and Captain Hadraeth hates me *and* you." I looked at Elaran. "Why would they let us go?"

Gravel tumbled down the hill as the three of us scrambled down it as fast as we could without tripping.

"Wow," Shade said. "Feelings really are a total mystery to you, aren't they?"

"What?" I threw my arms out, both to steady myself and as a show of exasperation.

"Lady Nelyssae is in love with Hadraeth, so she will do whatever he tells her. And the captain is in love with Princess Illeasia." The Master Assassin managed a shrug as we rounded the final bend in the path. "And the princess wanted him to let us go. So he did."

"Oh." I shook my head. "Man, feelings are so complicated."

Shade offered a slight chuckle in reply.

Waves crashed onto the shore before us when we finally cleared the hill. The smell of seaweed and salt filled my lungs. I set course for the rowboat waiting in the sand. Home. Soon we would be home.

A figure straightened in front of the boat. I skidded to a halt. Sand crunched underneath his boots as the lone star elf advanced on us. Moonlight fell across Niadhir's sad face.

"I suspected that you might be coming here. Why are you doing this?" Hurt dripped from his voice. "Why are you leaving me? We talked about our future! Getting married, having children, buying a house in the city. How could you string me along like that?"

Having finally recovered enough from the surprise of finding him here, I shook my head. "I didn't string you along."

"You have to stay," he pleaded.

Guilt twisted in my gut. "I can't stay. I'm not happy here."

"But you have to!" His voice was laced with pain and tears glistened in his eyes. "I can never be happy without you. You have to stay. For me."

His words stirred up a torrent of guilt and deep feelings of selfishness inside me. How was I supposed to leave after he had said something like that? He obviously needed me. What kind of villain was I to put my own health and happiness ahead of someone else? I took a step towards him.

"You were my happily ever after," he mumbled between sobs. "Do not leave me. I will never be happy without you."

In a few rapid strides, I closed the distance between us. Hope glittered in his eyes.

"Oh, Niadhir." I punched a hard fist into his gut. "Emotional blackmail doesn't work on someone who doesn't have a heart."

The scholar crumpled to the ground. He sucked in a couple of deep breaths while trying to recover from the hit. I jerked my chin at Shade and Elaran who stood staring at me further behind. Surprise and a little admiration swirled in their eyes.

"What a shame."

Whirling back around at the sound, I found Niadhir climbing to his feet. His manners were completely changed. Gone was the sad scholar and instead, a man with a cold voice and calculating eyes dusted himself off and drew up to his full height.

"You were such an interesting research object," he continued in the same emotionless voice. "So very resilient but at the same time, so insecure."

Shocked, I took a step back. "What?"

"You never stood a chance, though." His cold eyes glittered. "As soon as I drugged you and convinced you to tell me about your friend Rain that you got killed, I knew I had everything I needed to break you into tiny little pieces. When Queen Nimlithil finally authorized me to begin my experiment, I was ecstatic."

My mouth was suddenly very dry. I worked my tongue around it a couple of times before I could form a word. "Experiment?"

"Yes, making you believe you killed another friend." A detached smile stretched his lips. "After that, I could simply watch you descend into madness and all I needed was a hallucinogenic and to say a few strategic things to fuel your guilt and pain."

Water crashed against stone further away and mixed with the noise of blood rushing in my ears. I shook my head but the scholar pressed on.

"Making you feel small and stupid. Telling you that you were cursed. Reminding you of all the awful things you have done. Convincing you that you were a villain by hinting that you could still be saved. Saying that you were beautiful and pretending like I cared about you and wanted to have a future with you." He lifted his shoulders in a light shrug. "It was so easy. You were like a child. So gullible and lost. Desperate for someone to love you and want you."

Stumbling back another step, I shook my head again. "You're a psychopath."

Niadhir raised his chin defiantly. "I am a scholar."

"You did that to her?" a dark voice growled behind me.

"Yes." The lunatic scholar arched an eyebrow at the assassin responsible for the comment. "Were you not paying attention just now?"

"I will make you beg for death," Shade threatened, drawing out each word.

Without turning around to watch the lightning storm flash in the Master Assassin's black eyes, I held up a hand. "No. He is mine."

"Oh!" Niadhir held up a finger in the air and then dug around inside his white suit until he found a small notepad.

A knife-covered Storm Caster and the Master of the Assassins' Guild had just threatened to kill him but he seemed to completely disregard that fact as another scientific query jumped to the front of his mind. He pulled out the notepad while excitement bounced in his eyes.

"Tell me," he began, "did you ever notice the white mist in the Spirit Garden?"

I was too fascinated by how completely crazy he was so I answered honestly because I kind of wanted to see where he was going with this. "Well, yeah."

"Did you notice anything specific about it?"

"No?"

"Excellent!" His eyes lit up and he scrawled something on the piece of paper. "It induces hallucinations. It kept you in a constant drugged state since you received your daily dose by going to the Spirit Garden. Hence the nightmares and the slight hallucinations."

My mouth dropped open. That was what had caused the nightmares and the dead people popping up at the ball and other places? Niadhir finished writing and jerked up from the notepad. He tapped the pen to it.

"But I was so curious to see what would happen if you were dosed twice. I knew I just had to send you back there twice in one day to study what would happen." He drew a hand over his chin. "The breakdown you had when you thought all the people you had killed were there to punish you was fascinating. That was my planned breaking point for you. The moment when I stripped you of everything you were and made you into someone else. Into the kind of person I wanted you to be."

Completely lost for words, I just stared at him. He had drugged me. Given me nightmares for weeks and made me see dead people. He had orchestrated the breakdown that had crushed me into a thousand shards of glass that very nearly left irreparable damage. Anger surged through me. That damn psychopath had tried to change the core of who I was.

The darkness ripped from my soul. Tendrils of black smoke snaked around me while my eyes went black as death. I threw my arms out. Lightning crackled as storm clouds gathered around me. Rage and insanity danced in my eyes as I leveled a withering glare on the scholar before me.

"After everything I've been through, you thought you would be the one to break me?" Thunder punctuated my words. "I have survived on the streets as a child. I have been beaten, betrayed, tortured, and hanged. I have been forced to betray allies. Assassinate innocents. I have been called heartless, cold, and cruel. I got my best friend, my sister in all but blood, killed when I was eleven. When I was a child!" Lightning flashed around me as the dark clouds grew. "After all of that, after everything I have survived, did you really think that you would be the one to break me? I am smoke and steel and lightning. I cannot be broken."

Niadhir took a step back, fear coloring his eyes, but it was too late. Sand sprayed into the air as I shot forward. Desperate pleas fell on deaf ears when I caught up to the scholar. I rammed a hunting knife through his heart.

A strained gasp cut through the noise of the storm. Niadhir pressed his hands to his chest as I withdrew a blade smeared with blood. Grabbing the back of his neck, I drew him towards me.

"You cannot break me," I whispered in his ear.

When I released my grip on his neck and took a step back, his knees buckled. Black sand ruined his spotless suit as he slumped to the ground. Well, that and the large red stain spreading across his chest. I watched the light die in his pale violet eyes before pulling the darkness into my soul again. Drawing a deep breath of sea air, I let the rage subside. No one would break me.

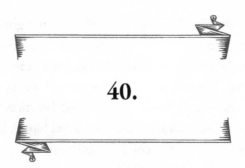

40.

S hade chuckled behind me. "It's good to have you back."
I turned around to find the assassin giving me a lopsided smile while Elaran nodded next to him.

"I agree," the auburn-haired ranger announced. "Moping doesn't suit you."

"Right?" Shade said before shifting his amused gaze back to me. "Threatening to kill people in a cloud of black smoke and lightning is so much more your style."

"I wasn't moping," I muttered and drew my eyebrows down in a halfhearted attempt at a scowl.

Another bout of rippling laughter drifted through the night air. I shook my head. Damn assassin. After wiping off my knife and returning it to the small of my back, I strode across the black sand.

"Come on," I called over my shoulder. "Help me get the rowboat in the water."

Together, we pushed the small boat across the beach until we finally reached the dark blue water. The vessel wobbled slightly as the three of us climbed aboard. With powerful strokes, we made our way out to sea.

"What now?" Elaran waved a hand at the vast expanse of water around us. "We're going to row back to Pernula?"

"Oh come on, have a little faith." I grinned at the confounded elf. "When I stage a rescue, I do it properly."

Waves crashed against the sides of the boat, sending sprays of salt water over us as we made our way further out. Before long, a hulking shape became visible on the horizon. It grew larger at a rapid rate.

Shade narrowed his eyes at it. "Is that...?"

A smirk decorated my face. "Yep."

"How did you even arrange that?"

"It's the only reason I agreed to that damn ritual in the first place." I shrugged. "I knew they'd never let me send a letter to someone outside otherwise."

The Master Assassin arched an eyebrow at me. "And they didn't read it?"

"Of course they did." I gave him a short shake of my head as if that should've been obvious. "Which is why I wrote two letters. One for Niadhir to read and one for me to send." Another grin flashed over my mouth. "Come on, sleight of hand is kinda my thing, remember?"

"Underworlders," Elaran muttered and shook his head ruefully.

The assassin and I both chuckled at that.

While we waited for the dark shape to get closer, I filled them in on what had happened while they'd been locked away. They listened mostly without interrupting but there were some parts where I could almost see the anger dancing in their eyes. I contemplated giving them a censored version but after everything we'd been through together these past few months, I figured that they deserved the truth.

I had already finished when at last a wall of dark wood blocked out the horizon.

"Someone arrange for a pickup?" a cheerful voice called above us.

Looking up, we found Zaina grinning down at us from her pirate ship. Wood clattered as she threw down the ladder.

"When you stage a rescue, you do it properly indeed." Shade chuckled and then nodded at the ladder. "After you."

Shooting him a satisfied grin, I grabbed the closest rung and started the climb. Zaina reached down and helped me the final bit onto deck.

"On the night of the full moon, huh?" She chuckled. "You didn't give me a lot of time to get here."

"I know. I'm sorry."

Once I had both feet on the wooden planks, she clapped a hand to my shoulder and gave me a warm smile. "Don't be. It's good to see you." She nodded at the assassin and the elf as they climbed onto the deck as well. "All of you. A lot of people have been really worried about you."

"Yeah, uhm, sorry about that." I scratched the back of my neck. "It's kinda my fault that we got caught up in this."

The pirate leveled observant black eyes on me. "And later, we're gonna have a very long drink while you tell me all about whatever this thing you got caught up in is."

"Promise." I let out a small laugh. "But we're gonna need more than one drink."

"It's a deal." She winked at me. "Now, let's get out of here."

While snapping orders to her crew, Zaina strode across the deck. Shade nodded at me before following the pirate and firing off a whole bunch of questions about the state of Pernula. I turned to Elaran. He was leaning against the wooden railing, staring at the gleaming City of Glass across the dark water. The damp material groaned as I moved over and rested my arms on the railing next to him.

"She's a good person." He let out a long sigh. "A rare person."

Already knowing that he was talking about Princess Illeasia, I just nodded. "Yeah."

"Do you think we ever had a chance?"

"I think you still do." I motioned at the world around us. "One day, all this craziness with her mother will be over. And then, there's nothing stopping you from being together."

Mixed feelings of sadness and determination washed over his face. "I still need to protect my people."

"When this war is over, there won't be anything to protect them from." I bumped his shoulder with mine. "Don't forget that you deserve to be happy too."

For a long moment, we just stood there, listening to the waves slosh against the hull. A cool night wind ruffled our hair and brought another waft of seaweed and salt to our lungs. Sails snapped above us.

"You're not fooling anyone, by the way," Elaran suddenly declared.

I frowned at him. "Fooling anyone with what?"

"It might be covered in black ice and metal spikes but you do have a heart."

My eyebrows shot up as I stared at him. A warm feeling spread through my chest and I gave him a small smile. The grumpy elf seemed to notice the expression on my face because he crossed his arms and drew his eyebrows down.

"Don't look at me like that," he huffed. "You're still the most disagreeable person I've ever met."

I snorted. "Right back at you."

After another few moments of amused looks and stifled chuckles, we left the railing and drifted across the ship.

In the shadows of the raised part of the deck, Shade caught up with me. With my back against the wooden planks, I studied the assassin. Strange feelings swirled in his dark eyes.

"I lied before," he stated. "Back in Travelers' Rest."

"The Master of the Assassins' Guild lied about something?" I drew my hands in a dramatic arc. "Shocker."

A hand on my collarbone pushed me into the wall while his athletic body pressed against me. His lips met mine with ferocious passion. I blinked in surprise. After one more second of trying to figure out what was going on, I gave up the futile attempt and instead leaned into his embrace and returned the kiss.

There on that pirate ship under the stars, time stood still as everything else dropped away and Shade and I became the only two people in the whole world. His heartbeat against my chest. His lips against mine.

After an eternity of timelessness, he drew back just enough to place his lips next to my ear. "I do care what happens to you." His breath was hot against my neck. "I care about you."

Strange feelings, feelings I didn't even knew I was capable of, sparkled like fireworks in my chest. A shiver rippled through my body as he drew his fingers along my throat before placing his strong hand behind my neck. Lightning crackled inside me. His lean muscles shifted against me as he ran his other hand down my body before he drew me into another ravenous kiss.

When he at last pulled back and the press of his muscled body no longer kept me upright, I slumped back against the wooden planks behind me. I felt as though my brain had been blown clear out of my head and had sailed up into the heavens.

"Wow," I breathed. "That was... wow."

Putting two fingers under my chin, he tilted my head up to meet his eyes. "I do care about you," he repeated.

Before I completely lost myself in his intense dark eyes again, I raked my hands through my hair and cracked a rueful smile. "You know, as much as it annoys me, I care about you too."

A lopsided smile quirked his lips. I ran my fingers along his jaw while my own smile turned sad.

"But love is not for people like us."

Some of Zaina's sailors blundered into our momentous moment so Shade took me by the hand and led us towards the railing instead. Leaning a hip against the wood, he gazed down at me.

"Your body seemed to disagree just now," he said with a grin.

Chuckling, I grabbed the collar of his shirt and drew him in for another quick kiss. Satisfaction coursed through me when a small moan escaped his lips. I drew back.

"If only it were that simple." Twisting away slightly, I leaned against the railing and stared out at the darkened sea.

He propped up his elbows on the damp wood next to me. "What do you mean?"

"When we get back to Pernula, you're gonna have to regain power you've lost while you've been away. And..." I blew out a short chuckle. "You're not satisfied just being the General, are you? If I know anything about you, you've already started manipulating your way into becoming the sole ruler of Pernula.

But to do that, you need the support of the nobles and the merchants. No matter how reformed they think you are, I am still a thief from the Underworld. So, if you want to become the sole ruler of Pernula, you can't do it with me by your side." I glanced at him from the corner of my eye. "Tell me I'm wrong."

Dropping his head into his hands, he raked his fingers through his thick black hair before looking up again. A heavy sigh rose from his chest. "You're not."

"And besides, when we get back to Pernula, I'm leaving again. I finally know where the Storm Casters are and I have to go find them."

His intense black eyes searched my face. "Are you coming back?"

"Do you want me to?"

"Yeah."

"Good." A smirk spread across my lips. "I was always planning on coming back. I just wanted to hear you say it."

The Master Assassin chuckled and shook his head. For a while, Shade and I just stood there, arms brushing against each other as we watched the waves in comfortable silence. The white city was growing smaller in the distance.

"And when I get back," I said at last, "I'm sure you will have married some strategically important daughter."

Shade nodded next to me. "Yeah, I probably will. And you will have fallen for some powerful Storm Caster who can teach you everything you want to know."

I tipped my head to the side. "Probably."

"But then again, maybe we won't have."

Casting a glance at him from the corner of my eye, I found him watching me. "Maybe we won't have indeed." Strong waves slapped against the ship as I turned to face him again. Trying to suppress the mess of emotions in my chest, I lifted my eyebrows at him. "Hold on, didn't we agree that feelings were a bloody inconvenience?"

A surprised chuckle bubbled from his throat but then he gave me a grave nod. "Yes, we did. And they are."

Matching his dead serious look, I pretended to hoist a cup in the air. "Well, then. To a cold black heart."

Shade lifted his own pretend cup into the night air. "To a cold black heart. That we may or may not actually have."

Laughing, I shot the assassin a knowing look. "May we one day find out which."

After drawing soft fingers along my neck, Shade made his way back into the ship. My skin still tingled from his touch. The two of us together, what a force we would've been. I shook my head. If only our lives weren't so bloody complicated. Maybe one day they wouldn't be, and what would happen then, only the gods knew.

As we sailed on to the open sea, I gazed back at Starhaven and the City of Glass. It had been one of the most emotionally draining experiences of my life but I had also found out some very important things. In addition to, well, whatever it was that Shade and I now were, I had also learned quite a lot about myself and about the Storm Casters.

Thanks to Maesia, I didn't have to search blindly anymore. I knew where the other Ashaana were and I could now start my journey to understand how my powers worked.

Straightening, I swept my gaze over the vast dark blue sea filled with glittering stars. Wind whipped through my hair.

The loss of identity and the confused feelings of rootlessness were gone as well. My unshakable sense of self was back and stronger than ever.

What do you want? At last, I knew the answer to that question. What did I want? I smiled at the open horizon. Freedom.

Acknowledgements

This was an emotionally draining book to write, but one I wanted to write. There will always be people who will try to change you. People who will try to turn you into someone you're not just so that you will fit into their narrow view of how everyone should live their life. Don't let them. Be you. Live your life in a way that makes you happy. Unless, you know, you're someone like Niadhir who enjoys breaking people and driving them insane in the name of research. Then maybe don't be that guy. But otherwise, be you.

As always, I would like to say a huge thank you to my family and loved ones. Mom, Dad, Mark, thank you for the enthusiasm, love, and encouragement. I truly don't know what I would do without you. Lasse, Ann, Karolina, Axel, Martina, thank you for continuing to take such an interest in my books. It really means a lot.

Another group of people I would like to once again express my gratitude to is my wonderful team of beta readers: Deshaun Hershel, Jennifer Nicholls, Luna Lucia Lawson, and Orsika Petér. Thank you for the time and effort you put into reading the book and providing helpful feedback. Your suggestions and encouragement truly makes the book better.

To my fantastic copy editor and proofreader Julia Gibbs, thank you for all the hard work you always put into making my books shine. Your attention to detail is amazing and makes me feel confident that I'm publishing the very best version of my books.

Dane Low is another person I'm very fortunate to have found. He is the extraordinary designer from ebooklaunch.com who made the stunning cover for this book. Dane, thank you for the effort you put into making yet another gorgeous cover for me. You knock it out of the park every time.

I am also very fortunate to have friends both close by and from all around the world. My friends, thank you for everything you've shared with me. Thank you for the laughs, the tears, the deep discussions, and the unforgettable memories. My life is a lot richer with you in it.

Before I go back to writing the next book, I would like to once again say thank you to you, the reader. Thank you for being so invested in the world of the Oncoming Storm that you continued the series. If you have any questions or comments about the book, I would love to hear from you. You can find all the different ways of contacting me on my website, www.marionblackwood.com. There you can also sign up for my newsletter to receive updates about coming novels. Lastly, if you liked this book and want to help me out so that I can continue writing books, please consider leaving a review. It really does help tremendously. I hope you enjoyed the adventure!